Anonymous

The First Book of the Hitopadesa

containing the Sanskrit text with interlinear transliteration, grammatical analysis and English translation

Anonymous

The First Book of the Hitopadesa
containing the Sanskrit text with interlinear transliteration, grammatical analysis and English translation

ISBN/EAN: 9783337188573

Printed in Europe, USA, Canada, Australia, Japan

Cover: Foto ©Andreas Hilbeck / pixelio.de

More available books at **www.hansebooks.com**

THE

FIRST BOOK OF THE HITOPADEŚA:

CONTAINING

THE SANSKRIT TEXT,

WITH

INTERLINEAR TRANSLITERATION, GRAMMATICAL ANALYSIS, AND ENGLISH TRANSLATION.

SECOND EDITION

LONDON
LONGMANS, GREEN, AND CO.
1884.

PREFACE.

A SERIES of Handbooks for the study of Sanskrit seems to be required at the present moment by two classes of readers; by those who, as candidates for the Indian Civil Service, are anxious to acquire that amount of familiarity with the grammar and literature of the classical language of India, which is not only useful for an honourable acquitment at the public examinations, but serves as the best foundation for the subsequent study of the spoken vernaculars; and by that steadily increasing number of scholars who wish to gain an elementary, yet accurate, knowledge of a language which is the key to the secrets of Comparative Philology.

There is, indeed, no lack of books in English for those who make Sanskrit the study of their life; and even continental scholars who wish to acquire a sound and profound knowledge of the ancient language and literature of India, must still have recourse to the masterworks of English scholars such as Colebrooke, Prinsep, and Wilson. The first volume of Colebrooke's Sanskrit Grammar, published sixty years ago, is a monument of English scholarship which has never been surpassed by any subsequent Grammar, whether in English, German, or French. Professor Benfey's large Sanskrit Grammar, published at Leipzig in 1852, is the only work that rivals it in comprehensiveness and authoritativeness.* The Dictionary of Wilson, to which is mainly due the rapid progress which Sanskrit scholarship has made in the Universities of Europe, is still the only complete thesaurus of the language of ancient India. There are the *editiones principes*, the original translations, the comprehensive essays, due to the honest industry of such men as Sir W. Jones, Wilkins, Colebrooke, Wilson, and Ballantyne, which will always keep their place of honour in the library of every student of Sanskrit. But these works are available to advanced scholars only, while the elementary books now accessible to English students who wish to begin the study of Sanskrit, and who, in many cases, have to begin it without the help of a master, are, with rare exceptions, edited in such a manner that they fail in the very elements of grammar, and unnecessarily retard the progress even of the most painstaking pupils. It has been said, indeed, with some apparent truth, that the race of *bonâ fide* Sanskrit scholars seemed for a time extinct in England; but the late publications of Mr. J. Muir of Edinburgh, and Professor E. B. Cowell of Calcutta, bear witness that in Sanskrit scholarship, too, England will always hold her own, and that, with the

* The same author has lately published a 'Practical Grammar of the Sanskrit Language for the Use of early Students,' London, 1863.

advantages enjoyed by the members of the Civil Service in India, there will never be wanting worthy successors of Colebrooke and Wilson—men who have not only mastered the intricacies of Sanskrit grammar, but who are capable of reading Sanskrit MSS., and contributing towards the progress of Sanskrit scholarship by editing texts that have never been edited before, and translating texts that have never been translated before.

The present series of elementary handbooks is intended to comprise an elementary Grammar for English students, a Sanskrit-English Dictionary, and the ordinary text-books, the Hitopadeśa, the Laws of Manu, the play of Śakuntalâ, the Nala, and such other works as may hereafter seem to be called for either in England or in India. A Manual of Comparative Philology, written with special reference to Greek and Latin, is likewise in preparation. The cooperation of several eminent Sanskrit scholars has been secured.

The first volume of the series contains the First Book of the Hitopadeśa, a work which, since the days of Sir William Jones, has been used as the text-book in all Colleges and Public Examinations. The Sanskrit text has been so arranged that even those who are not able to command the assistance of an efficient teacher will be able by themselves to read, parse, and translate every word of this ancient collection of Indian fables.

The first line contains the Sanskrit text in Devanâgarî letters, the words properly joined according to the rules of Sandhi.

The second line gives every word transcribed in Roman letters. The system of transliteration is that of Sir W. Jones, with a few modifications which are now generally adopted by Sanskrit scholars. The words are separated, and the final and initial letters allowed to remain unaffected by the rules of Sandhi. Compound words have been divided, and the single words which enter into composition are given in their crude forms. Thus *saṁskṛitoktishu* is printed *saṁskṛita-uktishu*, but not *sam-kṛita-uktishu*, because it is *saṁskṛita*, as a ready-made word, that enters into composition with *ukti*. *Saṁskâras*, on the contrary, is divided into *sam-kâras*, thus showing the reader that the insertion of the *s*, and the change of *m* into Anusvâra, are the result of the composition of *kâras* with *sam*. According to the same system *samunnatim* is printed *sam-ud-natim*, *râjaputrâs* appears as *râjan-putrâs*, *upaiti* as *upa-eti*, &c. Two advantages are thus secured: the pupil is warned against reading the Devanâgarî text too mechanically by the aid of the transliteration, and his attention is from the first attracted to the rules which govern the composition of words.

The third line contains a grammatical analysis of every word. The space that could be spared for this being very limited, it was necessary to use abbreviations, a complete list of which will be found at the end of the preface.

The fourth line supplies an English interlinear translation. As far as possible each Sanskrit word is here rendered by an English word, the succession of words in Sanskrit being preserved throughout in English. Any attempt at English idiom was out of the question; yet it is hoped that, by the help of the grammatical analysis, this English transvocabulation (*sit venia verbo*) may be intelligible and useful to a diligent student.

From page 38 the transliteration is discontinued. The student, after having worked his way through the first thirty-eight pages, ought to be sufficiently familiarised with the Devanâgarî alphabet to be able to dispense henceforth with the Roman transcript. In order to mark the end of words which in the Devanâgarî text are joined together with the next following words, a dot has been placed beneath the final letter, an expedient which, it is hoped, will prove useful to the beginner, and do away with the necessity of separating the final and initial letters of words which, according to the genius of the Sanskrit language, cannot be conceived as separated from each other.

From page 68 the grammatical analysis too has been discontinued. The student, after having read so far, may reasonably be supposed to have acquired such a knowledge of the elements of Sanskrit grammar as to be able to read the rest of the first book of the Hitopadeśa with the help of a literal interlinear translation.

The Sanskrit text is chiefly based on that of Lakshami Náráyan Nyálankár, in his edition of the Hitopadeśa, with a Bengali and English translation, Calcutta, 1830. Deviations from that text were only resorted to where grammar, regard for the difficulties of beginners, or decency, seemed to require it. That text was chosen as an authority, partly because it was desirable to have, as far as possible, the same text in the examinations in India and in England, partly because an eclectic text, even one so carefully elaborated as that of Schlegel and Lassen, seemed to be incompatible with those principles of diplomatic criticism which are now adopted by all sound scholars, not only in Greek and Latin, but likewise in Sanskrit and Oriental literature. No attempt has yet been made to arrange the numerous MSS. of the Hitopadeśa genealogically, and there is hardly another work with which each copyist has ventured to take such liberties as with this, the most popular story-book of India. Until MSS. have been genealogically arranged, a selection of certain plausible readings from this or that MS. is worse than useless. In my translation of the Hitopadeśa, published in the year 1844, I pointed out that an eclectic restoration of the text, even if carried out by men of taste and profound scholarship, could never satisfy the demands of modern criticism. As the labour of collating and classifying the MSS. of the Hitopadeśa would have been very great, and as, owing to the nature of this popular work, the result would always have been problematical, I determined to make no attempt at a critical restoration of the text, but to adhere throughout to some one native authority. The reason why I preferred the text of Lakshami Náráyan Nyálankár, the Bengali editor and translator of this Indian school-book, to any single MS. of the Hitopadeśa, was, as I stated before, of a purely practical nature—I wished there should be, as far as possible, a certain uniformity in the text-books used in England and in India. I have also to confess that in cases where such common phrases as *tathâ cha, aparam cha, tathâ cha uktam* ('and thus it is said') would have entailed a blank space of four lines, they have sometimes been omitted, and that the same consideration has occasionally required the omission of certain portions in the grammatical analysis of the text.

The manuscript of the First Book of the Hitopadeśa, as here printed, was carefully prepared for me, according to the principles just explained, by Dr. F. Kielhorn, and I hope that the labour bestowed upon it by him and by myself will prove useful to that daily-increasing class of scholars who wish to acquire an accurate knowledge of the classical language of ancient India, whether as a preparation for the study of the spoken vernaculars, or as an introduction to the science of language.

Transliteration of the Devanâgarî Alphabet.

अ	a	औ	au	ठ	ṭh	भ	bh
आ	â	क	k	ड	ḍ	म	m
इ	i	ख	kh	ढ	ḍh	य	y
ई	î	ग	g	ण	ṇ	र	r
उ	u	घ	gh	त	t	ल	l
ऊ	û	ङ	ṅ	थ	th	व	v
ऋ	ṛi	च	ch	द	d	श	ś
ॠ	ṛî	छ	chh	ध	dh	ष	sh
ऌ	ḷi	ज	j	न	n	स	s
ए	e	झ	jh	प	p	ह	h
ऐ	ai	ञ	ñ	फ	ph	अं	aṁ
ओ	o	ट	ṭ	ब	b	अः	aḥ

List of Abbreviations.

N. = Nominative.	Pres. = Present.	Ind. = Indeclinable.
G. = Genitive.	Impf. = Imperfect.	Adv. = Adverb.
D. = Dative.	Perf. = Perfect.	Prep. = Preposition.
Ac. = Accusative.	Aor. = Aorist.	rt. = root.
V. = Vocative.	Fut. = Future.	aff. = affix.
Ab. = Ablative.	Pot. = Potential.	Compar. = Comparative.
I. = Instrumental.	Imp. = Imperative.	Superl. = Superlative.
L. = Locative.	Ptc. = Participle.	Ttp. = Tatpurusha.
m. = masculine.	Inf. = Infinitive.	Karm. = Karmadhâraya.
f. = feminine.	Ger. = Gerund.	Bahuv. = Bahuvrîhi.
n. = neuter.	Par. = Parasmaipada.	Dvand. = Dvandva.
sg. = singular.	Âtm. = Âtmanepada.	Avyay. = Avyayîbhâva.
pl. = plural.	Pass. = Passive.	cf. = compare.
du. = dual.	Caus. = Causative.	id. = the same.

The Anusvâra and the Nasal Dot.

Another abbreviation which I have adopted in the Sanskrit text requires a few words of explanation.

According to Pâṇini (viii. 3, 23), every *m* at the end of a word (*pada*), may, before any consonant, be pronounced as Anusvâra. Hence we find the following combinations —

तं करोति, 1. taṁ karoti,	तं खादति, 2. taṁ khâdati,	तं गच्छति, 3. taṁ gachchhati,	तं घोषयति 4. taṁ ghoshayati,	तं ङकारं, 5. taṁ ṅakâram,
तं चिनोति, 6. taṁ chinoti,	तं छिनत्ति, 7. taṁ chhinatti,	तं जयति, 8. taṁ jayati,	तं झकारं, 9. taṁ jhakâram,	तं ञकारं, 10. taṁ ñakâram,
तं टकारं, 11. taṁ ṭakâram,	तं ठकारं, 12. taṁ ṭhakâram,	तं डकारं, 13. taṁ ḍakâram,	तं ढकारं, 14. taṁ ḍhakâram,	तं णकारं, 15. taṁ ṇakâram.
तं तुदति, 16. taṁ tudati,	तं थकारं, 17. taṁ thakâram,	तं ददाति, 18. taṁ dadâti,	तं धमति, 19. taṁ dhamati,	तं नयति, 20. taṁ nayati,
तं पिबति, 21. taṁ pibati,	तं फलं, 22. taṁ phalam,	तं बोधति, 23. taṁ bodhati,	तं भिनत्ति, 24. taṁ bhinatti,	तं मोचयति, 25. taṁ mochayati,

तं याति, 26. taṁ yâti,	तं रक्षति, 27. taṁ rakshati,	तं लभते, 28. taṁ labhate,	तं वहति, 29. taṁ vahati,
तं शृणोति, 30. taṁ śṛiṇoti,	तं षकारं, 31. taṁ shakâram,	तं सरति, 32. taṁ sarati,	तं हरति. 33. taṁ harati.

According to the same Pâṇini, however (viii. 4, 59), this Anusvâra, at the end of words, may be (not *must be*) pronounced like the nasal corresponding to the initial letter of the following word, unless that initial letter be *ś*, *sh*, *s*, *h*; to which may be added *r*. Hence we find

in 1–5, तङ्करोति or तं करोति, taṅ karoti or taṁ karoti;

in 6–10, तञ्चिनोति or तं चिनोति, tañ chinoti or taṁ chinoti;

in 11–15, तण्टकारं or तं टकारं, taṇ ṭakâram or taṁ ṭakâram;

in 16–20, तन्तुदति or तं तुदति, tan tudati or taṁ tudati;

in 21–25, तम्पिबति or तं पिबति, tam pibati or taṁ pibati.

Of the semivowels, *r* only has no corresponding nasal, but य, ल, व, y, l, v, have their corresponding nasals, written यं, लं, वं, or यँ, लँ, वँ, ỹ, l̃, ṽ. Hence,

in 26, तय्ँयाति or तं याति, taỹ yâti or taṁ yâti;

in 28, तल्ँलभते or तं लभते, tal̃ labhate or taṁ labhate;

in 29, तव्ँवहति or तं वहति, taṽ vahati or taṁ vahati.

In 30–36, before ś, sh, s, h, and in 27, before r, the change of *m* into Anusvâra is absolute.

All cases * are thus provided for in which an *m* at the end of words is followed by a consonant. The only case not provided for is when *m* stands *in pausâ*. Here, according to the strict interpretation of Pâṇini, as no change of *m* into Anusvâra is prescribed, *m* ought to be pronounced *m*.

We now come to *m* in the middle of words. Here Pâṇini prescribes, first (viii. 3, 24), that *m* is pronounced as Anusvâra before any consonant except *y*, *r*, *l*, *v*, and *ṅ*, *ñ*, *ṇ*, *n*, *m*. But this, in the peculiar style of his grammar, is only a step to a further rule (viii. 4, 58), according to which every Anusvâra that has thus been enjoined, must be (not *may be*) pronounced like the nasal belonging to the consonant following, except before *ś*, *sh*, *s*, *h*, where it remains Anusvâra. The long and short of these rules is, that *m*, in the middle of a word, is pronounced like the nasal of the consonant following, except before *y*, *r*, *l*, *v*, *ṅ*, *ñ*, *ṇ*, *n*, *m* (where no change is enjoined by viii. 3, 24), and except before *ś*, *sh*, *s*, *h* (where the change of *m* into Anusvâra, prescribed by viii. 3, 24, is not repealed by viii. 4, 58).

It is absolutely necessary, therefore, to pronounce:

(1) अङ्किता aṅkitâ, अञ्चिता añchitâ, कुण्डिता kuṇḍitâ, नन्दिता nanditâ, कम्पिता kampitâ.

It is absolutely necessary to pronounce:

(2) गम्यते gamyate, नम्रः namraḥ, अम्लः amlaḥ;

And it is absolutely necessary to pronounce:

(3) आक्रंस्यते âkraṁsyate, संस्कृतः saṁskṛita [likewise यशांसि yaśâṁsi, धनूंषि dhanûṁshi, where Pâṇini treats the inserted nasal as *n* (*num*)].

All these rules will be found carefully observed in the text of the Hitopadeśa, with one exception. In apparent defiance of Pâṇini, the best MSS., and I would particularly instance the MSS. of the Saṁhitâ and Pada texts of the Rig-Veda, write, not अङ्किता, but अंकिता; not अञ्चिता, but अंचिता; not कुण्डिता, but कुंडिता; not नन्दिता, but नंदिता; not

* A few exceptions mentioned by Pâṇini serve only to confirm these general rules as far as the *m* at the end of words is concerned. Thus (Pâṇ. viii. 3, 25), in the compound *sam-râṭ*, a great king, the *m* of *sam*, though according to Sanskrit grammarians, standing at the end of a word (*padânte*), must be pronounced as *m*, not as Anusvâra. Hence, सम्राट् samrâṭ, not संराट् saṁrâṭ. But this applies to this one compound only; hence संराजिता, saṁrâjitâ, not सम्राजिता samrâjitâ.

Again (Pâṇ. viii. 3, 26), if initial *h* is followed by *m*, the final *m* of the preceding word may either, according to the general rule, be pronounced as Anusvâra, or remain *m*. Thus: किं ह्मलयति or किम्ह्मलयति, *kiṁ hmalayati* or *kim hmalayati*. The reason of this must be found in the slight pronunciation of *h* before *m*; so that *m*, not *h*, seems to be sounded as the initial of *hmalayati*. The same option is given by some grammarians with regard to words beginning with *hy*, *hl*, *hv*. Natives very commonly write *Bramha*, instead of *Brahma*, i.e. they pronounce *mh* instead of *hm*. Pâṇini (viii. 3, 27), gives a similar option with regard to words beginning with *hn*. Hence, *kiṁ hnute*, or *kin hnute*.

कम्पिता, but कंपिता. The reason of this is palpable: it is easier to write अंकिता than अङ्किता. What applies to writing applies with still greater force to printing, and I have, therefore, in all my Sanskrit publications, preferred the more compendious system of representing the five nasals before the consonants of their own classes by the dot above the line. It should be clearly understood, however, that whether we write अङ्किता or अंकिता, the rule of Pâṇini, which refers to pronunciation and not to writing, is equally absolute, and that in the middle of a word the only nasals that can be sounded before *k, kh, g, gh, ch, chh, j, jh, ṭ, ṭh, ḍ, ḍh, t, th, d, dh, p, ph, b, bh,* are the nasals of the five classes to which these consonants belong (ङ्, ञ्, ण्, न्, म्). The dot, therefore, used in writing and printing is here a mere graphic substitute for these five nasals, and in no way to be confounded with the dot as the sign of the Anusvâra.

At the end of words, as the pronunciation in cases 1–25, 26, 28, 29, is optional, the dot, which in accordance with most MSS. I always prefer, may either be pronounced as Anusvâra or looked upon as the graphic substitute for any of the five class-nasals and of the three nasalised semi-vowels. Only, if it precedes words beginning with *r, ś, sh, s, h,* the final dot must be pronounced as Anusvâra. Lastly, if words ending in *m* stand *in pausâ,* the final dot, according to the strict interpretation of Pâṇini, is to be pronounced as *m.*

Though this matter is in itself simple enough, it has been much complicated by grammarians who did not perceive that the rules given by Pâṇini refer to pronunciation and not to writing, and that in Sanskrit MSS. and native publications the dot has really two quite distinct functions:

1. It marks the sound of Anusvâra at the end of words before *ś, sh, s, h,* and *r* (optionally before any consonant), and in the middle of words before *ś, sh, s, h.*

2. It graphically replaces in the middle of words the five nasals before the twenty mutes, and the *m* at the end of words *in pausâ.*

In an elementary book like the present, the consistent use of the dot instead of the five class-nasals in the cases described above, has the advantage that while it removes any doubt as to the original nature of final *ñ, ṇ,* and *n,* when followed by initial sonant Palatals, Linguals, and Dentals,* it forces the student to practice the phonetic rules in order to be able to judge for himself whether the dot represents the sound of Anusvâra or whether it is used as an abbreviation in place of one of the five class-nasals.

MAX MÜLLER.

WEYMOUTH: *September* 1864.

* Thus ताञ्जयति, tâñ jayati, always represents an original ताम् जयति, he conquers them; while तां जयति, tâṁ jayati, stands for an original ताम् जयति, he conquers her. The nasal dot never represents an original *n* except in the middle of words before *t, th, d, dh.* In cases like तांश्च, *taṁś cha*, or मिमांसा, *mimâṁsâ,* the dot is meant for Anusvâra.

CONTENTS.

BOOK I.

FRIEND-ACQUISITION, ILLUSTRATED BY THE STORY OF THE CROW, THE PIGEONS, THE MOUSE, THE TORTOISE, AND THE DEER.

॥ श्रीगणेशाय नमः ॥

TO THE BLESSED GAṆEŚA, SALUTATION!

॥ अथ हितोपदेशः ॥

HERE BEGINS THE HITOPADEŚA.

सिद्धिः साध्ये सतामस्तु प्रसादात्तस्य धूर्जटेः ।

siddhis	sâdhye	satâm	astu	pra-sâdât	tasya	dhûrjaṭes
-dhi, *N. sg.*	-ya, *L. sg. n.*	-t, *G. pl.*	as, 3 *sg. Imp. Par.*	-da, *Ab. sg.*	tad, *G. sg. m.*	-ṭi, *G. sg.*
Success	in what is to be accomplished	of the good	may be	through the favour	of that	Dhûrjaṭi,

जाह्नवीफेनलेखेव यन्मूर्ध्नि शशिनः कला ॥ १ ॥

Jâhnavî-phena-lekhâ	iva	yad-mûrdhni	śaśinas	kalâ.	(1)
Ttp. -khâ, *N. sg.*	*Ind.*	*Ttp.* -dhan, *L. sg.*	-śin, *G. sg.*	-lâ, *N. sg.*	
Ganges-froth-streak	- like	on whose-head	the moon's	sixteenth part.	

श्रुतो हितोपदेशो ऽयं पाटवं संस्कृतोक्तिषु ।

śrutas	hita-upadeśas	ayam	pâṭavam	saṁskṛita-uktishu
śru, *N. sg. m. past Ptc. Pass.*	*Karm.* -śa, *N. sg.*	idam, *N. sg. m.*	-va, *Ac. sg.*	*Karm.* -ti, *L. pl.*
Heard	friendly-advice	this,	skill	in polished-expressions,

वाचां सर्वत्र वैचित्र्यं नीतिविद्यां ददाति च ॥ २ ॥

vâchâm	sarvatra	vaichitryam	nîti-vidyâm	dadâti	cha.	(2)
-ch, *G. pl.*	*Ind.*	-ya, *Ac. sg.*	*Ttp.* -yâ, *Ac. sg.*	dâ, 3 *sg. Pres. Par.*	*Ind.*	
of words	everywhere	variety,	behaviour-knowledge	gives	and.	

अजरामरवत्प्राज्ञो विद्यामर्थं च चिंतयेत् ।

ajara-amara-vat	prâjñas	vidyâm	artham	cha	chintayet
Ind.	-ña, *N. sg. m.*	-yâ, *Ac. sg.*	-tha, *Ac. sg.*	*Ind.*	chint, 3 *sg. Pot. Par.*
Not-growing old, not-dying-like,	the wise	knowledge	gain	and	should consider,

गृहीत इव केशेषु मृत्युना धर्ममाचरेत् ॥ ३ ॥

gṛihîtas	iva	keśeshu	mṛityunâ	dharmam	â-charet.	(3)
grah, *N. sg. m. past Ptc. Pass.*	*Ind.*	-śa, *L. pl.*	-yu, *I. sg.*	-ma, *Ac. sg.*	char *with* â, 3 *sg. Pot. Par.*	
seized	as if	by the hairs	by death,	virtue	he should practise.	

सर्वद्रव्येषु विद्यैव द्रव्यमाहुरनुत्तमं ।

sarva-dravyeshu	vidyâ	eva	dravyam	âhus	an-uttamam
Karm. -ya, L.pl.	-yâ, N.sg.	Ind.	-ya, N.sg.	ah, 3 pl. Perf. Par.	Bahuv. -ma, N.sg.n.
Among all-things	knowledge	only	a thing,	they say,	having nothing-beyond :

अहार्यत्वादनर्घ्यत्वादक्षयत्वाच्च सर्वदा ॥ ४ ॥

ahâryatvât	anarghyatvât	akshayatvât	cha	sarvadâ.	(4)
-tva, Ab.sg.	-tva, Ab.sg.	-tva, Ab.sg.	Ind.	Ind.	
from the irremov-ability,	from the inestima-bleness,	from the imperish-ableness,	and	always.	

संगमयति विद्यैव नीचगापि नरं सरित् ।

sam-gamayati	vidyâ	eva	nîcha-gâ	api	naram	sarit
gam with sam, 3 sg. Pres. Par. Caus.	-yâ, N.sg.	Ind.	-gâ, N.sg.f.	Ind.	-ra, Ac.sg.	-t, N.sg.
It causes to meet	knowledge	only,	low-going	even	a man	a stream

समुद्रमिव दुर्धर्षं नृपं भाग्यमतः परं ॥ ५ ॥

samudram	iva	dus-dharsham	nṛi-pam	bhâgyam	atas	param. (5)
-dra, Ac.sg.	Ind.	-sha, Ac.sg.m.	-pa, Ac.sg.	-ya, N.sg.	Ind.	-ra, Ac.sg.n. Adv.
the ocean	as,	a difficult to be approached	prince ;	happiness	thence	further.

विद्या ददाति विनयं विनयाद्याति पात्रतां ।

vidyâ	dadâti	vi-nayam	vi-nayât	yâti	pâtratâm
-yâ, N.sg.	dâ, 3 sg. Pres. Par.	-ya, Ac.sg.	-ya, Ab.sg.	yâ, 3 sg. Pres. Par.	-tâ, Ac.sg.
Knowledge	gives	good behaviour,	from good behav.	one goes	to worthiness,

पात्रत्वाद्धनमाप्नोति धनाद्धर्मं ततः सुखं ॥ ६ ॥

pâtratvât	dhanam	âpnoti	dhanât	dharmam	tatas	sukham. (6)
-tva, Ab.sg.	-na, Ac.sg.	âp, 3 sg. Pres. Par.	-na, Ab.sg.	-ma, Ac.sg.	Ind.	-kha, Ac.sg.
from worthiness	wealth	one obtains,	from wealth	religious merit,	thence	happiness.

विद्या शस्त्रस्य शास्त्रस्य द्वे विद्ये प्रतिपत्तये ।

vidyâ	śastrasya	śâstrasya	dve	vidye	prati-pattaye
-yâ, N.sg.	-tra, G.sg.	-tra, G.sg.	dvi, N.du.f.	-yâ, N.du.	-tti, D.sg.
The knowledge	of the weapon (and)	of a learned book,	two	kinds of knowledge	for acquirement,

आद्या हास्याय वृद्धत्वे द्वितीयाद्रियते सदा ॥ ७ ॥

âdyâ	hâsyâya	vṛiddhatve	dvitîyâ	â-driyate	sadâ. (7)
-yâ, N.sg.f.	-ya, D.sg.	-tva, L.sg.	-yâ, N.sg.f.	dṛi with â, 3 sg. Pres. Pass.	Ind.
the first	for ridicule	in old age,	the second	is respected	always.

यन्नवे भाजने लग्नः संस्कारो नान्यथा भवेत् ।

yad	nave	bhâjane	lagnas	sam-kâras	na	anyathâ	bhavet
Ind.	-va, L.sg.n.	-na, L.sg.	lag, N.sg.m. past Part. Pass.	-ra, N.sg.	Ind.	Ind.	bhû, 3 sg. Pot. Par.
Because	on a new	vessel	impressed	an ornament	not	otherwise	may be,

कथाछलेन बालानां नीतिस्तदिह कथ्यते ॥ ८ ॥

kathâ-chhalena	bâlânâm	nîtis	tad	iha	kathyate. (8)
Ttp. -la, I.sg.	-la, G.pl.	-ti, N.sg.	Ind.	Ind.	kath, 3 sg. Pres. Pass.
Through story-disguise	of children	prudence	therefore	here	is told.

मित्रलाभः सुहृद्भेदो विग्रहः संधिरेव च ।

mitra - lâbhas	suhṛid - bhedas	vi-grahas	sam-dhis	eva	cha
Tp. -bha, N. sg.	Tp. -da, N. sg.	-ha, N. sg.	-dhi, N. sg.	Ind.	Ind.
Friend-acquisition,	friend-separation,	war,	conciliation	even	and

पंचतंत्रात्तथान्यस्माद्ग्रंथादाकृष्य लिख्यते ॥ ९ ॥

pañcha-tantrât	tathâ	anyasmât	granthât	â-kṛishya	likhyate. (9)
Dvigu. -tra, Ab. sg.	Ind.	-ya, Ab. sg. m.	-tha, Ab. sg	kṛish, with â, Ger.	likh, 3 sg. Pres. Pass.
from the Pañchat.	and likewise	from another	book	having drawn	is written.

अस्ति भागीरथीतीरे पाटलिपुत्रनामधेयं नगरं । तत्र

asti	bhâgîrathî-tîre	pâṭaliputra-nâmadheyam	nagaram.	tatra
as, 3 sg. Pres. Par.	Tp. -ra, L. sg.	Bahuv. -ya, N. sg. n.	-ra, N. sg.	Ind.
There is	on the Bhâgîrathî-bank	Pâṭaliputra-named	a town.	Therein

सर्वस्वामिगुणोपेतः सुदर्शनो नाम नरपतिरासीत् ।

sarva-svâmin-guṇa -upetas	su-darśanas	nâma	nara-patis	âsît.
Tp. -ta, N. sg. m.	-na, N. sg.	-man, Ac. sg. Adv.	Tp. -ti, N. sg.	as, 3 sg. Impf. Par.
with all-lord's-qualities-endowed,	Sudarśana	by name	a man-lord	was.

स भूपतिरेकदा केनापि पठ्यमानं

sas	bhû-patis	ekadâ	kena-api	paṭhyamânam
tad, N. sg. m.	Tp. -ti, N. sg.	Ind.	kim, I. sg. m. Ind.	paṭh, Ac. sg. n. Pres. Ptc. Pass.
That	earth-lord	one day	by somebody	being recited

श्लोकद्वयं शुश्राव ।

śloka-dvayam	śuśrâva :
Tp. -ya, Ac. sg.	śru, 3 sg. Perf. Par.
a verse-couple	heard :

अनेकसंशयोच्छेदि परोक्षार्थस्य दर्शकं ।

aneka-saṁśaya-uchchhedi	paroksha-arthasya	darśakam
Tp. -din, N. sg. n.	Karm. -tha, G. sg.	-ka, N. sg. n.
Many-doubts-dispelling,	of invisible-matter	showing,

सर्वस्य लोचनं शास्त्रं यस्य नास्त्यंध एव सः ॥ १० ॥

sarvasya	lochanam	śâstram	yasya	na	asti	andhas	eva	sas. (10)
-va, G. sg. n.	-na, N. sg.	-tra, N. sg.	yad, G. sg. m.	Ind.	as, 3 sg. Pres. Par.	-dha, N. sg. m.	Ind.	tad, N. sg. m.
of everything	the eye,	learning	whose	not	is,	blind	indeed	he.

यौवनं धनसंपत्तिः प्रभुत्वमविवेकता ।

yauvanam	dhana-sampattis	prabhutvam	a-vivekatâ
-na, N. sg.	Tp. -ti, N. sg.	-tva, N. sg.	-tâ, N. sg.
Youth,	wealth-acquisition,	lordship,	want of judgment,

एकैकमप्यनर्थाय किमु यत्र चतुष्टयं ॥ ११ ॥

eka-ekam	api	an-arthâya	kim-u	yatra	chatushṭayam. (11)
-ka, N. sg. n.	Ind.	-tha, D. sg.	Ind.	Ind.	-ya, N. sg.
one-by-one	even	to disadvantage,	how much more	where	a tetrad.

इत्याकर्ण्यात्मनः पुत्राणामनधिगतशास्त्राणां नित्यम्

iti	â-karṇya	âtmanas	putrâṇâm	an-adhigata-śâstrâṇâm	nityam
Ind.	karṇ *with* â, *Ger.*	-man, *G. sg.*	-ra, *G. pl.*	*Bahuv.* -ra, *G. pl. m.*	-ya, *Ac. sg. n. Adv.*
Thus	having heard,	of himself	of the sons	who had not-read-books	constantly

उन्मार्गगामिनां शास्त्राननुष्ठानेनोद्विग्नमनाः स राजा चिंतयामास ।

unmârga-gâminâm	śâstra-ananushṭhânena	udvigna-manâs	sas	râjâ	chintayâm-âsa:
Ttp. -min, *G. pl. m.*	*Ttp.* -na, *I. sg.*	*Bahuv.* -nas, *N. sg. m.*	tad, *N. sg. m.*	-jan, *N. sg.*	chint, 3 *sg. Perf. Par.*
wrong-ways-going	by the book-neglect	with afflicted-mind,	that	king	was reflecting:

को ऽर्थः पुत्रेण जातेन यो न विद्वान्न धार्मिकः ।

kas	arthas	putreṇa	jâtena	yas	na	vidvân	na	dhârmikas
kim, *N. sg. m.*	-tha, *N. sg.*	-ra, *I. sg.*	jan, *I. sg. m. past Ptc. Pass.*	yad, *N. sg. m.*	*Ind.*	-vas, *N. sg. m.*	*Ind.*	-ka, *N. sg. m.*
What	use	by a son	born,	who	not	learned,	not	virtuous?

काणेन चक्षुषा किं वा चक्षुःपीडैव केवलं ॥ १२ ॥

kâneṇa	chakshushâ	kim	vâ	chakshus-pîḍâ	eva	kevalam. (12)
-ṇa, *I. sg. n.*	-shus, *I. sg.*	kim, *N. sg. n.*	*Ind.*	*Ttp.* -ḍâ, *N. sg.*	*Ind.*	-la, *Ac. sg. n. Adv.*
with an injured	eye	what	or?	an eye-pain	indeed	merely.

अजातमृतमूर्खाणां वरमाद्यौ न चांतिमः ।

ajâta-mṛita-mûrkhânâm	varam	âdyau	na	cha	antimas
Dvandva, -kha, *G. pl.*	-ra, *N. sg. n.*	-ya, *N. du. m.*	*Ind.*	*Ind.*	-ma, *N. sg. m.*
Of unborn-dead-foolish-ones	better	the two first	not	and	the last,

सकृद्दुःखकरावाद्यावंतिमस्तु पदे पदे ॥ १३ ॥

sakṛit	duḥkha-karau	âdyau	antimas	tu	pade	pade. (13)
Ind.	*Ttp.* -ra, *N. du. m.*	-ya, *N. du. m.*	-ma. *N. sg. m.*	*Ind.*	-da, *L. sg.*	-da, *L. sg.*
once	pain-causing	the two first,	the last	but	at step	at step.

किंच । स जातो येन जातेन याति वंशः समुन्नतिं ।

kim-cha,	sas	jâtas	yena	jâtena	yâti	vaṁśas	sam-ud-natim
Ind.	tad, *N. sg. m.*	jan, *N. sg. m. past Ptc. Pass.*	yad, *I. sg. m.*	jan, *I. sg. m. past Ptc. Pass.*	yâ, 3 *sg. Pres. Par.*	-śa, *N. sg.*	-ti, *Ac. sg.*
Moreover,	He	is born	through whom	born	goes	the family	to exaltation,

परिवर्तिनि संसारे मृतः को वा न जायते ॥ १४ ॥

pari-vartini	sam-sâre	mṛitas	kas	vâ	na	jâyate. (14)
-tin, *L. sg. m.*	-ra, *L. sg.*	mṛi, *N. sg. m. past Ptc. Pass.*	kim, *N. sg. m.*	*Ind.*	*Ind.*	jan, 3 *sg. Pres. Âtm.*
in the revolving	world	dead	who	or	not	is born?

गुणिगणगणनारंभे न पतति कठिनी सुसंभ्रमाद्यस्य ।

guṇin-gaṇa-gaṇanâ-ârambhe	na	patati	kaṭhinî	su-sambhramât	yasya
Ttp.- bha, *L. sg.*	*Ind.*	pat, 3 *sg. Pres. Par.*	-nî, *N. sg.*	*Karm*, -ma, *Ab. sg.*	yad, *G. sg. m.*
In the virtuous-multitude-enumerating-attempt	not	falls	the chalk	through great-haste	of whom,

तेनांबा यदि सुतिनी वद बंध्या कीदृशी नाम ॥ १५ ॥

tena	ambâ	yadi	sutinî	vada	bandhyâ	kîdṛiśî	nâma. (15)
tad, *I. sg. m.*	-bâ, *N. sg.*	*Ind.*	-nî, *N. sg.*	vad, 2 *sg. Imp. Par.*	-yâ, *N. sg.*	-dṛiś, *N. sg. f.*	-man, *Ac. sg. Adv.*
through him	the mother	if	son-possessed,	say,	barren	which (wife)	in truth?

अपि च। दाने तपसि शौर्ये च यस्य न प्रथितं मनः।

api cha,	dâne	tapasi	śauryo	cha	yasya	na	prathitam	manas
Ind. Ind.	-na, L.sg.	-pas, L.sg.	-ya, L.sg.	Ind.	yad, G. sg.m.	Ind.	prath, N.sg.n. past Ptc.Pass.	-nas, N. sg.n.
Also and,	In liberality,	in penance,	in heroism	and,	whose	not	praised	mind,

विद्यायामर्थलाभे च मातुरुच्चार एव सः॥ १६॥

vidyâyâm	artha-lâbhe	cha	mâtus	ud-châras	eva	sas. (16)
-yâ, L. sg.	Ttp. -bha, L. sg.	Ind.	-tṛi, G. sg.	-ra, N. sg.	Ind.	tad, N. sg. m.
in knowledge,	in wealth-acquisition	and,	a mother's	discharge	merely	he.

अपरं च। वरमेको गुणी पुत्रो न च मूर्खशतैरपि।

aparam	cha,	varam	ekas	guṇî	putras	na	cha	mûrkha-śatais	api
-ra, N.sg.n.	Ind.	-ra, N. sg. n.	-ka, N. sg. m.	-ṇin, N. sg. m.	-ra, N.sg.	Ind.	Ind.	Ttp. -ta, I. pl.	Ind.
Again	and,	Better	one	virtuous	son,	not	and	of fools-hundreds	even;

एकश्चंद्रस्तमो हंति न च तारागणैरपि॥ १७॥

ekas	chandras	tamas	hanti	na	cha	târâ-gaṇais	api. (17)
-ka, N. sg. m.	-ra, N. sg.	-mas, Ac. sg.	han, 3 sg. Pres. Par.	Ind.	Ind.	Ttp. -ṇa, I. pl.	Ind.
the one	moon	darkness	dispels,	not	and	star-heaps	even.

पुण्यतीर्थे कृतं येन तपः क्वाप्यतिदुष्करं।

puṇya-tîrthe	kṛitam	yena	tapas	kva-api	ati-dus-karam
Karm. -tha, L. sg.	kṛi, N. sg. n. past. Ptc. Pass.	yad, I. sg. m.	-pas, N. sg.	Ind. Ind.	Karm. -ra, N. sg. n.
At a holy-bathing place	performed	by whom	penance	where-ever	very-difficult

तस्य पुत्रो भवेद्वश्यः समृद्धो धार्मिकः सुधीः॥ १८॥

tasya	putras	bhavet	vaśyas	sam-ṛiddhas	dhârmikas	su-dhîs. (18)
tad, G. sg. m.	-ra, N. sg.	bhû, 3. sg. Pot. Par.	-ya, N. sg. m.	-dha, N. sg. m.	-ka, N. sg. m.	Bahuv. -dhî, N. sg. m.
of him	a son	will be	obedient,	prosperous,	righteous,	wise.

अर्थागमो नित्यमरोगिता च प्रियस्य भार्या प्रियवादिनी च।

artha-âgamas	nityam	a-rogitâ	cha	priyas	cha	bhâryâ	priya-vâdinî	cha
Ttp. -ma, N. sg.	-ya, Ac. sg. n. Adv.	-tâ, N. sg.	Ind.	-ya, N. sg. m.	Ind.	-yâ, N. sg.	Ttp. -din, N. sg. f.	Ind.
Wealth-affluence,	constantly	not-illness	and,	a friend	and,	a wife	kind-speaking	and,

वश्यश्च पुत्रोऽर्थकरी च विद्या षड्जीवलोकस्य सुखानि राजन्॥ १९॥

vaśyas	cha	putras	artha-karî	cha	vidyâ,	shaṭ	jîva-lokasya	sukhâni	râjan. (19)
-ya, N. sg. m.	Ind.	-ra, N. sg.	Ttp. -ra, N. sg. f.	Ind.	-yâ, N. sg.	shash, N.	Ttp. -ka, G. sg.	-kha, N. pl.	-jan, V. sg.
obedient	and	a son,	useful	and	a craft,	the six	of man-kind	pleasures,	O king.

को धन्यो बहुभिः पुत्रैः कुशूलापूरणाढकैः।

kas	dhanyas	bahubhis	putrais	kuśûla-âpûraṇa-âḍhakais,
kim, N. sg. m.	-ya, N. sg. m.	-hu, I. pl. m.	-ra, I. pl.	Karm. -ka, I. pl.
Who	wealthy	through many	sons,—	granary-filling-measures?

वरमेकः कुलालंबी यत्र विश्रूयते पिता॥ २०॥

varam	ekas	kula-âlambî	yatra	vi-śrûyate	pitâ (20)
-ra, N. sg. n.	-ka, N. sg. m.	Ttp. -bin, N. sg. m.	Ind.	śru with vi, 3 sg. Pres. Pass.	-tṛi, N. sg.
better	one	family-upholding,	in whom	is renowned	the father.

ऋणकर्ता पिता शत्रुर्माता च व्यभिचारिणी ।

ṛiṇa-kartâ	pitâ	śatrus	mâtâ	cha	vi-abhi-châriṇî
Ttp. -tṛi, *N. sg. m.*	-tṛi, *N. sg.*	-ru, *N. sg.*	-tṛi, *N. sg.*	*Ind.*	-rin, *N. sg. f.*
A debt-contracting	father	an enemy,	a mother	and	wanton,

भार्या रूपवती शत्रुः पुत्रः शत्रुरपंडितः ॥ २१ ॥

bhâryâ	rûpavatî	śatrus	putras	śatrus	a-paṇḍitas.	(21)
-yâ, *N. sg.*	-vat, *N. sg. f.*	-ru, *N. sg.*	-ra, *N. sg.*	-ru, *N. sg.*	*Karm.* -ta, *N. sg. m.*	
a wife	beautiful	an enemy,	a son	an enemy	not-learned.	

अनभ्यासे विषं विद्या अजीर्णे भोजनं विषं ।

an-abhyâse	visham	vidyâ	a-jîrṇe	bhojanam	visham
Karm. -sa, *L. sg.*	-sha, *N. sg.*	-yâ, *N. sg.*	*Karm.* -ṇa, *L. sg.*	-na, *N. sg.*	-sha, *N. sg.*
In want of practice	poison	knowledge,	in indigestion	food	poison,

विषं सभा दरिद्रस्य वृद्धस्य तरुणी विषं ॥ २२ ॥

visham	sabhâ	daridrasya	vṛiddhasya	taruṇî	visham.	(22)
-sha, *N. sg.*	-bhâ, *N. sg.*	-ra, *G. sg. m.*	-dha, *G. sg. m.*	-ṇa, *N. sg. f.*	-sha, *N. sg.*	
poison	company	of the poor,	of an old man	a young wife	poison.	

यस्य कस्य प्रसूतो ऽपि गुणवान्पूज्यते नरः ।

yasya	kasya	pra-sûtas	api	guṇavân	pûjyate	naras
yad, *G. sg. m.*	kim, *G. sg. m.*	sû *with* pra, *N. sg. m. past Ptc. Pass.*	*Ind.*	-vat, *N. sg. m.*	pûj, 3 *sg. Pres. Pass.*	-ra, *N. sg.*
Of whom	- soever	engendered	also,	virtuous	is honoured	a man,

धनुर्वंशविशुद्धो ऽपि निर्गुणः किं करिष्यति ॥ २३ ॥

dhanus	vaṁśa-viśuddhas	api	nis-guṇas	kim	karishyati.	(23)
-nu, *N. sg.*	*Ttp.* -dha, *N. sg. m.*	*Ind.*	*Bahuv.* -ṇa, *N. sg. m.*	kim, *Ac. sg. n.*	kṛi, 3 *sg. Fut. Par.*	
a bow	stem-faultless	also,	stringless	what	will it do?	

हा हा पुत्रक नाधीत सुगतैतासु रात्रिषु ।

hâ	hâ	putraka	na adhi-ita	su-gata	etâsu	râtrishu
Ind.	*Ind.*	-ka, *V. sg.*	*Ind.* i *with* adhi, *V. sg. m. past Ptc. Pass.*	*Karm.* -ta, *V. sg. m.*	etad, *L. pl. f.*	-ri, *L. pl.*
Ah,	ah,	O boy,	not-learned,	pleasantly-faring	in these	nights!

तेन त्वं विदुषां मध्ये पंके गौरिव सीदसि ॥ २४ ॥

tena	tvam	vidushâm	madhye	paṅke	gaus iva	sîdasi.	(24)
tad, *I. sg. n.*	yushmad, *N. sg.*	-vas, *G. pl. m.*	-ya, *L. sg.*	-ka, *L. sg.*	go, *N. sg.* *Ind.*	sad, 2 *sg. Pres. Par.*	
therefore	thou	of the learned	in the midst,	in a mire	cow-like,	thou sittest.	

तत्कथमिदानीमेते मम पुत्रा गुणवंतः क्रियंतां ।

tad	katham	idânîm	ete	mama	putrâs	guṇavantas	kriyantâm?
Ind.	*Ind.*	*Ind.*	etad, *N. pl. m.*	asmad, *G. sg.*	-ra, *N. pl.*	-vat, *N. pl. m.*	kṛi, 3 *pl. Imp. Pass.*
Then	how	now	these	of me	the sons	virtuous	shall be made?

आहारनिद्राभयमैथुनं च सामान्यमेतत्पशुभिर्नराणां ।

âhâra-nidrâ-bhaya-maithunam	cha	sâmânyam	etad	paśubhis	narâṇâm
Dvandva. -na, *N. sg.*	*Ind.*	-ya, *N. sg.*	etad, *N. sg. n.*	-śu, *I. pl.*	-ra, *G. pl.*
Feeding-sleep-fear-love	and	common property	this	with animals	of men,

धर्मो हि तेषामधिको विशेषो धर्मेण हीनाः पशुभिः समानाः ॥ २५ ॥

dharmas	hi	teshâm	adhikas	vi-śeshas	dharmeṇa	hînâs	paśubhis	samânâs. (25)
-ma, *N. sg.*	*Ind.*	tad, *G. pl. m.*	-ka, *N. sg. m.*	-sha, *N. sg.*	ma, *I. sg.*	hâ, *N. pl. m. past. Ptc. Pass.*	-śu, *I. pl.*	-na, *N. pl. m.*
Virtue	for	of them	the additional	special property;	of virtue	deprived	with animals	equal.

यतः । धर्मार्थकाममोक्षाणां यस्यैको ऽपि न विद्यते ।

yatas,	dharma-artha-kâma-mokshâṇâm	yasya	ekas	api	na	vidyate
Ind.	*Dvandva.* -sha, *G. pl.*	yad, *G. sg. m.*	-ka, *N. sg. m.*	*Ind.*	*Ind.*	vid, 3 *sg. Pres. Pass.*
For,	Of virtue-wealth-desire-final liberation	of whom	one	even	not	is known,

अजगलस्तनस्येव तस्य जन्म निरर्थकं ॥ २६ ॥

aja-gala-stanasya	iva	tasya	janma	nis-arthakam. (26)
Ttp. -na, *G. sg.*	*Ind.*	tad, *G. sg. m.*	-man, *N. sg.*	*Bahuv.* -ka, *N. sg. n.*
of the he-goat-throat-nipple	like	of him	the birth	useless.

यच्चोच्यते । आयुः कर्म च वित्तं च विद्या निधनमेव च ।

yad	cha	uchyate,	âyus	karma	cha	vittam	cha	vidyâ	ni-dhanam	eva	cha
yad, *N. sg. n.*	*Ind.*	vach, 3 *sg. Pres. Pass.*	-yus, *N. sg.*	-man, *N. sg.*	*Ind.*	-ta, *N. sg.*	*Ind.*	-yâ, *N. sg.*	-na, *N. sg.*	*Ind.*	*Ind.*
What	and	is said,	Life,	action	and,	riches	and,	knowledge,	death	even	and,

पंचैतान्यपि सृज्यंते गर्भस्थस्यैव देहिनः ॥ २७ ॥

pañcha	etâni	api	sṛijyante	garbha-sthasya	eva	dehinas. (27)
-chan, *N.*	etad, *N. pl. n.*	*Ind.*	sṛij, 3 *pl. Pres. Pass.*	*Ttp.* -stha, *G. sg. m.*	*Ind.*	-hin, *G. sg. m.*
five	these	also	are produced	of the in the womb-standing	even	being.

किंच । अवश्यंभाविनो भावा भवंति महतामपि ।

kim-cha	avaśyam-bhâvinas	bhâvâs	bhavanti	mahatâm	api
Ind.	-vin, *N. pl. m.*	-va, *N. pl.*	bhû, 3 *pl. Pres. Par.*	-hat, *G. pl. m.*	*Ind.*
Moreover,	Necessarily-becoming	the conditions	are	of the great	even;—

नग्नत्वं नीलकंठस्य महाहिशयनं हरेः ॥ २८ ॥

nagnatvam	nîla-kaṇṭhasya	mahâ-ahi-śayanam	hares. (28)
-tva, *N. sg.*	*Bahuv.* -ṭha, *G. sg. m.*	*Ttp.* -na, *N. sg.*	-ri, *G. sg.*
the nakedness	of the blue-necked,	the on the great-serpent-lying	of Hari.

अपि च । यदभावि न तद्भावि भावि चेन्न तदन्यथा ।

api cha,	yad	a-bhâvi	na	tad	bhâvi	bhâvi	ched	na	tad	anyathâ
Ind. Ind.	yad, *N. sg. n.*	*Karm.* -vin, *N. sg. n.*	*Ind.*	tad, *N. sg. n.*	-vin, *N. sg. n.*	-vin, *N. sg. n.*	*Ind.*	*Ind.*	tad, *N. sg. n.*	*Ind.*
Also and,	What	not-to be,	not	that	to be;	to be	if,	not	that	otherwise,

इति चिंताविषघ्नो ऽयमगदः किं न पीयते ॥ २९ ॥

iti	chintâ-visha-ghnas	ayam	a-gadas	kim	na	pîyate? (29)
Ind.	*Ttp.* -ghna, *N. sg. m.*	idam, *N. sg. m.*	-da, *N. sg.*	*Ind.*	*Ind.*	pâ, 3 *sg. Pres. Pass.*
thus	reflection-poison-destroying	this	medicine	why	not	is drunk?

एतत्कार्याक्षमाणां केषांचिदालस्यवचनं ।

etad	kârya-akshamâṇâm	keshâm-chid	âlasya-vachanam.
etad, *N. sg. n.*	*Ttp.* -ma, *G. pl. m.*	kim, *G. pl. m. Ind.*	*Ttp.* -na, *N. sg. n.*
This	of duty-incapable	of some	the laziness-speech !

न दैवमपि संचिंत्य त्यजेदुद्योगमात्मनः ।

na	daivam	api	sam-chintya	tyajet	ud-yogam	âtmanas
Ind.	-va, *Ac. sg.*	*Ind.*	chint with sam, *Ger.*	tyaj, 3 *sg. Pot. Par.*	-ga, *Ac. sg.*	-man, *G. sg.*
Not,	fate	even	reflecting on,	one should give up	the exertion	of one self,

अनुद्योगेन तैलानि तिलेभ्यो नाप्तुमर्हति ॥ ३० ॥

an-udyogena	tailâni	tilebhyas	na	âptum	arhati. (30)
Karm. -ga, *I. sg.*	-la, *Ac. pl.*	-la, *Ab. pl.*	*Ind.*	âp, *Inf.*	arh, 3 *sg. Pres. Par.*
with no-exertion	sesamum oil	from sesamum seeds	not	obtain	one can.

अन्यच्च । उद्योगिनं पुरुषसिंहमुपैति लक्ष्मीः

anyad cha,	udyoginam	purusha-siṁham	upa-eti	lakshmîs,
-ya, *N. sg. n. Ind.*	-gin, *Ac. sg. m.*	*Karm.* -ha, *Ac. sg.*	i with upa, 3 *sg. Pres. Par.*	-mî, *N. sg.*
Again and,	The exerting himself	man-lion	approaches	Fortune,

दैवेन देयमिति कापुरुषा वदंति ।

daivena	deyam	iti	kâ-purushâs	vadanti,
-va, *I. sg.*	dâ, *N. sg. n. Fut. Ptc. Pass.*	*Ind.*	*Karm.* -sha, *N. pl.*	vad, 3 *pl. Pres. Par.*
'by Fate	it must be given,'	thus	weak-men	say;

दैवं निहत्य कुरु पौरुषमात्मशक्त्या

daivam	ni-hatya	kuru	paurusham	âtman-śaktyâ,
-va, *Ac. sg.*	han with ni, *Ger.*	kṛi, 2 *sg. Imp. Par.*	-sha, *Ac. sg.*	*Ttp.* -ti, *I. sg.*
Fate	down-striking	do	a man's work	with thy own-power,

यत्ने कृते यदि न सिध्यति कोऽत्र दोषः ॥ ३१ ॥

yatne	kṛite	yadi	na	sidhyati	kas	atra	doshas ? (31)
-na, *L. sg.*	kṛi, *L. sg. m. past Ptc. Pass.*	*Ind.*	*Ind.*	sidh, 3 *sg. Pres. Par.*	kim, *N. sg. m.*	*Ind.*	-sha, *N. sg.*
The effort	having been made,	if	not	there is success,	what	therein	fault ?

यथा ह्येकेन चक्रेण न रथस्य गतिर्भवेत् ।

yathâ	hi	ekena	chakreṇa	na	rathasya	gatis	bhavet
Ind.	*Ind.*	-ka, *I. sg. n.*	-ra, *I. sg.*	*Ind.*	-tha, *G. sg.*	-ti, *N. sg.*	bhû, 3 *sg. Pot. Par.*
As	for	with a single	wheel	not	of a carriage	movement	can be,

एवं पुरुषकारेण विना दैवं न सिध्यति ॥ ३२ ॥

evam	purusha-kâreṇa	vinâ	daivam	na	sidhyati. (32)
Ind.	*Ttp.* -ra, *I. sg.*	*Ind.*	-va, *N. sg.*	*Ind.*	sidh, 3 *sg. Pres. Par.*
thus	a man's-work	without,	fate	not	does succeed.

तथा च । पूर्वजन्मकृतं कर्म तद्दैवमिति कथ्यते ।

tathâ	cha,	pûrva-janman-kṛitam	karma	tad	daivam	iti	kathyate
Ind.	*Ind.*	*Ttp.* -ta, *N. sg. n.*	-man, *N. sg.*	tad, *N. sg. n.*	-va *N. sg.*	*Ind.*	kath, 3 *sg. Pres. Pass.*
Thus	and,	In a former-birth-done	action	that	'fate'	thus	is called,

तस्मात्पुरुषकारेण यत्नं कुर्यादतंद्रितः ॥ ३३ ॥

tasmât	purusha-kâreṇa	yatnam	kuryât	a-tandritas. (33)
tad, *Ab. sg. n. Adv.*	*Ttp.* -ra, *I. sg.*	-na, *Ac. sg.*	kṛi, 3 *sg. Pot. Par.*	*Karm.* -ta, *N. sg. m.*
therefore	with man's-work	effort	one should make	unwearied.

यथा मृत्पिंडतः कर्ता कुरुते यद्यदिच्छति ।

yathâ	mṛid-piṇḍa-tas	kartâ	kurute	yad-yad	ichchhati
Ind.	*Ttp.* -ḍa, *with Ab. aff.* tas	-tṛi, *N. sg. m.*	kṛi, 3 *sg. Pres. Âtm.*	yad, *Ac. sg. n.*	ish, 3 *sg. Pres. Par.*
As	from a clay-lump	the worker	makes for himself	whatever	he wishes,

एवमात्मकृतं कर्म मानवः प्रतिपद्यते ॥ ३४ ॥

evam	âtman-kṛitam	karma	mânavas	prati-padyate. (34)
Ind.	*Ttp.* -ta, *Ac. sg. n.*	-man, *Ac. sg.*	-va, *N. sg.*	pad *with* prati, 3 *sg. Pres. Âtm.*
thus	the by himself-done	action	man	obtains.

काकतालीयवत्प्राप्तं दृष्ट्वापि निधिमग्रतः ।

kâka-tâlîya-vat	pra-âptam	dṛishṭvâ	api	ni-dhim	agra-tas
Ind.	âp *with* pra, *Ac. sg. m. past Ptc. Pass.*	dṛiś, *Ger.*	*Ind.*	-dhi, *Ac. sg.*	-ra *with Ab. aff.* tas
As-in (the story of) the Crow-and the Palmfruit,	reached	having seen	even	a treasure	in front,

न स्वयं दैवमादत्ते पुरुषार्थमपेक्षते ॥ ३५ ॥

na	svayam	daivam	â-datte	purusha-artham	apa-îkshate. (35)
Ind.	*Ind.*	-va, *N. sg.*	dâ *with* â, 3 *sg. Pres. Âtm.*	*Ttp.* -tha, *Ac. sg.*	îksh *with* apa, 3 *sg. Pres. Âtm.*
not	of itself	fate	takes (it) up,	man's-exertion	it expects.

उद्यमेन हि सिध्यंति कार्याणि न मनोरथैः ।

ud-yamena	hi	sidhyanti	kâryâṇi	na	manas-rathais
-ma, *I. sg.*	*Ind.*	sidh, 3 *pl. Pres. Par.*	-ya, *N. pl.*	*Ind.*	*Ttp.* -tha, *I. pl.*
Through exertion	indeed	succeed	works,	not	through wishes,

न हि सुप्तस्य सिंहस्य प्रविशंति मुखे मृगाः ॥ ३६ ॥

na	hi	suptasya	siṁhasya	pra-viśanti	mukhe	mṛigâs. (36)
Ind.	*Ind.*	svap, *G. sg. m. past. Ptc. Pass.*	-ha, *G. sg.*	viś *with* pra, 3 *pl. Pres. Par.*	-kha, *L. sg.*	-ga, *N. pl.*
not	indeed	of the sleeping	lion	enter	into the mouth	the deer.

मातृपितृकृताभ्यासो गुणितामेति बालकः ।

mâtṛi-pitṛi-kṛita-abhyâsas	guṇitâm	eti	bâlakas
Bahuv. -sa, *N. sg. m.*	-tâ, *Ac. sg.*	i, 3 *sg. Pres. Par.*	-ka, *N. sg.*
By mother-and father-made-to study	to the state of a virtuous man	comes	a child,

न गर्भच्युतिमात्रेण पुत्रो भवति पंडितः ॥ ३७ ॥

na	garbha-chyuti-mâtreṇa	putras	bhavati	paṇḍitas. (37)
Ind.	*Ttp.* -ra, *I. sg.*	-ra, *N. sg.*	bhû, 3 *sg. Pres. Par.*	-ta, *N. sg. m.*
not	by birth-alone	a son	becomes	learned.

माता शत्रुः पिता वैरी येन बालो न पाठितः ।

mâtâ	śatrus	pitâ	vairî	yena	bâlas	na	pâṭhitas
-tṛi, *N. sg.*	-ru, *N. sg.*	-tṛi, *N. sg.*	-rin, *N. sg. m.*	yad, *I. sg. m.*	-la, *N. sg.*	*Ind.*	paṭh, *N. sg. m. past Ptc. Pass. Caus.*
The mother	an enemy,	the father	hostile,	by whom	a boy	not	made to study,

न शोभते सभामध्ये हंसमध्ये वको यथा ॥ ३८ ॥

na	śobhate	sabhâ-madhye	haṁsa-madhye	vakas	yathâ. (38)
Ind.	śubh, 3 *sg. Pres. Âtm.*	*Ttp.* -ya, *L. sg.*	*Ttp.* -ya, *L. sg.*	-ka, *N. sg.*	*Ind.*
not	does he shine	in an assembly-midst,	in the flamingo-midst	a crane	like.

रूपयौवनसंपन्ना विशालकुलसंभवाः ।

rûpa-yauvana-sampannâs — viśâla-kula-sambhavâs
Ttp. -na, *N. pl. m.* (*rt.* pad *with* sam, *past Ptc. Pass.*) — *Bahuv.* -va, *N. pl. m.*
Beauty-youth-endowed — of noble-race-sprung,

विद्याहीना न शोभंते निर्गंधा इव किंशुकाः ॥ ३९ ॥

vidyâ-hînâs — na — śobhante — nis-gandhâs — iva — kiṁśukâs. (39)
Ttp. -na, *N. pl. m.* (*rt.* hâ) — *Ind.* — śubh, 3 *pl. Pres. Âtm.* — *Bahuv.* -dha, *N. pl. m.* — *Ind.* — -ka, *N. pl.*
knowledge-destitute ones — not — shine, — scent-less — like — kiṁśuka flowers.

मूर्खो ऽपि शोभते तावत्सभायां वस्त्रवेष्टितः ।

mûrkhas — api — śobhate — tâvat — sabhâyâm — vastra-veshṭitas
-kha, *N. sg. m.* — *Ind.* — śubh, 3 *sg. Pres. Âtm.* — -vat, *Ac. sg. n. Adv.* — -bhâ, *L. sg.* — *Ttp.* -ta, *N. sg. m.* (*rt.* veshṭ).
A fool — also — shines — so long — in an assembly — garment-dressed,

तावच्च शोभते मूर्खो यावत्किंचिन्न भाषते ॥ ४० ॥

tâvat — cha — śobhate — mûrkhas — yâvat — kim - chid — na — bhâshate. (40)
-vat, *Ac. sg. n. Adv.* — *Ind.* — śubh, 3 *sg. Pres. Âtm.* — -kha, *N. sg. m.* — -vat, *Ac. sg. n. Adv.* — kim, *Ac. sg. n.* — *Ind.* — *Ind.* — bhâsh, 3 *sg. Pres. Âtm.*
So long — and — shines — a fool — as long as — anything — not — he says.

एतच्चिंतयित्वा स राजा पंडितसभां कारितवान् ।

etad — chintayitvâ — sas — râjâ — paṇḍita-sabhâm — kâritavân.
etad, *Ac. sg. n.* — chint, *Ger.* — tad, *N. sg. m.* — -jan, *N. sg. m.* — *Ttp.* -bhâ, *Ac. sg.* — kṛi, *N. sg. m. past Ptc. Par. Caus.*
This — having thought — that — King — a wise men-assembly — caused to be made.

राजोवाच । भो भोः पंडिताः श्रूयतां । अस्ति

râjâ — uvâcha: — bho — bhos — paṇḍitâs, — śrûyatâm; — asti
-jan, *N. sg.* — vach, 3 *sg. Perf. Par.* — *Ind.* — *Ind.* — -ta, *V. pl. m.* — śru, 3 *sg. Imp. Pass.* — as, 3 *sg. Pres. Par.*
The King — said: — O — ye — wise, — be it heard; — Is there

कश्चिदेवंभूतो विद्वान्यो मम पुत्राणां नित्यमु-

kas-chid — evam-bhûtas — vidvân — yas — mama — putrâṇâm — nityam
kim, *N. sg. m., Ind.* — *Karm.* -ta, *N. sg. m.* — -vas, *N. sg. m.* — yad, *N. sg. m.* — asmad, *G. sg.* — -ra, *G. pl.* — *Ind.*
any one — such a — sage, — who — of me — of the sons — constantly

न्मार्गगामिनामनधिगतशास्त्राणामिदानीं नीतिशास्त्रोपदेशेन पुनर्जन्म

unmârga-gâminâm — an-adhigata-śâstrâṇâm — idânîm — nîti-śâstra-upadeśena — punar-janma
Ttp. -min, *G. pl. m.* — *Bahuv.* -ra, *G. pl. m.* — *Ind.* — *Ttp.* -śa, *I. sg.* — *Karm.* -man, *Ac. sg.*
wrong-ways-going, — who have not-read-books, — now — by behaviour-book-instruction — again-birth

कारयितुं समर्थः ।

kârayitum — sam-arthas?
kṛi, *Inf. Caus.* — -tha, *N. sg. m.*
to effect — (is) capable?

यतः । काचः कांचनसंसर्गाद्धत्ते मारकतीं द्युतिं ।

yatas, — kâchas — kâñchana-saṁsargât — dhatte — mârakatîm — dyutim
Ind. — -cha, *N. sg.* — *Ttp.* -ga, *Ab. sg.* — dhâ, 3 *sg. Pres. Âtm.* — -ta, *Ac. sg. f.* — -ti, *Ac. sg.*
For, — Glass — from gold-proximity — accepts — emerald — splendour;

तथा सत्संनिधानेन मूर्खो याति प्रवीणतां ॥ ४१ ॥

tathâ	sat-sannidhânena	mûrkhas	yâti	praviṇatâm.	(41)
Ind.	*Ttp.* -na, *I. sg.*	-kha, *N. sg. m.*	yâ, 3 *sg. Pres. Par.*	-tâ, *Ac. sg.*	
thus	through the good-vicinity	a fool	goes	to cleverness.	

उक्तं च । हीयते हि मतिस्तात हीनैः सह समागमात् ।

uktam	cha,	hîyate	hi	matis	tâta	hînais	saha	sam-â-gamât
vach, *N. sg. n. past Ptc. Pass.*	*Ind.*	hâ, 3 *sg. Pres. Pass.*	*Ind.*	-ti, *N. sg.*	-ta, *V. sg.*	hâ, *I. pl. m. past Ptc. Pass.*	*Ind. Prep.*	-ma, *Ab. sg.*
Said	and,	It is lowered	truly	the intelligence,	my dear,	low persons	with	through intercourse,

समैश्च समतामेति विशिष्टैश्च विशिष्टतां ॥ ४२ ॥

samais	cha	samatâm	eti	vi-śishṭais	cha	viśishṭatâm.	(42)
-ma, *I. pl. m.*	*Ind.*	-tâ, *Ac. sg.*	i, 3 *sg. Pres. Par.*	-ta, *I. pl. m.*	*Ind.*	-tâ, *Ac. sg.*	
with equals	and	to equality	it goes,	with distinguished	and	to distinction.	

अत्रांतरे विष्णुशर्मनामा महापंडितः सकलनीतिशास्त्रतत्त्वज्ञो

atra	antare	vishṇuśarman-nâmâ	mahâ-paṇḍitas	sakala-nîti-śâstra-tattva-jñas
Ind.	-ra, *L. sg.*	*Bahuv.* -man, *N. sg. m.*	*Karm.* -ta, *N. sg. m.*	*Ttp.* -jña, *N. sg. m.*
There	meanwhile	Vishṇuśarman-named	a great-scholar	of all-behaviour-books-the essence-knowing

बृहस्पतिरिवाब्रवीत् । देव महाकुलसंभूता एते राजपुत्राः ।

bṛihas-patis	iva	abravît:	deva,	mahâ-kula-sambhûtâs	ete	râjan-putrâs;
Ttp. -ti, *N. sg.*	*Ind.*	brû, 3 *sg. Impf. Par.*	-va, *V. sg.*	*Ttp.* -ta, *N. pl. m.*	etad, *N. pl. m.*	*Ttp.* -ra, *N. pl.*
Bṛihaspati	like	spoke:	Sire,	from a great-family-sprung	these	king's-sons;

तन्मया नीतिं ग्राहयितुं शक्यंते ।

tad	mayâ	nîtim	grâhayitum	śakyante.
Ind.	asmad, *I. sg.*	-ti, *Ac. sg.*	grah, *Inf. Caus.*	śak, 3 *pl. Pres. Pass.*
therefore	by me	behaviour	to accept	they can be made.

यतः । नाद्रव्ये निहिता काचित्क्रिया फलवती भवेत् ।

yatas,	na	a-dravye	ni-hitâ	kâ-chid	kriyâ	phalavatî	bhavet
Ind.	*Ind.*	*Karm.* -ya, *L. sg.*	dhâ *with* ni, *N. sg. f. past Ptc. Pass.*	kim, *N. sg. f.* *Ind.*	-yâ, *N. sg.*	-vat, *N. sg. f.*	bhû, 3 *sg. Pot. Par.*
For,	Not	on a worthless-object	bestowed	any	labour	fruitful	can be,

न व्यापारशतेनापि शुकवत्पाठ्यते बकः ॥ ४३ ॥

na	vyâpâra-śatena	api	śuka-vat	pâṭhyate	vakas	(43)
Ind.	*Ttp.* -ta, *I. sg.*	*Ind.*	*Ind.*	paṭh, 3 *sg. Pres. Pass. Caus.*	-ka, *N. sg.*	
not	by a hundred of exertions	even	parrot-like	is made to talk	a crane.	

अन्यच्च । अस्मिंस्तु निर्गुणं गोत्रे नापत्यमुपजायते ।

anyad	cha,	asmin	tu	nis-guṇam	gotre	na	apatyam	upa-jâyate
-ya, *N. sg. n.*	*Ind.*	idam, *L. sg. n.*	*Ind.*	*Bahuv.* -ṇa, *N. sg. n.*	-ra, *L. sg.*	*Ind.*	-ya, *N. sg.*	jan *with* upa, 3. *sg. Pres. Pass.*
Again	and,	In this	but	void-of virtue	family	not	offspring	is born,

आकरे पद्मरागाणां जन्म काचमणेः कुतः ॥ ४४ ॥

â-kare	padma-râgâṇâm	janma	kâcha-maṇes	kutas.	(44)
-ra, *L. sg.*	*Bahuv.* -ga, *G. pl.*	-man, *N. sg.*	*Karm.* -ṇi, *G. sg.*	*Ind.*	
In a mine	of rubies	the production	of crystal	whence?	

अतो ऽहं षण्मासाभ्यंतरे तव पुत्रान्नीतिशास्त्राभिज्ञान्करिष्यामि ।

atas	aham	shash-mâsa-abhyantare	tava	putrân	nîti-śâstra-abhijñân	karishyâmi.
Ind.	asmad, *N. sg.*	*Ttp.* -ra, *L. sg.*	yushmad, *G. sg.*	-ra, *Ac. pl.*	*Ttp.* -jña, *Ac. pl. m.*	kṛi, 1 *sg. Fut. Par.*
Therefore	I	in a six-months-interval	of thee	the sons	behaviour-book-knowing	will make.

राजा सविनयं पुनरुवाच ।

râjâ	sa-vinayam	punar	uvâcha:
-jan, *N. sg.*	*Avyay.*	*Ind.*	vach, 3 *sg. Perf. Par.*
The king	graciously	again	spoke:

कीटो ऽपि सुमनःसंगादारोहति सतां शिरः ।

Kîṭas	api	sumanas-saṅgât	â-rohati	satâm	śiras
-ṭa, *N. sg.*	*Ind.*	*Ttp.* -ga, *Ab. sg.*	ruh *with* â, 3 *sg. Pres. Par.*	-t, *G. pl.*	-ras, *Ac. sg.*
A worm	even	through flower-attachment	ascends	of the noble	the head,

अश्मापि याति देवत्वं महद्भिः सुप्रतिष्ठितः ॥ ४५ ॥

aśmâ	api	yâti	devatvam	mahadbhis	su-pratishṭhitas. (45)
-man, *N. sg.*	*Ind.*	yâ, 3 *sg. Pres. Par.*	-tva, *Ac. sg.*	-hat, *I. pl. m.*	*Karm.* -ta, *N. sg. m.* (*rt.* sthâ)
a stone	even	goes	to divinity	by the great	well-set up.

अन्यच्च । यथोदयगिरेर्द्रव्यं संनिकर्षेण दीप्यते ।

anyad	cha,	yathâ	udaya-gires	dravyam	sam-ni-karsheṇa	dîpyate
-ya, *N. sg. n*	*Ind.*	*Ind.*	*Ttp.* -ri, *L. sg.*	-ya, *N. sg.*	-sha, *I. sg.*	dîp, 3 *sg. Pres. Âtm.*
Again	and,	As	of the sunrise-mountain	a thing	through the proximity	shines,

तथा सत्संनिधानेन हीनवर्णो ऽपि दीप्यते ॥ ४६ ॥

tathâ	sat-sannidhânena	hîna-varṇas	api	dîpyate. 46
Ind.	*Ttp.* -na, *I. sg.*	*Bahuv.* -ṇa, *N. sg. m.*	*Ind.*	dîp, 3 *sg. Pres. Âtm.*
thus	through the noble-vicinity	one of low-caste	even	shines.

गुणा गुणज्ञेषु गुणा भवंति

guṇâs	guṇa-jñeshu	guṇâs	bhavanti
-ṇa, *N. pl.*	*Ttp.* -jña, *L. pl. m.*	-ṇa, *N. pl.*	bhû, 3 *pl. Pres. Par.*
Virtues	in virtue-knowers	virtues	are,

ते निर्गुणं प्राप्य भवंति दोषाः ।

te	nis-guṇam	pra-âpya	bhavanti	doshâs;
tad, *N. pl. m.*	*Bahuv.* -ṇa, *Ac. sg. m.*	âp *with* pra, *Ger.*	bhû, 3 *pl. Pres. Par.*	-sha, *N. pl.*
they	to a virtue-void	having come	become	vices;

आस्वाद्यतोयाः प्रभवंति नद्यः

âsvâdya-toyâs	pra-bhavanti	nadyas
Bahuv. -ya, *N. pl. f.*	bhû *with* pra, 3 *pl. Pres. Par.*	-dî, *N. pl.*
savoury-water holding	rise	rivers,

समुद्रमासाद्य भवंत्यपेयाः ॥ ४७ ॥

samudram	â-sâdya	bhavanti	a-peyâs (47)
-ra, *Ac. sg.*	sad *with* â, *Ger. Caus.*	bhû, 3 *pl. Pres. Par.*	*Karm.* -ya, *N. pl. f.*
the sea	having reached,	they are	undrinkable.

तदेतेषामस्मत्पुत्राणां नीतिशास्त्रोपदेशाय भवंतः प्रमाणं।

tad	eteshâm	asmat-putrâṇâm	nîti-śâstra-upadeśâya	bhavantas	pra-mâṇam.
Ind.	etad, *G. pl. m.*	*Ttp.* -ra, *G. pl.*	*Ttp.* -śa, *D. sg.*	-vat, *N. pl. m.*	-ṇa, *N. sg.*
Therefore	of these	of us-the sons	for the behaviour- book-instruction	you	the authority.

इत्युक्त्वा तस्य विष्णुशर्मणो बहुमानपुरःसरं पुत्रान्

iti	uktvâ	tasya	vishṇu-śarmaṇas	bahumâna-puraḥsaram	putrân
Ind.	vach, *Ger.*	tad, *G. sg. m.*	-man, *G. sg.*	*Ind.*	-ra, *Ac. pl*
Thus	having said	of that	Vishṇuśarman	by respect preceded	the sons

समर्पितवान्। अथ प्रासादपृष्ठे सुखोपविष्टानां राजपुत्राणां

sam-arpitavân.	atha	prâsâda-pṛishṭhe	sukha-upavishṭânâm	râjan-putrâṇâm
ṛi, *with* sam, *N. sg. m.* *past. Ptc. Par. Caus.*	*Ind.*	*Ttp.* -ṭha, *L. sg.*	*Karm.* -ṭa, *G. pl. m.* (*rt.* viś *with* upa).	*Tpt.* -ra, *G. pl.*
he made over.	Now	on the palace- terrace	of the comfortably- seated	king's-sons

पुरस्तात्प्रस्तावक्रमेण स पंडितोऽब्रवीत्।

purastât	prastâva-krameṇa	sas	paṇḍitas	abravît:
Ind.	*Ttp.* -ma, *I. sg*	tad, *N. sg. m.*	-ta, *N. sg. m.*	brû, 3 *sg. Impf. Par.*
in front	of introduction-by way	that	learned man	said:

काव्यशास्त्रविनोदेन कालो गच्छति धीमतां।

kâvya-śâstra-vinodena	kâlas	gachchhati	dhîmatâm
Ttp. -da, *I. sg.*	-la, *N. sg.*	gam, 3 *sg. Pres. Par.*	-mat, *G. pl. m.*
Through poem-book-entertainment	the time	passes away	of the wise,

व्यसनेन च मूर्खाणां निद्रया कलहेन वा ॥ ४८ ॥

vyasanena	cha	mûrkhâṇâm	nidrayâ	kalahena	vâ	(48)
-na. *I. sg.*	*Ind.*	-kha, *G. pl. m.*	-drâ, *I. sg.*	-ha, *I. sg.*	*Ind.*	
through vice	and	of fools,	through sleep,	through quarrel	or.	

तद्भवतां विनोदाय काककूर्मादीनां विचित्रां

tad	bhavatâm	vi-nodâya	kâka-kûrma-âdinâm	vichitrâm
Ind.	-vat, *G. pl. m.*	-da, *D. sg.*	*Bahuv.* -di, *G. pl, m.*	-tra, *Ac. sg. f.*
Therefore	of you	for the entertainment	of the crow-the tortoise-etc.	the wonderful

कथां कथयामि। राजपुत्रैरुक्तं। आर्य कथ्यतां।

kathâm	kathayâmi.	râjan-putrais	uktam:	ârya	kathyatâm.
-thâ, *Ac. sg.*	kath, 1 *sg.* *Pres. Par.*	*Ttp.* -ra, *I. pl.*	vach, *N. sg. n. past* *Ptc. Pass.*	-ya, *V. sg.*	kath, 3 *sg. Imp. Pass*
story	I tell.	By the princes	said:	Reverend Sir,	it may be told.

विष्णुशर्मोवाच। शृणुत। संप्रति मित्रलाभः प्रस्तूयते यस्या-

vishṇu-śarmâ	uvâcha:	śṛiṇuta;	samprati	mitra-lâbhas	pra-stûyate,	yasya
-man, *N. sg.*	vach, 3 *sg.* *Perf. Par.*	śru, 2 *pl. Imp.* *Par.*	*Ind.*	*Ttp.* -bha, *N. sg.*	stu *with* pra, 3 *sg.* *Pres. Pass.*	yad, *G. sg. m.*
Vishṇuśarman	said:	Listen;	now	the friend- acquisition	is introduced,	of which

यमाद्यः श्लोकः ॥

ayam	âdyas	ślokas:
idam, *N. sg. m*,	-ya, *N. sg. m.*	-ka, *N. sg.*
this	the first	verse:

॥ मित्रलाभः ॥

MITRA-LÂBHAS.

Ttp. -bha, *N. sg.*

FRIEND-ACQUISITION.

असाधना वित्तहीना बुद्धिमंतः सुहृत्तमाः ।

a-sâdhanâs	vitta-hînâs	buddhimantas	suhṛittamâs
Bahuv. -na, *N. pl. m.*	*Ttp.* -na, *N. pl. m.* (*rt.* hâ).	-mat, *N. pl. m.*	su-hṛid, *N. pl. m. Superl.*
Having no-means,	of wealth-destitute,	the wise,	(if) very friendly,

साधयंत्याशु कार्याणि काककूर्ममृगाखुवत् ॥ १ ॥

sâdhayanti	âśu	kâryâṇi	kâka-kûrma-mṛiga-âkhu-vat.	(1)
sâdh, 3 *pl. Pres. Par. Caus.*	*Ac. sg. n.*, *Adv.*	-ya, *Ac. pl.*	*Dvandva, with aff.* vat, *Ind.*	
accomplish	quickly	purposes	like-the crow-the tortoise-the deer-the mouse.	

राजपुत्रा ऊचुः । कथमेतत् । विष्णुशर्मा कथयति ।

râjan-putrâs	ûchus:	katham	etad?	vishṇu-śarmâ	kathayati:
Ttp. -ra, *N. pl.*	vach, 3 *pl. Perf. Par.*	*Ind.*	etad, *N. sg. n.*	-man, *N. sg.*	kath, 3 *sg. Pres. Par.*
The princes	said:	'How	that?'	Vishṇuśarman	relates:

अस्ति गोदावरीतीरे विशालः शाल्मलीतरुः । तत्र

asti	godâvarî-tîre	viśâlas	śâlmalî-tarus;	tatra
as, 3 *sg. Pres. Par.*	*Ttp.* -ra, *L. sg.*	-la, *N. sg. m.*	*Karm.* -ru, *N. sg.*	*Ind.*
There is	on the Godâvarî-bank	a large	silk cotton-tree;	thereon

नानादिग्देशादागत्य रात्रौ पक्षिणो निवसंति । अथ

nânâ-diś-deśât	â-gatya	râtrau	pakshiṇas	ni-vasanti.	atha
Ttp. -śa, *Ab. sg.*	gam *with* â, *Ger.*	-ri, *L. sg.*	-shin, *N. sg. m.*	vas *with* ni, 3 *pl. Pres. Par.*	*Ind.*
from various-region-country	having arrived	at night	birds	dwell.	Now

कदाचिदवसन्नायां रात्रावस्ताचलचूडावलंबिनि भगवति

kadâ-chid	ava-sannâyâm	râtrau	astâchala-chûḍâ-avalambini	bhagavati
Ind. *Ind.*	sad *with* ava, *L. sg. f. past Ptc. Pass.*	-ri, *L. sg.*	*Ttp.* -bin, *L. sg. m.*	-vat, *L. sg. m.*
once,	being ended	the night,	while on setting-mountain-crest-resting	the venerable

कुमुदिनीनायके चंद्रमसि लघुपतनकनामा वायसः प्रबुद्धः

kumudinî-nâyake	chandramasi	laghupatanaka-nâmâ	vâyasas	pra-buddhas
Ttp. -ka, *L. sg. m.*	-mas, *L. sg.*	*Bahuv.* -man, *N. sg. m.*	-sa, *N. sg.*	budh *with* pra, *N. sg. m. past Ptc. Pass.*
lotus-lover	the moon,	Laghupatanaka-named	a crow,	being awake,

कृतांतमिव द्वितीयमायांतं व्याधमपश्यत् । तम-

kṛitântam	iva	dvitiyam	â-yântam	vyâdham	apaśyat.	tam
-ta, Ac. sg.	*Ind.*	*-ya, Ac. sg. m.*	yâ *with* â. *Ac. sg. m. Ptc. Pres. Par.*	*-dha, Ac. sg.*	dṛiś, *3 sg. Impf. Par.*	tad, *Ac. sg. m.*
Death	like	a second,	approaching	a hunter	saw.	Him

वलोक्याचिंतयत् । अद्य प्रातरेवानिष्टदर्शनं

ava-lokya	achintayat:	adya	prâtar	eva	anishṭa-darśanam
lok *with* ava, *Ger.*	chint, *3 sg. Impf. Par.*	*Ind.*	*Ind.*	*Ind.*	*Ttp. -na. N. sg.*
having seen	he reflected:	To day	early	indeed	of unwished-the sight

जातं । न जाने किमनभिमतं दर्शयिष्यति ।

jâtam;	na	jâne	kim	an-abhimatam	darśayishyati
jan, *N. sg. n. past Ptc. Pass.*	*Ind.*	jñâ, *1 sg. Pres. Âtm.*	*Ac. sg. n.*	*Karm. -ta, Ac. sg. n. (rt.* man *with* abhi)	dṛiś, *3 sg. Fut. II. Par. Caus.*
produced;	not	do I know,	what	disagreeable	it will show.

इत्युक्त्वा तदनुसरणक्रमेण व्याकुलश्चलितः ।

iti	uktvâ	tad-anusaraṇa-krameṇa	vyâkulas	chalitas.
Ind.	vach, *Ger.*	*Ttp.-ma, I. sg.*	*-la, N. sg. m.*	chal, *N. sg. m. past Ptc. Pass.*
Thus	having said	by way-of following-him	perplexed	he moved about.

यतः । शोकस्थानसहस्राणि भयस्थानशतानि च ।

yatas,	śoka-sthâna-sahasrâṇi	bhaya-sthâna-śatâni	cha
Ind.	*Ttp. -ra, N. pl.*	*Ttp. -ta, N. pl.*	*Ind.*
For,	Of sorrow-occasions-thousands,	of fear-occasions-hundreds	and

दिवसे दिवसे मूढमाविशंति न पंडितं ॥ २ ॥

divase	divase	mûḍham	â-viśanti	na	paṇḍitam.	(2)
-sa, L. sg.	*-sa, L. sg.*	muh, *Ac. sg. m. past Ptc. Pass.*	viś, *with* â, *3 pl. Pres. Par.*	*Ind.*	*-ta, Ac. sg. m.*	
by day	by day	the fool	approach,	not	the wise.	

अन्यच्च । विषयिणामिदमवश्यं कर्तव्यं ।

anyad	cha,	vishayiṇâm	idam	avaśyam	kartavyam.
-ya N. sg. n.	*Ind.*	*-yin, G. pl. m.*	idam, *N. sg. n.*	*Ind.*	kṛi, *N. sg. n. Ptc. Fut. Pass.*
Again	and;	Of men of the world	this	surely	to be done.

उत्थायोत्थाय बोद्धव्यं महद्भयमुपस्थितं ।

ud-sthâya	ud-sthâya	boddhavyam	mahat	bhayam	upa-sthitam,
sthâ *with* ud, *Ger.*	sthâ, *with* ud, *Ger.*	budh, *N. sg. n. Ptc. Fut. Pass.*	*-t, N. sg. n.*	*-ya, N. sg.*	sthâ, *with* upa, *N. sg. n. past Ptc. Pass.*
Having risen,	having risen,	it is to be thought,	great	danger	impending,

मरणव्याधिशोकानां किमद्य निपतिष्यति ॥ ३ ॥

maraṇa-vyâdhi-śokânâm	kim	adya	ni-patishyati?	(3)
Dvandva. -ka, G. pl.	kim, *N. sg. n.*	*Ind.*	pat, *with* ni, *3 sg. Fut. II. Par.*	
of death-sickness-sorrow	which	to-day	will fall down?	

अथ तेन व्याधेन तंडुलकणान्विकीर्य जालं

atha	tena	vyâdhena	taṇḍula-kaṇân	vi-kîrya	jâlam
Ind.	tad, *I. sg. m.*	*-dha, I. sg.*	*Ttp. -ṇa, Ac. pl.*	kṛî, *with* vi, *Ger.*	*-la, N. sg.*
Then	by that	hunter	rice-grains	having scattered,	a net

विस्तीर्णं । स च प्रच्छन्नो भूत्वा स्थितः ।

vi-stîrṇam ;	sas	cha	pra-chhannas	bhûtvâ	sthitas.
stṛî, with vi, *N. sg. n. past Ptc. Pass.*	tad, *N. sg. m.*	*Ind.*	chhad, *with* pra, *N. sg. m. past Ptc. Pass.*	bhû, *Ger.*	sthâ, *N. sg. m. past Ptc. Pass.*
was spread ;	he	and	hidden	having been	stood.

तस्मिन्नेव काले चित्रग्रीवनामा कपोतराजः सपरिवारो

tasmin	eva	kâle	chitragrîva-nâmâ	kapota-râjas	sa-parivâras
tad, *L. sg. m.*	*Ind.*	-la, *L. sg.*	*Bahuv.* -man, *N. sg. m.*	*Ttp.* -ja, *N. sg.*	*Bahuv.* -ra, *N. sg. m.*
At that	very	time	Chitragrîva-named	a pigeon-king	with-retinue

वियति विसर्पंस्तांस्तंडुलकणानवलोकयामास । ततः

viyati	vi-sarpan	tân	taṇḍula-kaṇân	ava-lokayâm-âsa.	tatas
-t, *L. sg.*	sṛip, *with* vi, *N. sg. m. Ptc. Pres. Par.*	tad, *Ac. pl. m.*	*Ttp.* -ṇa, *Ac. pl.*	lok, *with* ava, 3 *sg. Perf. Par.*	*Ind.*
in the air	flying-about	those	rice-grains	espying-was.	Then

कपोतराजस्तंडुलकणलुब्धान्कपोतान्प्रत्याह । कुतो ऽत्र

kapota-râjas	taṇḍula-kaṇa-lubdhân	kapotân	prati-âha :	kutas	atra
Ttp. -ja, *N. sg.*	*Ttp.* -dha, *Ac. pl. m.* (*rt.* lubh)	-ta, *Ac. pl.*	ah, *with* prati, 3 *sg.*	*Ind.*	*Ind.*
the pigeon-king	the rice-grains desiring	pigeons	addressed :	Whence	here

निर्जने वने तंडुलकणानां संभवः । तन्निरूप्यतां तावत् ।

nis-jane	vane	taṇḍula-kaṇânâm	sam-bhavas?	tad	ni-rûpyatâm	tâvat !
Bahuv. -na, *L. sg. n.*	-na, *L. sg.*	*Ttp.* -ṇa, *G. pl.*	-va, *N. sg.*	tad, *N. sg. n.*	rûp, *with* ni, 3 *sg. Imp. Pass.*	*Ind.*
in the lonely	wood	of rice-grains	the production?	That	may be investigated,	first !

भद्रमिदं न पश्यामि । प्रायेणानेन तंडुलकणलोभेना-

bhadram	idam	na	paśyâmi.	prâyeṇa	anena	taṇḍula-kaṇa-lobhena
-ra, *Ac. sg. n.*	idam, *Ac. sg. n.*	*Ind.*	driś, 1 *sg. Pres. Par.*	-ya, *I. sg. Adv.*	idam, *I. sg. m.*	*Ttp.* -bha, *I. sg.*
Fortunate	this	not	I do consider.	Possibly	through this	rice-grain-desire

स्माभिरपि तथा भवितव्यं ।

asmâbhis	api	tathâ	bhavitavyam,
asmad, *I. pl.*	*Ind.*	*Ind.*	bhû, *N. sg. n. Ptc. Fut. Pass.*
by us	also	thus	to be fared,

कंकणस्य तु लोभेन मग्नः पंके सुदुस्तरे ।

kaṅkaṇasya	tu	lobhena	magnas	paṅke	su-dustare
-ṇa, *G. sg.*	*Ind.*	-bha, *I. sg.*	majj, *N. sg. m. past Ptc. Pass.*	-ka, *L. sg.*	*Karm.* -ra, *L. sg. n.* or *m.*
of gold	(but)	through desire	plunged	in a mire	very-difficult-to be crossed,

वृद्धव्याघ्रेण संप्राप्तः पथिकः स मृतो यथा ॥ ४ ॥

vṛiddha-vyâghreṇa	sam-pra-âptas	pathikas	sas	mṛitas	yathâ.	(4)
Karm. -ra, *I. sg.*	âp, *with* sam *and* pra, *N. sg. m. past Ptc. Pass.*	-ka, *N. sg.*	tad, *N. sg. m.*	mṛi, *N. sg. m. past Ptc. Pass.*	*Ind.*	
by an old-tiger	seized	wanderer	that	dead	as.	

कपोता ऊचुः । कथमेतत् । सो ऽब्रवीत् ।

kapotâs	ûchus :	katham	etad?	sas	abravît :
-ta, *N. sg.*	vach, 3 *pl. Perf. Par.*	*Ind.*	etad, *N. sg. n.*	tad, *N. sg. m.*	brû, 3 *sg. Impf. Par.*
The pigeons	said :	how	that?	He	said :

अहमेकदा दक्षिणारण्ये चरन्नपश्यं। एको वृद्धव्याघ्रः स्नातः

aham	ekadâ	dakshiṇa-aranye	charan	apaśyam,	ekas	vṛiddha-vyâghras	snâtas
asmad, *N. sg.*	*Ind.*	*Karm.* -ya, *L. sg.*	char, *N. sg m. Pres. Ptc. Par.*	driś, 1 *sg. Impf. Par.*	eka, *N. sg. m.*	*Karm.* -ra, *N. sg.*	snâ, *N. sg. m. past Ptc. Pass.*
I	once	in the southern-wood	roaming	saw,	An	old-tiger	bathed

कुशहस्तः सरस्तीरे ब्रूते। भो भोः पांथ इदं

kuśa-hastas	saras-tîre	brûte:	bho	bhos	pântha,	idam
Bahuv. -ta, *N. sg. m.*	*Ttp.* -ra, *L. sg.*	brû, 3 *sg. Pres. Âtm.*	*Ind.*	*Ind.*	-tha, *V. sg.*	idam, *N. sg. n.*
with kuśa grass-in his hand	on a lake-bank	says:	Ho,	ho,	wanderer,	this

सुवर्णकंकणं गृह्यतां। ततो लोभाकृष्टेन केनचित्पांथेना-

suvarṇa-kaṅkaṇam	gṛihyatâm!	tatas	lobha-âkṛishṭena	kena-chid	pânthena
Ttp. -ṇa, *N. sg.*	grah, 3 *sg. Imp. Pass.*	*Ind.*	*Ttp.* -ta *I. sg. m.* (*rt.* krish *with* â)	kim, *Ind. I. sg. m.*	-tha, *I. sg.*
gold-bracelet	may be taken!	Then	by a desire-attracted	some	wanderer

लोचितं। भाग्येनैतत्संभवति। किंत्वस्मिन्नात्मसंदेहे

â-lochitam:	bhâgyena	etad	sam-bhavati;	kim-tu	asmin	âtman-sandehe
loch *with* â, *N. sg. n. past Ptc. Pass.*	-ya, *I. sg.*	etad, *N. sg. n.*	bhû *with* sam, 3 *sg. Pres. Par.*	*Ind. Ind.*	idam, *L. sg. m.*	*Ttp.* -ha, *L. sg.*
it was considered:	luckily	this	happens;	but	in this	life-risk

प्रवृत्तिर्न विधेया।

pra-vṛittis	na	vi-dheyâ;
-ti, *N. sg.*	*Ind.*	dhâ *with* vi, *N. sg. f. Ptc. Fut. Pass.*
engagement	not	to be made;

यतः। अनिष्टादिष्टलाभेऽपि न गतिर्जायते शुभा।

yatas,	an-ishṭât	ishṭa-lâbhe	api	na	gatis	jâyate	śubhâ,
Ind.	*Karm.* -ṭa, *Ab. sg.* (*rt.* ish).	*Ttp.* -bha, *L. sg.*	*Ind.*	*Ind.*	-ti, *N. sg.*	jan, 3 *sg. Pres. Âtm.*	-bha, *N. sg. f.*
For,	From an unpleasant one	on pleasure-reception	even	not	a result	is produced	prosperous,

यत्रास्ते विषसंसर्गोऽमृतं तदपि मृत्यवे ॥ ५ ॥

yatra	âste	visha-saṁsargas	a-mṛitam	tad	api	mṛityave.	(5)
Ind.	âs, 3 *sg. Pres. Âtm.*	*Ttp.* -ga, *N. sg.*	*Bahuv.* -ta, *N. sg.*	tad, *N. sg. n.*	*Ind.*	-yu, *D. sg.*	
where	there lies	poison-mixture,	Ambrosia	that	even	for death.	

किंतु सर्वत्रार्थार्जने प्रवृत्तिः संदेह एव।

kim-tu	sarvatra	artha-arjane	pra-vṛittis	sam-dehas	eva.
Ind. Ind.	*Ind.*	*Ttp.* -na, *L. sg.*	-ti, *N. sg.*	-ha, *N. sg.*	*Ind.*
However	everywhere	in wealth-acquisition	engaging	risk	certainly.

तथा चोक्तं। न संशयमनारुह्य नरो भद्राणि पश्यति।

tathâ	cha	uktam,	na	sam-śayam	an-âruhya	naras	bhadrâṇi	paśyati
Ind.	*Ind.*	vach, *N. sg. n. past Ptc. Pass.*	*Ind.*	-ya, *Ac. sg.*	an *before* ruh *with* â, *Ger.*	-ra, *N. sg.*	-ra, *Ac. pl. n.*	driś, 3 *sg. Pres. Par.*
Thus	and	said,	Not	risk	not-having encountered	a man	prosperity	beholds,

संशयं पुनरारुह्य यदि जीवति पश्यति ॥ ६ ॥

sam-śayam	punar	â-ruhya	yadi	jîvati	paśyati.	(6)
-ya, *Ac. sg.*	*Ind.*	ruh *with* â, *Ger.*	*Ind.*	jîv, 3 *sg. Pres. Par.*	driś, 3 *sg. Pres. Par.*	
risk	on the contrary	having encountered,	if	he lives,	he sees (it).	

तन्निरूपयामि तावत्। प्रकाशं ब्रूते। कुत्र तव कंकणं।

tad	ni-rûpayâmi	tâvat.	pra-kâśam	brûte:	kutra	tava	kaṅkaṇam?
tad, *Ac. sg. n.*	rûp *with* ni, 1 *sg. Pres. Par.*	*Ind.*	*Ind.*	brû, 3 *sg. Pres. Âtm.*	*Ind.*	yushmad, *G. sg.*	-ṇa, *N. sg.*
That	I investigate	then.	Aloud	he says:	Where	of thee	the bracelet?

व्याघ्रो हस्तं प्रसार्य दर्शयति। पांथो ऽवदत्। कथं

vyâghras	hastam	pra-sârya	darśayati.	pânthas	avadat:	katham
-ra, *N. sg.*	-ta, *Ac. sg.*	sri *with* pra, *Ger. Caus.*	driś 3 *sg. Pres. Par. Caus.*	-tha, *N. sg.*	vad, 3 *sg. Impf. Par.*	*Ind.*
The tiger	the paw	having stretched-forth	shows.	The wanderer	said:	How

मारात्मके त्वयि विश्वासः। व्याघ्र उवाच। शृणु रे पांथ।

mâra-âtmake	tvayi	vi-śvâsas?	vyâghras	uvâcha:	śṛiṇu	re	pântha!
Bahuv. -ka, *L. sg. m.* (âtman)	yushmad, *L. sg.*	-sa, *N. sg.*	-ra, *N. sg.*	vach, 3 *sg. Perf. Par.*	śru, 2 *sg. Imp. Par.*	*Ind.*	-tha, *V. sg.*
in the murder-minded	in thee	confidence?	The tiger	said:	Listen	O	wanderer!

प्रागेव यौवनदशायामतिदुर्वृत्त आसं। अनेकगोमानुषाणां बधान्मे

prâk	eva	yauvana-daśâyâm	ati-durvṛittas	âsam.	aneka-go-mânushâṇâm	badhât	me
prâch, *Ac. sg. n. Adv.*	*Ind.*	*Ttp.* -śâ, *L. sg.*	*Karm.* -tta, *N. sg. m.*	as, 1 *sg. Impf. Par.*	*Karm.* -sha, *G. pl.*	-dha, *Ab. sg.*	asmad, *G. sg.*
Formerly	indeed	in the youth-period	exceedingly-wicked	I was.	Of many-cows-(and)-men	because of the murder,	of me

पुत्रा मृता दाराश्च वंशहीनश्चाहं। ततः केनचिद्धार्मिकेण-

putrâs	mṛitâs	dârâs	cha	vaṁśa-hînas	cha	aham.	tatas	kena-chid	dhârmikeṇa
-ra, *N. pl.*	mṛi, *N. pl. m. past Ptc. Pass.*	-ra, *N. pl.*	*Ind.*	*Ttp.* -na, *N. sg. m.* (hâ)	*Ind.*	asmad, *N. sg.*	*Ind.*	kim, *I. sg. m. Ind.*	-ka, *I. sg. m.*
the sons	dead,	wife	and,	family-deprived	and	I.	Then	by some	virtuous

ऽहमादिष्टः। दानधर्मादिकं चरतु भवान्। तदुपदेशादिदानीमहं

aham	â-dishṭas:	dâna-dharma-âdikam	charatu	bhavân.	tad-upadeśât	idânîm	aham
asmad, *N. sg.*	diś *with* â, *N. sg. m. past Ptc. Pass.*	*Bahuv.* -ka, *Ac. sg. n.* (âdi)	char, 3 *sg. Imp. Par.*	-vat, *N. sg. m.*	*Ttp.* -śa, *Ab. sg.*	*Ind.*	asmad, *N. sg.*
I	was advised:	Liberality-virtue, etc.	should practise	you.	Of him-because of the advice	now	I

स्नानशीलो दाता वृद्धो गलितनखदंतो न कथं विश्वासभूमिः।

snâna-śîlas	dâtâ	vṛiddhas	galita-nakha-dantas	na	katham	viśvâsa-bhûmis?
Bahuv. -la, *N. sg. m.*	-tṛi, *N. sg. m.*	-dha, *N. sg. m.*	*Bahuv.* -ta, *N. sg. m.*	*Ind.*	*Ind.*	*Ttp.* -mi, *N. sg.*
ablution-observing,	charitable,	old,	having lost-claws-(and)-teeth	not	how	a confidence-object?

यतः। इज्याध्ययनदानानि तपः सत्यं धृतिः क्षमा।

yatas,	ijyâ-adhyayana-dânâni	tapas	satyam	dhṛitis	kshamâ
Ind.	*Dvandva.* -na, *N. pl.*	-as, *N. sg.*	-ya, *N. sg.*	-ti, *N. sg.*	-mâ, *N. sg.*
For,	Sacrificing-study-charity,	penance,	truth,	firmness,	forgiveness,

अलोभ इति मार्गो ऽयं धर्मस्याष्टविधः स्मृतः॥ ७॥

a-lobhas	iti	mârgas	ayam	dharmasya	ashṭan-vidhas	smṛitas; (7)
Karm. -bha, *N. sg.*	*Ind.*	-ga, *N. sg.*	idam, *N. sg.*	-ma, *G. sg.*	*Bahuv.* -dha, *N. sg. m.*	smṛi, *N. sg. m. past Ptc. Pass.*
want-of desire,	thus	way	this	of virtue	the eight-fold	is recorded;

तत्र पूर्वश्चतुर्वर्गो दंभार्थमपि सेव्यते ।

tatra	pûrvas	chatur-vargas	dambha-artham	api	sevyate;
Ind.	-va, *N. sg. m.*	*Drigu.* -ga, *N. sg. m.*	*Ind.* (-tha, *Ac. sg.*)	*Ind.*	sev, 3 *sg. Pres. Pass.*
There	the former	four-collection	for simulation's sake	also	is attended to;

उत्तरस्तु चतुर्वर्गो महात्मन्येव तिष्ठति ॥ ८ ॥

uttaras	tu	chatur-vargas	mahâ-âtmani	eva	tishṭhati (8)
-ra, *N. sg. m.*	*Ind.*	*Drigu.* -ra, *N. sg.*	*Bahuv.* -man, *L. sg. m.*	*Ind.*	sthâ, 3 *sg. Pres. Par.*
the latter	but	four-collection	in the great-minded	only	stands.

मम चैतावांल्लोभविरहो येन स्वहस्तस्थमपि सुवर्णकंकणं

mama	cha	etâvân	lobha-virahas	yena	sva-hasta-stham	api	suvarṇa-kaṅkaṇam
asmad, *G. sg.*	*Ind.*	-vat, *N. sg. m.*	*Tip.* -ha, *N. sg.*	yad, *I. sg. n. Adv.*	*Tip.* -stha, *Ac. sg. n.*	*Ind.*	*Tip.* -ṇa, *Ac. sg.*
Of me	and	such	desire-freedom	that	in the own-hand-standing	even	the gold-bracelet

यस्मै कस्मैचिद्दातुमिच्छामि । तथापि व्याघ्रो मानुषं खादती-

yasmai kasmai-chid	dâtum	ichchhâmi.	tathâ	api	vyâghras	mânusham	khâdati
yad, *D. sg. m.* kim, *D. sg. m.* *Ind.*	dâ, *Inf.*	ish, 1 *sg. Pres. Par.*	*Ind.*	*Ind.*	-ra, *N. sg.*	-sha, *Ac. sg.*	khâd, 3 *sg. Pres. Par.*
to any-body	to give	I wish.	So	even,	'the tiger	the man	devours,'

ति लोकप्रवादो दुर्निवारः ।

iti	loka-pravâdas	dus-nivâras.
Ind.	*Tip.* -da, *N. sg.*	-ra, *N. sg. m.*
thus	the world-report	difficult-to be overcome.

यतः । गतानुगतिको लोकः कुट्टनीमुपदेशिनीं ।

yatas,	gata-anugatikas	lokas	kuṭṭanîm	upa-deśinîm
Ind.	*Bahuv.* -ka, *N. sg. m.*	-ka, *N. sg.*	-nî, *Ac. sg.*	-šin, *Ac. sg. f.*
For,	The predecessor-following	world	a bawd	as instructress

प्रमाणयति नो धर्मे यथा गोघ्नमपि द्विजं ॥ ९ ॥

pramâṇayati	nas	dharme	yathâ	go-ghnam	api	dvi-jam. (9)
pramâṇaya, 3 *sg. Pres. Par.*	asmad, *D. pl.*	-ma, *L. sg.*	*Ind.*	*Tip.* -na, *Ac. sg. m.*	*Ind.*	-ja, *Ac. sg. m.*
holds up as a model	to us	in virtue,	as	a cow-killing	also	a twice-born.

मया च धर्मशास्त्राण्यधीतानि । शृणु ।

mayâ	cha	dharma-śâstrâṇi	adhi-itâni.	śriṇu!
asmad, *I. sg.*	*Ind.*	*Tip.* -ra, *N. pl.*	i *with* adhi, *N. pl. n. past Ptc. Pass.*	śru, 2 *sg. Imp. Par.*
By me	and	of religion-the books	read.	Listen;

मरुस्थल्यां यथा वृष्टिः क्षुधार्ते भोजनं तथा ।

maru-sthalyâm	yathâ	vṛishṭis	kshudhâ-ârte	bhojanam	tathâ,
Tip. -lî, *L. sg.*	*Ind.*	-ṭi, *N. sg.*	*Tip.* -ta, *L. sg. m.*	-na, *N. sg.*	*Ind.*
In a desert-place	as	rain,	in the hunger-pained	food	thus,

दरिद्रे दीयते दानं सफलं पांडुनंदन ॥ १० ॥

daridre	dîyate	dânam	sa-phalam	pâṇḍu-nandana. (10)
-ra, *L. sg. m.*	dâ, 3 *sg. Pres. Pass.*	-na, *N. sg.*	*Bahuv.* -la, *N. sg. n.*	*Tip.* -na, *V. sg.*
Unto a poor	is given	a gift	fruitful,	O Pâṇḍu-son.

प्राणा यथात्मनो ऽभीष्टा भूतानामपि ते तथा ।

prâṇâs	yathâ	âtmanas	abhi-ishṭâs	bhûtânâm	api	te	tathâ
-ṇa, *N. pl.*	*Ind.*	-man, *G. sg.*	ish *with* abhi, *N. pl. m. past Ptc. Pass.*	-ta, *G. pl. n.*	*Ind.*	tad, *N. pl. m.*	*Ind.*
Life	as	of oneself	dear,	of living beings	also	it	thus,

आत्मौपम्येन भूतेषु दयां कुर्वंति साधवः ॥ ११ ॥

âtman-aupamyena	bhûteshu	dayâm	kurvanti	sâdhavas.	(11)
Ttp. -ya, *I. sg.*	-ta, *L. pl. n.*	-yâ, *Acc. sg.*	kri, 3 *pl. Pres. Par.*	-dhu, *N. pl. m.*	
Through self-comparison	unto living beings	sympathy	bestow	the good.	

अपरं च । प्रत्याख्याने च दाने च सुखदुःखे प्रियाप्रिये ।

aparam	cha,	prati-â-khyâne	cha	dâne	cha	sukha-duḥkhe	priya-apriye
-ra, *N. sg. n.*	*Ind.*	-na, *L. sg.*	*Ind.*	-na, *L. sg.*	*Ind.*	*Dvandva.* -kha, *L. sg.*	*Dvandva.* -ya, *L. sg.*
Another	and,	In refusing	and,	in granting	and,	in pleasure-(and) pain,	in pleasing-(and) displeasing,

आत्मौपम्येन पुरुषः प्रमाणमधिगच्छति ॥ १२ ॥

âtman-aupamyena	purushas	pra-mâṇam	adhi-gachchhati.	(12)
Ttp. -ya, *I. sg.*	-sha, *N. sg.*	-ṇa, *Ac. sg.*	gam *with* adhi, 3 *sg. Pres. Par.*	
through self-comparison	a man	a scale	obtains.	

अन्यच्च । मातृवत्परदारेषु परद्रव्येषु लोष्टवत् ।

anyad	cha,	mâtṛi-vat	para-dâreshu	para-dravyeshu	loshta-vat
-ya, *N. sg. n.*	*Ind.*	*Ind.*	*Ttp.* -ra, *L. pl.*	*Ttp.* -ya, *L. pl.*	*Ind.*
Again	and,	As-on a mother	on another's-wife,	on another's-possessions	as-on a lump of earth,

आत्मवत्सर्वभूतेषु यः पश्यति स पंडितः ॥ १३ ॥

âtman-vat	sarva-bhûteshu	yas	paśyati	sas	paṇḍitas.	(13)
Ind.	*Karm.* -ta, *L. pl. n.*	yad, *N. sg. m.*	dṛiś 3 *sg. Pres. Par.*	tad, *N. sg. m.*	-ta, *N. sg. m.*	
as-on himself	on all-beings	who	looks,	he	wise.	

त्वं चातीव दुर्गतस्तेन तत्तुभ्यं

tvam	cha	ati-iva	dus-gatas,	tena	tad	tubhyam
yushmad, *N. sg.*	*Ind.*	*Ind. Ind.*	*Karm.* -ta, *N. sg. m.*	tad, *I. sg. n. Adv.*	tad, *Ac. sg. n.*	yushmad, *D. sg.*
Thou	and	exceedingly	bad-circumstanced,	therefore	this	to thee

दातुं सयत्नो ऽहं । तथा चोक्तं ।

dâtum	sa-yatnas	aham.	tathâ	cha	uktam.
dâ, *Inf.*	*Bahuv.* -na, *N. sg. m.*	asmad, *N. sg.*	*Ind.*	*Ind.*	vach, *N. sg. n. past Ptc. Pass.*
to give	endeavouring	I.	Thus	and	said,

दरिद्रान्भर कौंतेय मा प्रयच्छेश्वरे धनं ।

daridrân	bhara	kaunteya	mâ	pra-yachchha	îśvare	dhanam,
-ra, *Ac. pl. m.*	bhri, 2 *sg. Imp. Par.*	-ya, *V. sg.*	*Ind.*	yam *with* pra, 2 *sg. Imp. Par.*	-ra, *L. sg.*	-na, *Ac. sg.*
The poor	support,	O son of Kunti,	not	bestow	on a lord	wealth,

व्याधितस्यौषधं पथ्यं नीरुजस्य किमौषधैः ॥ १४ ॥

vyâdhitasya	aushadham	pathyam,	nis-rujasya	kim	aushadhais?	(14)
-ta, *G. sg. m.*	-dha, *N. sg.*	-ya, *N. sg. n.*	*Bahuv.* -ja, *G. sg. m.*	kim *Ac. sg. n.*	-dha, *I. pl.*	
Of the diseased	medicine	wholesome,	of the un-diseased	what	with drugs?	

अन्यच्च । दातव्यमिति यद्दानं दीयतेऽनुपकारिणे ।

anyad	cha,	dâtavyam	iti	yad	dânam	diyate	an-upakâriṇe
-ya, *N. sg. n.*	*Ind.*	dâ, *N. sg. n. Ptc. Fut. Pass.*	*Ind.*	yad, *N. sg. n.*	-na, *N. sg.*	dâ, *3 sg. Pres. Pass.*	*Karm.* -rin, *D. sg. m.*
Again	and,	'It ought to be given,'	thus	what	gift	is given	to one not-conferring benefits,

देशे काले च पात्रे च तद्दानं सात्त्विकं विदुः ॥ १५ ॥

deśe	kâle	cha	pâtre	cha	tad	dânam	sâttvikam	vidus. (15)
-śa, *L. sg.*	-la, *L. sg.*	*Ind.*	-ra, *L. sg.*	*Ind.*	-tad, *Ac. sg. n.*	-na, *Ac. sg.*	-ka, *Ac. sg. n.*	vid, *3 pl. Perf. Par.*
In place,	in time	and,	unto a worthy person	and,	that	gift	a true one	they record.

तदत्र सरसि स्नात्वा सुवर्णकंकणं गृहाण । ततो यावद्-

tad	atra	sarasi	snâtvâ	suvarṇa-kaṅkaṇam	gṛihâṇa.	tatas	yâvat
Ind.	*Ind.*	-ras, *L. sg.*	snâ, *Ger.*	*Ttp.* -ṇa, *Ac. sg.*	grah, *2 sg. Imp. Âtm.*	*Ind.*	*Ind.*
Therefore	here	in the lake	having bathed	the gold-bracelet	accept.	Thereupon	while

सौ तद्वचः प्रतीतो लोभात्सरः स्नातुं प्रविशति तावन्म-

asau	tad-vachas	prati-itas	lobhât	saras	snâtum	pra-viśati,	tâvat
adas, *N. sg. m.*	*Ttp.* -chas, *Ac. sg.*	i *with* prati, *N. sg. m. past Ptc. Pass.*	-bha, *Ab. sg.*	-ras, *Ac. sg.*	snâ, *Inf.*	viś, *with* pra, *3 sg. Pres. Par.*	*Ind.*
he	his word	trusting	through desire	the lake	to bathe	enters,	then

हापंके निमग्नः पलायितुमक्षमः । पंके पतितं

mahâ-paṅke	ni-magnas	palâyitum	a-kshamas.	paṅke	patitam
Karm. -ka, *L. sg.*	majj *with* ni, *N. sg. m. past. Ptc. Pass.*	ay *with* parâ, *Inf.*	*Karm.* -ma, *N. sg. m.*	-ka, *L. sg.*	pat, *Ac. sg. m. past Ptc. Pass.*
into the great-mire	plunged	to escape	unable.	Into the mire	the fallen

दृष्ट्वा व्याघ्रोऽवदत् । अहह महापंके पतितोऽसि ।

dṛishṭvâ	vyâghras	avadat:	ahaha	mahâ-paṅke	patitas	asi;
dṛiś, *Ger.*	-ra, *N. sg.*	vad, *3 sg. Impf. Par.*	*Ind.*	*Karm.* -ka, *L. sg.*	pat, *N. sg. m. past Ptc. Pass.*	as, *2 sg. Pres. Par.*
having seen	the tiger	said:	'Ah, ah,	into the great-mire	fallen	thou art;

अतस्त्वामहमुत्थापयामि । इत्युक्त्वा शनैः शनै-

atas	tvâm	aham	ud-sthâpayâmi,	iti	uktvâ	śanais	śanais
Ind.	yushmad, *Ac. sg.*	asmad, *N. sg.*	sthâ *with* ud, *1 sg. Pres Par. Caus.*	*Ind.*	vach,	*Ind.*	*Ind.*
thence	thee	I	lift out,'	thus	having said,	slowly	slowly

रुपगम्य तेन व्याघ्रेण धृतः स पांथोऽचिंतयत् ।

upa-gamya	tena	vyâghreṇa	dhṛitas	sas	pânthas	achintayat:
gam *with* upa, *Ger.*	tad, *I. sg. m.*	-ra, *I. sg.*	dhṛi, *N. sg. m. past Pass. Ptc.*	tad, *N. sg. m.*	-tha, *N. sg.*	chint, *3 sg. Impf. Par.*
having approached,	by that	tiger	seized	that	wanderer	thought:

न धर्मशास्त्रं पठतीति कारणं

na	dharma-śâstram	paṭhati	iti	kâraṇam,
Ind.	*Ttp.* -ra, *Ac. sg.*	paṭh, *3 sg. Pres. Par.*	*Ind.*	-ṇa, *N. sg.*
Not	'the law-book	he reads,'	thus is	a reason,

न चापि वेदाध्ययनं दुरात्मनः ।

na	cha	api	veda-adhyayanam	dus-âtmanas
Ind.	*Ind.*	*Ind.*	*Ttp.* -na, *N. sg.*	*Bahuv.* -man, *G. sg. m.*
not	and	also	the Veda-study	of the wicked-minded,

स्वभाव एवात्र तथातिरिच्यते

sva-bhâvas	eva	atra	tathâ	ati-richyate
Karm. -va, *N. sg.*	*Ind.*	*Ind.*	*Ind.*	rich *with* ati, 3 *sg. Pres. Pass.*
the inborn-disposition	only	here	thus	prevails,

यथा प्रकृत्या मधुरं गवां पयः ॥ १६ ॥

yathâ	pra-kṛityâ	madhuram	gavâm	payas.	(16)
Ind.	-ti, *I. sg.*	-ra, *N. sg. n.*	go, *G. pl.*	-yas, *N. sg.*	
as	by nature	sweet	of cows	the milk.	

किंच । अवशेन्द्रियचित्तानां हस्तिस्नानमिव क्रिया ।

Kim-cha,	avaśa-indriya-chittânâm	hastin-snânam	iva	kriyâ,
Ind. Ind.	*Bahuv.* -tta, *G. pl. m.*	*Tîp.* -na. *N. sg.*	*Ind.*	-yâ, *N. sg.*
Moreover,	Of those with unsubdued senses-(and)-mind	elephant-bathing	like	the action,

दुर्भगाभरणप्रायो ज्ञानं भारः क्रियां विना ॥ १७ ॥

durbhagâ-âbharaṇa-prâyas	jñânam	bhâras	kriyâm	vinâ.	(17)
Bahuv. -ya, *N. sg. m.*	-na, *N. sg.*	-ra, *N. sg.*	-yâ, *Ac. sg.*	*Ind.*	
Unhappy women's-ornaments-resembling	knowledge	a burthen	action	without.	

तन्मया भद्रं न कृतं यदत्र मारात्मके विश्वासः कृतः ।

tad	mayâ	bhadram	na	kṛitam	yad	atra	mâra-âtmake	vi-śvâsas	kṛitas.
tad, *N. sg. n.*	asmad, *I. sg.*	-ra, *N. sg. n.*	*Ind.*	kri, *N. sg. n. p. Pt. Pass.*	*Ind.*	*Ind.*	*Bahuv.* -ka, *L. sg. m.* (âtman).	-sa, *N. sg.*	kri, *N. sg. m. past Ptc. Pass.*
This	by me	prosperous	not	done,	that	here	in the murderous-minded	confidence	placed.

तथा ह्युक्तं । नदीनां शस्त्रपाणीनां नखिनां शृङ्गिणां तथा ।

tathâ	hi	uktam,	nadînâm	śastra-pâṇinâm	nakhinâm	śṛiṅgiṇâm	tathâ,
Ind.	*Ind.*	vach, *N. sg. n. past Ptc. Pass.*	-dî, *G. pl.*	*Bahuv.* -ṇi, *G. pl. m.*	-in, *G. pl. m.*	-in, *G. pl. m.*	*Ind.*
Thus	for	said,	Of rivers,	of the weapon-in hand having,	of the claw possessing,	of the horn possessing	thus,

विश्वासो नैव कर्तव्यः स्त्रीषु राजकुलेषु च ॥ १८ ॥

vi-śvâsas	na	eva	kartavyas	strîshu	râjan-kuleshu	cha.	(18)
-sa, *N. sg.*	*Ind.*	*Ind.*	kṛi, *N. sg. m. Ptc. Fut. Pass.*	-rî, *L. pl.*	*Tîp.* -la, *L. pl.*	*Ind.*	
confidence	not	by any means	to be made,	in women,	in kings' families	and.	

अपरं च । सर्वस्य हि परीक्ष्यन्ते स्वभावा नेतरे गुणाः ।

aparam	cha,	sarvasya	hi	pari-ikshyante	sva-bhâvâs	na	itare	guṇâs;
-ra, *N. sg. n.*	*Ind.*	-va, *G. sg. m.*	*Ind.*	îksh *with* pari, 3. *pl. Pres. Pass.*	*Karm.* -va, *N. pl.*	*Ind.*	-ra, *N. pl. m.*	-ṇa, *N. pl.*
Another	and,	Of every one	indeed	are investigated	the natural-dispositions,	not	the other	qualities;

अतीत्य हि गुणान्सर्वान्स्वभावो मूर्ध्नि वर्तते ॥ १९ ॥

ati-itya	hi	guṇân	sarvân	sva-bhâvas	mûrdhni	vartate.	(19)
i *with* ati, *Ger.*	*Ind.*	-ṇa, *Ac. pl.*	-va, *Ac. pl. m.*	*Karm.* -va, *N. sg.*	-dhan, *L. sg.*	vṛit, 3. *sg. Pres. Âtm.*	
excelling	for	qualities	all	the natural-disposition	at the head	stands.	

अन्यच्च । स हि गगणविहारी कल्मषध्वंसकारी

anyad	cha,	sas	hi	gagaṇa-vihârî	kalmasha-dhvaṁsa-kârî
-ya, *N. sg. n.*	*Ind.*	tad, *N. sg. m.*	*Ind.*	*Tîp.* -rin, *N. sg. m.*	*Tîp.* -rin, *N. sg. m.*
Again	and,	This	indeed	in the sky-roaming	sin-destruction-causing

दशशतकरधारी ज्योतिषां मध्यचारी ।
daśan-śata-kara-dhârî jyotishâm madhya-chârî
Ttp. -rin, *N. sg. m.* -tis, *G. pl.* *Ttp.* -rin, *N. sg. m.*
ten-hundred-rays-bearing of the lights in the midst-wandering

विधुरपि विधियोगाद्ग्रस्यते राहुणासौ
vidhus api vidhi-yogât grasyate râhuṇâ asau;
-dhu, *N. sg.* *Ind.* *Ttp.* -ga, *Ab. sg.* gras, 3 *sg. Pres. Pass.* -hu, *I. sg.* adas, *N. sg. m.*
the moon even through fate-conjuncture is devoured by Râhu he;

लिखितमपि ललाटे प्रोज्झितुं कः समर्थः ॥ २० ॥
likhitam api lalâṭe pra-ujjhitum kas sam-arthas? (20)
likh, *Ac. sg. n. past Ptc. Pass.* *Ind.* -ṭa, *L. sg.* ujjh *with* pra, *Inf.* kim, *N. sg. m.* -tha, *N. sg. m.*
what is written even on the forehead to-escape who able?

इति चिंतयन्नेवासौ व्याघ्रेण व्यापादितः खादितश्च । अतो
iti chintayan eva asau vyâghreṇa vi-â-pâditas khâditas cha. atas
Ind. chint, *N. sg. m. Ptc. Pres. Par.* *Ind.* adas, *N. sg. m.* -ra, *I. sg.* pad *with* vi *and* â, *N. sg. m. past Ptc. Pass. Caus.* khâd, *N. sg. m. past Ptc. Pass.* *Ind.* *Ind.*
Thus reflecting even he by the tiger killed, eaten and. Therefore

ऽहं ब्रवीमि कंकणस्य तु लोभेनेत्यादि । अतः सर्वथाविचारितं
aham bravîmi: kaṅkaṇasya tu lobhena iti-âdi. atas sarvathâ a-vichâritam
asmad, *N. sg.* brû, 1 *sg. Pres. Par.* -ṇa, *G. sg.* *Ind.* -bha, *I. sg.* *Ind.* *Ind.* *Ind.* *Karm.* -ta, *N. sg. n.* (*rt.* char *with* vi)
I say: 'of gold but through desire, etc.' Therefore anyhow an inconsiderate

कर्म न कर्तव्यं । यतः ।
karma na kartavyam. yatas,
-man, *N. sg.* *Ind.* kri, *N. sg. n. Ptc. Fut. Pass.* *Ind.*
act not to be done. For,

सुजीर्णमन्नं सुविचक्षणः सुतः सुशासिता स्त्री नृपतिः सुसेवितः ।
su-jîrṇam annam su-vichakshaṇas sutas su-śâsitâ strî nṛi-patis su-sevitas
Karm. -ṇa, *N. sg. n.* -na, *N. sg.* *Karm.* -ṇa, *N. sg. m.* -ta, *N. sg.* *Karm.* -ta, *N. sg. f.* -rî, *N. sg.* *Ttp.* -ti, *N. sg.* *Karm.* -ta, *N. sg. m.*
Well-digested food, a well-discerning son, a well-governed wife, a prince well-served,

सुचिंत्य चोक्तं सुविचार्य यत्कृतं सुदीर्घकालेऽपि न
su-chintya cha uktam su-vichârya yad kṛitam su-dîrgha-kâle api na
chint, *with* su, *Ger.* *Ind.* vach, *N. sg. n. past Ptc. Pass.* char *with* vi, *Ger. Caus.* yad, *N. sg. n.* kri, *N. sg. n. past Ptc. Pass.* *Karm.* -la, *L. sg.* *Ind.* *Ind.*
Well-having reflected and spoken, well-having considered what done, in very-long-time even not

याति विक्रियां ॥ २१ ॥
yâti vi-kriyâm. (21)
yâ, 3. *sg. Pres. Par.* -yâ, *Ac. sg.*
goes to change.

एतद्वचनं श्रुत्वा कश्चित्कपोतः सदर्पमाह । आः किमेवमुच्यते ।
etad vachanam śrutvâ kas - chid kapotas sa-darpam âha: âḥ kim evam uchyate?
etad, *Ac. sg. n.* -na, *Ac. sg.* śru, *Ger.* kim, *N. sg. m.* *Ind.* -ta, *N. sg.* *Avyay.* ah, 3 *sg. Perf. Par.* *Ind.* *N. sg. n.* *Ind.* vach, 3 *sg. Pres. Pass.*
This speech having heard some pigeon haughtily said: Ha, what thus is said?

वृद्धानां वचनं ग्राह्यमापत्काले ह्युपस्थिते ।

vṛiddhânâm vachanam grâhyam âpad-kâle hi upa-sthite,

-dha, *G. pl. m.* -na, *N. sg.* grah, *N. sg. n. Ptc. Fut. Pass.* *Ttp.* -la, *L. sg.* *Ind.* sthâ *with* upa, *L. sg. m. past Ptc. Pass.*

Of the old the word to be accepted misfortune-time for having approached,

सर्वत्रैव विचारेण भोजने न प्रवर्तते ॥ २२ ॥

sarvatra eva vi-chârena bhojane na pra-vartate. (22)

Ind. *Ind.* -ra, *I. sg.* -na, *L. sg.* *Ind.* vṛit *with* pra, 3 *sg. Pres. Âtm.*

everywhere indeed with reflecting in eating not one engages.

यतः । शंकाभिः सर्वमाक्रांतमन्नं पानं च भूतले ।

yatas, śaṅkâbhis sarvam â-krântam annam pânam cha bhû-tale,

Ind. -kâ, *I. pl.* -va, *N. sg. n.* kram *with* â, *N. sg. n. past Ptc. Pass.* -na, *N. sg.* -na, *N. sg.* *Ind.* *Ttp.*-la, *L. sg.*

For, By apprehensions everything assailed, food, drink and, on the earth-surface,

प्रवृत्तिः कुत्र कर्तव्या जीवितव्यं कथं नु वा ॥ २३ ॥

pra-vṛittis kutra kartavyâ jîvitavyam katham nu vâ? (23)

-tti, *N. sg.* *Ind.* kṛi, *N. sg. f. Ptc. Fut. Pass.* jîv, *N. sg. n. Ptc. Fut. Pass.* *Ind.* *Ind.* *Ind.*

occupation where to be made, to be lived how now or?

ईर्ष्यी घृणी त्वसंतुष्टः क्रोधनो नित्यशंकितः ।

îrshyî ghṛiṇî tu a-santushṭas krodhanas nitya-śaṅkitas

-yin, *N. sg. m.* -ṇin, *N. sg. m.* *Ind.* *Karm.* -ta, *N. sg. m.* (*rt.* tush *with* sam) -na, *N. sg. m.* *Karm.* -ta, *N. sg. m.*

The envious, the censorious but, the dis-satisfied, the passionate, the constantly-suspicious,

परभाग्योपजीवी च षडेते दुःखभागिनः ॥ २४ ॥

para-bhâgya-upajîvî cha shaṭ ete duḥkha-bhâginas. (24)

Ttp. -vin, *N. sg. m.* *Ind.* shash, *N.* etad, *N. pl. m.* *Ttp.* -gin, *N. pl. m.*

the on another's-property-living and, six these misery-sharing.

एतच्छ्रुत्वा सर्वे कपोतास्तत्रोपविष्टाः ।

etad śrutvâ sarve kapotâs tatra upa-vishṭâs.

etad, *Ac. sg. n.* śru, *Ger.* -va, *N. pl. m.* -ta, *N. pl.* *Ind.* viś, *with* upa, *N. pl. m. past Ptc. Pass.*

This having heard all the pigeons there alighted.

यतः । सुमहांत्यपि शास्त्राणि धारयंतो बहुश्रुताः ।

yatas, su-mahânti api śâstrâṇi dhârayantas bahu-śrutâs

Ind. *Karm.* -hat, *Ac. pl. n.* *Ind.* -ra, *Ac. pl.* dhṛi, *N. pl. m. Ptc. Pres. Par. Caus.* *Bahuv.* -ta, *N. pl. m.* (*rt.* śru)

For, Very-great even sciences possessing, having learned-much,

छेत्तारः संशयानां च क्लिश्यंते लोभमोहिताः ॥ २५ ॥

chhettâras saṃ-śayânâm cha kliśyante lobha-mohitâs. (25)

-tṛi, *N. pl. m.* -ya, *G. pl.* *Ind.* kliś, 3 *pl. Pres. Âtm.* *Ttp.* -ta, *N. pl. m.* (*rt.* muh)

dispellers of doubts and, are pained by desire-infatuated.

अन्यच्च । लोभात्क्रोधः प्रभवति लोभात्कामः प्रजायते ।

anyad cha, lobhât krodhas pra-bhavati lobhât kâmas pra-jâyate,

-ya, *N. sg. n.* *Ind.* -bha, *Ab. sg.* -dha, *N. sg.* bhû *with* pra, 3 *sg. Pres. Par.* -bha, *Ab. sg.* -ma, *N. sg.* jan *with* pra, 3 *sg. Pres. Âtm.*

Again and, From desire passion springs, from desire lust is born,

लोभान्मोहश्च नाशश्च लोभः पापस्य कारणं ॥ २६ ॥

lobhât	mohas	cha,	nâśas	cha;	lobhas	pâpasya	kâraṇam.	(26)
-bha, *Ab. sg.*	-ha, *N. sg.*	*Ind.*	-śa, *N. sg.*	*Ind.*	-bha, *N. sg.*	-pa, *G. sg. n.*	-ṇa, *N. sg.*	
from desire	infatuation	and,	destruction	and;	desire	of evil	the cause.	

अन्यच्च । असंभवं हेममृगस्य जन्म तथापि रामो लुलुभे मृगाय ।

anyad	cha,	a-sambhavam	hema-mṛigasya	janma,	tathâ	api	râmas	lulubhe	mṛigâya;
-ya, *N. sg. n.*	*Ind.*	*Bahuv.* -va, *N. sg. n.*	*Ttp.* -ga, *G. sg.*	-man, *N. sg.*	*Ind.*	*Ind.*	-ma, *N. sg.*	lubh, 3 *sg. Perf. Âtm.*	-ga, *D. sg.*
Again	and,	Impossible	the gold-deer's	birth,	yet thus	even	Râma	had a desire	for the deer;

प्रायः समापन्नविपत्तिकाले धियोऽपि पुंसां मलिना भवंति ॥ २७ ॥

prâyas	samâpanna-vipatti-kâle	dhiyas	api	puṃsâm	malinâs	bhavanti.	(27)
Ind.	*Ttp.* -la, *L. sg.* (*rt.* pad *with* sam-â)	dhî, *N. pl.*	*Ind.*	puṃs, *G. pl.*	-na, *N. pl. f.*	bhû, 3 *pl. Pres. Par.*	
often	at the approached-misfortune's-time	the minds	even	of men	obscured	become.	

अनंतरं सर्वे जालेन बद्धा बभूवुः । ततो यस्य वचनात्

an-antaram	sarve	jâlena	baddhâs	babhûvus.	tatas	yasya	vachanât
Ind.	-va, *N. pl. m.*	-la, *I. sg.*	bandh, *N. pl. m. past Ptc. Pass.*	bhû, 3 *pl. Perf. Par.*	*Ind.*	yad, *G. sg. m.*	-na, *Ab. sg.*
Immediately	all	by the net	caught	were.	Then	whose	through speech

तत्रावलंबितास्तं सर्वे तिरस्कुर्वंति ।

tatra	ava-lambitâs	tam	sarve	tiras-kurvanti.
Ind.	lamb *with* ava, *N. pl. m. past. Ptc. Pass.*	tad, *Ac. sg. m.*	-va, *N. pl. m.*	kṛi *with* tiras, 3 *pl. Pres. Par.*
there	descended,	him	all	reproach.

यतः । न गणस्याग्रतो गच्छेत्सिद्धे कार्ये समं फलं ।

yatas,	na	gaṇasya	agratas	gachchhet,	siddhe	kârye	samam	phalam,
Ind.	*Ind.*	-ṇa, *G. sg.*	*Ind.*	gam, 3 *sg. Pot. Par.*	sidh, *L. sg. n. past Ptc. Pass.*	-ya, *L. sg.*	-ma, *N. sg. n.*	-la, *N. sg.*
For,	not	of a mass	in front	one should go;	succeeding	the action,	equal	the fruit,

यदि कार्यविपत्तिः स्यान्मुखरस्तत्र हन्यते ॥ २८ ॥

yadi	kârya-vipattis	syât	mukharas	tatra	hanyate.	(28)
Ind.	*Ttp.* -tti, *N. sg.*	as, 3 *sg. Pot. Par.*	-ra, *N. sg. m.*	*Ind.*	han, 3 *sg. Pres. Pass.*	
if	action-failure	should be,	the leader	there	is slain.	

तस्य तिरस्कारं श्रुत्वा चित्रग्रीव उवाच । नायमस्य दोषः ।

tasya	tiras-kâram	śrutvâ	chitra-grîvas	uvâcha:	na	ayam	asya	doshas;
tad, *G. sg. m.*	-ra, *Ac. sg.*	śru, *Ger.*	*Bahuv.* -va, *N. sg.*	vach, 3 *sg. Perf. Par.*	*Ind.*	idam, *N. sg. m.*	idam, *G. sg. m.*	-sha, *N. sg.*
Of him	the reproach	having heard	Chitragrîva	said:	Not	this	of him	the fault;

यतः । आपदामापतंतीनां हितोऽप्यायाति हेतुतां ।

yatas,	â-padâm	â-patantînâm	hitas	api	â-yâti	hetutâm;
Ind.	-pad, *G. pl.*	pat *with* â, *G. pl. f. Ptc. Pres. Par.*	-ta, *N. sg. m.*	*Ind.*	yâ *with* â, 3 *sg. Pres. Par.*	-tâ, *Ac. sg.*
For,	Of misfortunes	arriving	a friend	even	goes-to	the state of being the cause;

मातृजंघा हि वत्सस्य स्तंभीभवति बंधने ॥ २९ ॥

mâtṛi-jaṅghâ	hi	vatsasya	stambhî-bhavati	bandhane.	(29)
Ttp. -ghâ, *N. sg.*	*Ind.*	-sa, *G. sg.*	stambhî-bhû, 3 *sg. Pres. Par.*	-na, *L. sg.*	
the mother's-leg	for	of a calf	post-becomes	in the fastening.	

अन्यच्च । स बंधुर्यो विपन्नानामापदुद्धरणक्षमः ।

anyad	cha,	sas	bandhus	yas	vi-pannânâm	âpad-uddharaṇa-kshamas,
-ya, N. sg. n.	*Ind.*	*tad, N. sg. m.*	*-dhu, N. sg.*	*yad, N. sg. m.*	*pad with vi, G. pl. m. past Ptc. Pass.*	*Ttp. -ma, N. sg. m.*
Again	and,	He	a friend	who	of the afflicted	out of misfortune-to lift-able,

न तु भीतपरित्राणवस्तूपालंभपंडितः ॥ ३० ॥

na	tu	bhîta-paritrâṇa-vastu-upâlambha-paṇḍitas. (30)
Ind.	*Ind.*	*Ttp. -ta, N. sg. m.*
Not	but	the danger-deliverance-means-reproaching-clever.

विपत्काले विस्मय एव कापुरुषलक्षणं । तदत्र धैर्यम-

vipad-kâle	vi-smayas	eva	kâpurusha-lakshaṇam.	tad	atra	dhairyam
Ttp. -la, L. sg.	*-ya, N. sg.*	*Ind.*	*Ttp. -ṇa, N. sg.*	*Ind.*	*Ind.*	*-ya, Ac. sg.*
At misfortune-time	amazement	just	a weak-man's-mark.	Therefore	here	firmness

वलंब्य प्रतीकारश्चिंत्यतां ।

ava-lambya	pratî-kâras	chintyatâm.
lamb with ava, Ger.	*-ra, N. sg.*	*chint, 3 sg. Imp. Pass.*
embracing	a-remedy	let be thought of.

यतः । विपदि धैर्यमथाभ्युदये क्षमा

yatas,	vi-padi	dhairyam,	atha	abhi-ud-aye	kshamâ,
Ind.	*-pad, L. sg.*	*-ya, N. sg.*	*Ind.*	*-ya, L. sg.*	*-mâ, N. sg.*
For,	In misfortune	firmness,	further	in prosperity	moderation,

सदसि वाक्पटुता युधि विक्रमः ।

sadasi	vâch-paṭutâ,	yudhi	vi-kramas,
-das, L. sg.	*Ttp. -tâ, N. sg.*	*-dh, L. sg.*	*-ma, N. sg.*
in an assembly	word-cleverness,	in battle	heroism,

यशसि चाभिरुचिर्व्यसनं श्रुतौ

yaśasi	cha	abhi-ruchis,	vyasanam	śrutau,
-śas, L. sg.	*Ind.*	*-chi, N. sg.*	*-na, N. sg.*	*-ti, L. sg.*
in glory	and	contentment,	diligence	in sacred study,

प्रकृतिसिद्धमिदं हि महात्मनां ॥ ३१ ॥

prakṛiti-siddham	idam	hi	mahat-âtmanâm. (31)
Ttp. -dha, N. sg. n. (rt. sidh)	*idam, N. sg. n.*	*Ind.*	*Bahuv. -man, G. pl.*
by nature-accomplished	this	indeed	of the great-minded.

संपदि यस्य न हर्षो विपदि विषादो रणे च धीरत्वं ।

sam-padi	yasya	na	harshas,	vi-padi	vi-shâdas,	raṇe	cha	dhîratvam,
-pad, L. sg.	*yad, G. sg. m.*	*Ind.*	*-sha, N. sg.*	*-pad, L. sg.*	*-da, N. sg.*	*-ṇa, L. sg.*	*Ind.*	*-tva, N. sg.*
In happiness	whose	not	exultation,	in misfortune	despair,	in battle	and	firmness,

तं भुवनत्रयतिलकं जनयति जननी सुतं विरलं ॥ ३२ ॥

tam	bhuvana-traya-tilakam	janayati	jananî	sutam	viralam. (32)
tad, Ac. sg. m.	*Ttp. -ka, Ac. sg.*	*jan, 3 sg. Pres. Par. Caus.*	*-nî, N. sg.*	*-ta, Ac. sg. m.*	*-la, Ac. sg. n. Adv.*
him	a world-triad-ornament	bears	a mother	a son	rarely.

अन्यच्च। षड्दोषाः पुरुषेणेह हातव्या भूतिमिच्छता।

anyad	cha,	shaṭ	doshâs	purushеṇa	iha	hâtavyâs	bhûtim	ichchhatâ,
-ya, *N. sg. n.*	*Ind.*	shash, *N.*	-sha, *N. pl.*	-sha, *I. sg.*	*Ind.*	hâ, *N. pl. m. Ptc. Fut. Pass.*	-ti, *Ac. sg.*	ish, *I. sg. m. Ptc. Pres. Par.*
Again	and,	Six	faults	by a man	here	to be avoided,	prosperity	wishing,

निद्रा तंद्रा भयं क्रोध आलस्यं दीर्घसूत्रता ॥ ३३ ॥

nidrâ	tandrâ	bhayam	krodhas	âlasyam	dirgha-sûtratâ.	(33)
-râ, *N. sg.*	-râ, *N. sg.*	-ya, *N. sg.*	-dha, *N. sg.*	-ya, *N. sg.*	-tâ, *N. sg.*	
Sleep,	sloth,	fear,	anger,	laziness,	procrastination.	

इदानीमप्येवं क्रियतां। सर्वैरेकचित्तीभूय जालमादायोड्डीयतां।

idânîm	api	evam	kriyatâm;	sarvais	ekachittî-bhûya	jâlam	â-dâya	ud-ḍîyatâm.
Ind.	*Ind.*	*Ind.*	kṛi, 3 *sg. Imp. Pass.*	-va, *I. pl. m.*	ekachittî-bhû, *Ger.*	-la, *Ac. sg.*	dâ *with* â, *Ger.*	ḍî *with* ud, 3 *sg. Imp. Pass.*
At present	also	thus	may be acted;	by all	of one-mind-being,	the net	having taken,	up-may be flown.

यतः। अल्पानामपि वस्तूनां संहतिः कार्यसाधिका।

yatas,	alpânâm	api	vastûnâm	sam-hatis	kârya-sâdhikâ,
Ind.	-pa, *G. pl. n.*	*Ind.*	-tu, *G. pl.*	-ti, *N. sg.*	*Ttp.* -dhaka, *N. sg. f.*
For,	Of small	even	things	a combination	aim-accomplishing,

तृणैर्गुणत्वमापन्नैर्बध्यंते मत्तदंतिनः ॥ ३४ ॥

tṛiṇais	guṇatvam	â-pannais	badhyante	matta-dantinas.	(34)
-ṇa, *I. pl. m. or n.*	-tva, *Ac. sg.*	pad *with* â, *I. pl. m. or n. past Ptc. Pass.*	bandh, 3 *pl. Pres. Karm. Pass.*	-tin, *N. pl.* (*rt.* mad).	
with grass blades,	a rope's state	having attained,	are bound	furious-elephants.	

संहतिः श्रेयसी पुंसां स्वकुलैरल्पकैरपि।

sam-hatis	śreyasî	puṁsâm	sva-kulais	alpakais	api,
-ti, *N. sg.*	praśasya, *N. sg. f. Compar.*	puṁs, *G. pl.*	*Karm.* -la, *I. pl.*	-ka, *I. pl. n.*	*Ind.*
Combination	better	of men	with their-families	small	even,

तुषेणापि परित्यक्ता न प्ररोहंति तंडुलाः ॥ ३५ ॥

tushеṇa	api	pari-tyaktâs	na	pra-rohanti	taṇḍulâs.	(35)
-sha, *I. sg.*	*Ind.*	tyaj *with* pari, *N. pl. m. past Ptc. Pass.*	*Ind.*	ruh *with* pra, 3 *pl. Pres. Par.*	-la, *N. pl.*	
by the husk	merely	deserted	not	grow-up	rice-grains.	

इति विचिंत्य पक्षिणः सर्वे जालमादायोत्पतिताः।

iti	vi-chintya	pakshiṇas	sarve	jâlam	â-dâya	ud-patitâs.
Ind.	chint *with* vi, *Ger.*	-shin, *N. pl. m.*	-va, *N. pl. m.*	-la, *Ac. sg.*	dâ *with* â, *Ger.*	pat *with* ud, *N. pl. m. past Ptc. Pass.*
Thus	having considered,	the birds	all	the net	having taken,	flown-up.

अनंतरं स व्याधः सुदूराज्जालापहारकांस्तानवलोक्य

an-antaram	sas	vyâdhas	su-dûrât	jâla-apahârakân	tân	ava-lokya
Ind.	tad, *N. sg. m.*	-dha, *N. sg.*	*Ind.*	*Ttp.* -ka, *Ac. pl. m.*	tad, *Ac. pl. m.*	lok *with* ava, *Ger.*
Thereupon	that	hunter	from very-far	net-carrying off	them	having seen,

पश्चाद्धावन्नचिंतयत्।

paśchât	dhâvan	achintayat:
Ind.	dhâv, *N. sg. m. Ptc. Pres. Par.*	chint, 3 *sg. Impf. Par.*
after	running,	thought:

संहतास्तु हरंत्येते मम जालं विहंगमाः ।

sam-hatâs	tu	haranti	ete	mama	jâlam	viham-gamâs,
han *with* sam, *N. pl. m. past Ptc. Pass.*	*Ind.*	hṛi, 3 *pl. Pres. Par.*	etad, *N. pl. m.*	asmad, *G. sg.*	-la, *Ac. sg.*	-ma, *N. pl.*
Combined	indeed	take away	these	of me	the net	the birds,

यदा तु निपतिष्यंति वशमेष्यंति मे तदा ॥ ३६ ॥

yadâ	tu	ni-patishyanti	vaśam	eshyanti	me	tadâ.	(36)
Ind.	*Ind.*	pat *with* ni, 3 *pl. Fut.* ii. *Par.*	-śa, *Ac. sg.*	i, 3 *pl. Fut.* ii. *Par.*	asmad, *G. sg.*	*Ind.*	
if	but	down-they shall fall,	into the power	they will go	of me	then.	

ततस्तेषु चक्षुर्विषयातिक्रांतेषु पक्षिषु स व्याधो

tatas	teshu	chakshus-vishaya-atikrânteshu	pakshishu	sas	vyâdhas
Ind.	tad, *L. pl. m.*	*Tp.* -ta, *L. pl. m.* (*rt.* kram *with* ati)	-shin, *L. pl. m.*	tad, *N. sg. m.*	-dha, *N. sg.*
Then	those	the sight-confines-having passed	birds,	that	hunter

निवृत्तः । अथ लुब्धकं निवृत्तं दृष्ट्वा कपोता

ni-vṛittas.	atha	lubdhakam	ni-vṛittam	dṛishṭvâ	kapotâs
vṛit *with* ni, *N. sg. m. past Ptc. Pass.*	*Ind.*	-ka, *Ac. sg.*	vṛit *with* ni, *Ac. sg. m. past Ptc. Pass.*	dṛiś, *Ger.*	-ta, *N. pl.*
returned.	Now	the hunter	returned	having seen	the pigeons

ऊचुः । किमिदानीं कर्तुमुचितं । चित्रग्रीव उवाच ।

ûchus:	kim	idânîm	kartum	uchitam?	chitra-grîvas	uvâcha:
vach, 3 *pl. Perf. Par.*	kim, *Ac. sg. n.*	*Ind.*	kṛi, *Inf.*	-ta, *N. sg. n.*	*Bahuv.* -va, *N. sg.*	vach, 3 *sg. Perf. Par.*
said:	What	now	to do	proper?	Chitragrîva	said:

माता मित्रं पिता चेति स्वभावात्त्रितयं हितं ।

mâtâ	mitram	pitâ	cha	iti	sva-bhâvât	tritayam	hitam;
-tṛi, *N. sg.*	-ra, *N. sg.*	-tṛi, *N. sg.*	*Ind.*	*Ind.*	*Karm.* -va, *Ab. sg.*	-ya, *N. sg.*	-ta, *N. sg. n.*
A mother,	a friend,	a father	and,	thus	from inborn-disposition	a triad	friendly;

कार्यकारणतश्चान्ये भवंति हितबुद्धयः ॥ ३७ ॥

kârya-kâraṇa-tas	cha	anye	bhavanti	hita-buddhayas.	(37)
Dvandva. with tas.	*Ind.*	-ya, *N. pl. m.*	bhû, 3 *pl. Pres. Par.*	*Bahuv.* -dhi, *N. pl. m.*	
from effect-and-cause	and	others	become	friendly-minded.	

तदस्माकं मित्रं हिरण्यको नाम मूषिकराजो गंडकीतीरे

tad	asmâkam	mitram	hiraṇyakas	nâma	mûshika-râjas	gaṇḍakî-tîre
Ind.	asmad, *G. pl.*	-ra, *N. sg.*	-ka, *N. sg.*	-man, *Ac. sg. Adv.*	*Tp.* -ja, *N. sg.*	*Tp.* -ra, *L. sg.*
Now	of us	a friend	Hiraṇyaka	by name,	a mouse-king,	on the Gaṇḍakî-bank

चित्रवने निवसति । सो ऽस्माकं पाशांश्छेत्स्यति ।

chitra-vane	ni-vasati;	sas	asmâkam	pâśân	chhetsyati.
Karm. -na, *L. sg.*	vas *with* ni, 3 *sg. Pres. Par.*	tad, *N. sg. m.*	asmad, *G. pl.*	-śa, *Ac. pl.*	chhid, 3 *sg. Fut.* ii. *Par.*
in the Chitra-wood	dwells;	he	of us	the fetters	will cut.

इत्यालोच्य सर्वे हिरण्यकविवरसमीपं गताः । हिरण्यकश्च

iti	â-lochya	sarve	hiraṇyaka-vivara-samîpam	gatâs.	hiraṇyakas	cha
Ind.	loch *with* â, *Ger.*	-va, *N. pl. m.*	*Tp.* -pa, *Ac. sg. Adv.*	gam, *N. pl. m. past Ptc. Pass.*	-ka, *N. sg.*	*Ind.*
Thus	having reflected	all	Hiraṇyaka's-hole-near	gone.	Hiraṇyaka	and

सर्वदापायशंकया शतद्वारं विवरं कृत्वा निवसति ।

sarvadâ	apâya-śaṅkayâ	śata-dvâram	vi-varam	kṛitvâ	ni-vasati.
Ind.	Ttp. -kâ, I. sg.	Bahuv. -ra, Ac. sg. n.	-ra, Ac. sg.	kṛi, Ger.	vas with ni, 3 sg. Pres. Par.
always	through danger-dread	a hundred-doored	hole	having made	dwells.

ततो हिरण्यकः कपोतावपातभयाच्चकितस्तूष्णीं स्थितः ।

tatas	hiraṇyakas	kapota-avapâta-bhayât	chakitas	tûshṇîm	sthitas.
Ind.	-ka, N. sg.	Ttp. -ya, Ab. sg.	-ta, N. sg. m.	Ind.	sthâ, N. sg. m. past Ptc. Pass.
Then	Hiraṇyaka	from the pigeon-descent-fear	timid	silently	stood.

चित्रग्रीव उवाच । सखे हिरण्यक किमस्मान्न संभाषसे ।

chitra-grîvas	uvâcha:	sakhe	hiraṇyaka,	kim	asmân	na	sam-bhâshase?
Bahuv. -va, N. sg.	vach, 3 sg. Perf. Par.	-khi, V. sg.	-ka, V. sg.	Ind.	asmad, Ac. pl.	Ind.	bhâsh with sam, 2 sg. Pres. Âtm.
Chitragrîva	said:	Friend	Hiraṇyaka,	why	us	not	dost thou greet?

ततो हिरण्यकस्तद्वचनं प्रत्यभिज्ञाय ससंभ्रमं

tatas	hiraṇyakas	tad-vachanam	prati-abhi-jñâya	sa-sambhramam
Ind.	-ka, N. sg.	Ttp. -na, Ac. sg.	jñâ with prati-abhi, Ger.	Avyay.
Then	Hiraṇyaka	of him-the voice	having recognised	hastily

बहिर्निःसृत्याब्रवीत् । आः पुण्यवानस्मि प्रियसुहृन्मे

vahis	nis-sṛitya	abravît:	âḥ	puṇyavân	asmi,	priya-suhṛid	me
Ind.	sṛi with nis, Ger.	brû, 3 sg. Impf. Par.	Ind.	-vat, N. sg. m.	as, 1 sg. Pres. Par.	Karm. -d, N. sg.	asmad, G. sg.
out	slipping	said:	Oh,	happy	I am,	the dear-friend	of me

चित्रग्रीवः समायातः ।

chitra-grîvas	sam-â-yâtas.
Bahuv. -va, N. sg.	yâ with sam and â, N. sg. m. past Ptc. Pass.
Chitragrîva	arrived.

यस्य मित्रेण संभाषा यस्य मित्रेण संस्थितिः ।

yasya	mitreṇa	sam-bhâshâ	yasya	mitreṇa	sam-sthitis
yad, G. sg. m.	-ra, I. sg.	-shâ, N. sg.	yad, G. sg. m.	-ra, I. sg.	-ti, N. sg.
Whose	with a friend	greeting,	whose	with a friend	staying,

यस्य मित्रेण संलापस्ततो नास्तीह पुण्यवान् ॥ ३८ ॥

yasya	mitreṇa	sam-lâpas	tatas	na	asti	iha	puṇyavân.	(38)
yad, G. sg. m.	-ra, I. sg.	-pa, N. sg.	tad with Abl. aff. tas	Ind.	as, 3 sg. Pres. Par.	Ind.	-vat, N. sg. m.	
whose	with a friend	chatting,	than he	not	is there	here	a happier one.	

पाशबद्धांश्चैतान्दृष्ट्वा सविस्मयः क्षणं

pâśa-baddhân	cha	etân	dṛishṭvâ	sa-vismayas	kshaṇam
Ttp. -dha, Ac. pl. m. (rt. bandh).	Ind.	etad, Ac. pl. m.	dṛiś, Ger.	Bahuv. -ya, N. sg. m.	-ṇa, Ac. sg. Adv.
Net-confined	and	them	having seen	with-amazement	a moment

स्थित्वोवाच । सखे किमेतत् । चित्रग्रीवोऽवदत् ।

sthitvâ	uvâcha:	sakhe	kim	etad?	chitra-grîvas	avadat:
sthâ, Ger.	vach, 3 sg. Perf. Par.	-khi, V. sg.	kim, N. sg. n.	etad, N. sg. n.	Bahuv. -va, N. sg.	vad, 3 sg. Impf. Par.
having stood	he said:	Friend,	what	this?	Chitragrîva	said:

सखे ऽस्माकं प्राक्तनजन्मकर्मणः फलमेतत् ।

sakhe	asmâkam	prâktana-janman-karmaṇas	phalam	etad.
-khi, *V. sg.*	asmad, *G. pl.*	*Ttp.* -man, *G. sg.*	-la, *N. sg.*	etad, *N. sg. n.*
Friend,	of us	of a former-birth's-action	the fruit	this.

यस्माच्च येन च यथा च यदा च यच्च

yasmât	cha	yena	cha	yathâ	cha	yadâ	cha	yad	cha
yad, *Ab. sg. n.*	*Ind.*	yad, *I. sg. n.*	*Ind.*	*Ind.*	*Ind.*	*Ind.*	*Ind.*	yad, *N. sg. n.*	*Ind.*
Wherefore	and,	by what	and,	how	and,	when	and,	as what	and,

यावच्च यत्र च शुभाशुभमात्मकर्म ।

yâvat	cha	yatra	cha	śubha-aśubham	âtman-karma,
-vat, *N. sg. n.*	*Ind.*	*Ind.*	*Ind.*	*Dvandva.* -bha, *N. sg. n.*	*Ttp.* -man, *N. sg.*
how great	and,	where	and,	good-(and) evil	one's own-action,

तस्माच्च तेन च तथा च तदा च तच्च

tasmât	cha	tena	cha	tathâ	cha	tadâ	cha	tad	cha
tad, *Ab. sg. n.*	*Ind.*	tad, *I. sg. n.*	*Ind.*	*Ind.*	*Ind.*	*Ind.*	*Ind.*	tad, *N. sg. n.*	*Ind.*
therefore	and,	by that	and,	thus	and,	then	and,	as that	and,

तावच्च तत्र च विधातृवशादुपैति ॥ ३९ ॥

tâvat	cha	tatra	cha	vidhâtṛi-vaśât	upa-eti (39)
-vat, *N. sg. n.*	*Ind.*	*Ind.*	*Ind.*	*Ttp.* -śa, *Ab. sg.*	i *with* upa, 3 *sg. Pres. Par.*
so great	and,	there	and,	through fate's-power	it approaches.

रोगशोकपरीतापबंधनव्यसनानि च ।

roga-śoka-parîtâpa-bandhana-vyasanâni	cha
Dvandva. -na, *N. pl.*	*Ind.*
Sickness-sorrow-pain-bonds-affliction	and,

आत्मापराधवृक्षस्य फलान्येतानि देहिनां ॥ ४० ॥

âtman-aparâdha-vṛikshasya	phalâni	etâni	dehinâm. (40)
Ttp. -sha, *G. sg.*	-la, *N. pl.*	etad. *N. pl. n.*	-hin, *G. pl. m.*
of the self-transgressions'-tree	the fruits	these	of creatures.

एतच्छ्रुत्वा हिरण्यकश्चित्रग्रीवस्य बंधनं छेत्तुं

etad	śrutvâ	hiraṇyakas	chitra-grîvasya	bandhanam	chhettum
etad, *Ac. sg. n.*	śru, *Ger.*	-ka, *N. sg.*	*Bahuv.* -va, *G. sg.*	-na, *Ac. sg.*	chhid, *Inf.*
This	having heard	Hiraṇyaka	Chitragrîva's	bonds	to cut

सत्वरमुपसर्पति । चित्रग्रीव उवाच । मित्र मा मैवं ।

sa-tvaram	upa-sarpati.	chitra-grîvas	uvâcha:	mitra	mâ	mâ	evam;
Avyay.	sṛip, *with* upa, 3 *sg. Pres. Par.*	*Bahuv.* -va, *N. sg.*	vach, 3 *sg. Perf. Par.*	-ra, *V. sg.*	*Ind.*	*Ind.*	*Ind.*
with-haste	advances.	Chitragrîva	said:	Friend,	not,	not	thus;

अस्मदाश्रितानामेषां तावत्पाशांश्छिंधि तदा मम

asmad-âśritânâm	eshâm	tâvat	pâśân	chhindhi,	tadâ	mama
Ttp. -ta, *G. pl. m.* (ri, śri, *with* â)	etad, *G. pl. m.*	*Ind.*	-śa, *Ac. pl.*	chhid, 2 *sg. Imp. Par.*	*Ind.*	asmad, *G. sg.*
of my-dependants	of these,	first	the fetters	cut,	then	of me

पाशं पश्चाच्छेत्स्यसि। हिरण्यको ऽप्याह। अहमल्पशक्ति-

pâśam	paśchât	chhetsyasi.	hiraṇyakas	api	âha:	aham	alpa-śaktis,
-śa, *Ac. sg.*	*Ind.*	chhid, 2 *sg. Fut. ii. Par.*	-ka, *N. sg.*	*Ind.*	ah, 3 *sg. Perf. Par.*	asmad, *N. sg.*	*Bahuv.* -ti, *N. sg. m.*
the fetter	afterwards	thou wilt cut.	Hiraṇyaka	also	said:	I	of little-strength,

र्दंताश्च मे कोमलास्तदेतेषां पाशांश्छेत्तुं

dantâs	cha	me	komalâs,	tad	eteshâm	pâśân	chhettum
-ta, *N. pl.*	*Ind.*	asmad, *G. sg.*	-la, *N. pl. m.*	*Ind.*	etad, *G. pl. m.*	-śa, *Ac. pl.*	chhid, *Inf.*
the teeth	and	of me	delicate,	therefore	of these	the fetters	to cut

कथं समर्थः। तद्यावन्मे दंता न त्रुट्यंति

katham	samarthas?	tad	yâvat	me	dantâs	na	truṭyanti,
Ind.	-tha, *N. sg. m.*	*Ind.*	*Ind.*	asmad, *G. sg.*	-ta, *N. pl.*	*Ind.*	truṭ, 3 *pl. Pres. Par.*
how	able?	Therefore	as long as	of me	the teeth	not	break,

तावत्तव पाशं छिनद्मि तदनंतरमेषामपि

tâvat	tava	pâśam	chhinadmi;	tad-anantaram	eshâm	api
Ind.	yushmad, *G. sg.*	-śa, *Ac sg.*	chhid, 1 *sg. Pres. Par.*	*Ind.*	etad, *G. pl. m.*	*Ind.*
so long	of thee	the fetter	I cut;	thereafter	of these	also

बंधनं यावच्छक्यं छेत्स्यामि। चित्रग्रीव उवाच।

bandhanam	yâvat-śakyam	chhetsyâmi.	chitra-grîvas	uvâcha:
-na, *Ac. sg.*	*Avyay.*	chhid, 1 *sg. Fut. ii. Par.*	*Bahuv.* -va, *N. sg.*	vach, 3 *sg. Perf. Par.*
the bonds	as far as-possible	I shall cut.	Chitragrîva	said:

अस्त्वेवं तथापि यथाशक्त्येतेषां बंधनं

astu	evam,	tathâ	api	yathâ-śakti	eteshâm	bandhanam
as, 3 *sg. Imp. Par.*	*Ind.*	*Ind.*	*Ind.*	*Avyay.*	etad, *G. pl. m.*	-na, *Ac. sg.*
Be it	so,	thus	even	according to-strength	of these	the bonds

खंडय। हिरण्यकेनोक्तं। आत्मपरित्यागेन यदा-

khaṇḍaya.	hiraṇyakena	uktam:	âtman-parityâgena	yad
khaṇḍ, 2 *sg. Imp. Par.*	-ka, *I. sg.*	vach, *N. sg. n. past Ptc. Pass.*	*Ttp.* -ga, *I. sg.*	yad, *N. sg. n.*
divide.	By Hiraṇyaka	said:	by self-sacrifice	what

श्रितानां परिरक्षणं तन्न नीतिविदां संमतं।

â-śritânâm	pari-rakshaṇam	tad	na	nîti-vedinâm	sam-matam.
śri *with* â, *G. pl. m. past Ptc. Pass.*	-ṇa, *N. sg.*	tad, *N. sg. n.*	*Ind.*	*Ttp.* -din, *G. pl. m.*	man *with* sam, *N. sg. n. past Ptc. Pass.*
of dependants	preservation,	that	not	of the policy-knowing	approved of.

यतः। आपदर्थे धनं रक्षेद्दारान्रक्षेद्धनैरपि।

yatas,	âpad-arthe	dhanam	rakshet,	dârân	rakshet	dhanais	api,
Ind.	*Ttp.* -tha, *L. sg. Adv.*	-na, *Ac. sg.*	raksh, 3 *sg. Pot. Par.*	-ra, *Ac. pl.*	raksh, 3 *sg. Pot. Par.*	-na, *I. pl.*	*Ind.*
For,	For misfortune's-sake	riches	one should save,	the wife	one should save	through the riches	even,

आत्मानं सततं रक्षेद्दारैरपि धनैरपि ॥ ४१ ॥

âtmânam	satatam	rakshet	dârais	api	dhanais	api. (41)
-man, *Ac. sg.*	*Ac. sg. n. Adv.*	raksh, 3 *sg. Pot. Par.*	-ra, *I. pl.*	*Ind.*	-na, *I. pl.*	*Ind.*
oneself	constantly	one should save	through the wife	even,	through the riches	even.

अन्यच्च । धर्मार्थकाममोक्षाणां प्राणाः संस्थितिहेतवः ।

anyad	cha,	dharma-artha-kâma-mokshâṇâm	prâṇâs	saṁsthiti-hetavas,
-ya, N. sg. n.	*Ind.*	*Dvandva. -sha, G. pl.*	*-ṇa, N. pl.*	*Ttp. -tu, N. pl.*
Again	and,	Of virtue-wealth-desire-final liberation	life	the existence-cause,

तान्निघ्नता किं न हतं रक्षता किं न रक्षितं ॥ ४२ ॥

tân	ni-ghnatâ	kim	na	hatam,	rakshatâ	kim	na	rakshitam?	(42)
tad, Ac. pl. m.	*han with ni, I. sg. m. Pres. Ptc. Par.*	*kim, N. sg. n.*	*Ind.*	*han, N. sg. n. past Ptc. Pass.*	*raksh, I. sg. m. Pres. Ptc. Par.*	*id.*	*Ind.*	*raksh, past Ptc. Pass.*	
that	by one destroying	what	not	destroyed,	by one saving	what	not	saved?	

चित्रग्रीव उवाच । सखे नीतिस्तावदीदृश्येव किंतु-

chitra-grîvas	uvâcha:	sakhe	nîtis	tâvat	îdṛiśî	eva,	kim-	tu
Bahuv. -va, N. sg.	*vach, 3 sg. Perf. Par.*	*-khi, V. sg.*	*-ti, N. sg.*	*Ind.*	*-â, N. sg. f.*	*Ind.*	*Ind.*	*Ind.*
Chitragrîva	said:	Friend,	policy	certainly	such	just,	but	

अहमस्मदाश्रितानां दुःखं सोढुं सर्वथासमर्थः ।

aham	asmad-âśritânâm	duḥkham	soḍhum	sarvathâ	a-samarthas;
asmad, N. sg.	*Ttp. -ta, G. pl. m. (rt. śri with â)*	*-kha, Ac. sg.*	*sah, Inf.*	*Ind.*	*Karm. -tha, N. sg. m.*
I	of my-dependants	the affliction	to bear	wholly	un-able;

तेनेदं ब्रवीमि ।

tena	idam	bravîmi.
tad, I. sg. n. Adv.	*idam, Ac. sg. n.*	*brû, 1 sg. Pres. Par.*
therefore	this	I say.

यतः । धनानि जीवितं चैव परार्थे प्राज्ञ उत्सृजेत् ।

yatas	dhanâni	jîvitam	cha	eva	para-arthe	prâjñas	ud-sṛijet;
Ind.	*-na, Ac. pl.*	*-ta, Ac. sg.*	*Ind.*	*Ind.*	*Ttp. -tha, L. sg. Adv.*	*-ña, N. sg. m.*	*sṛij, with ud, 3 sg. Pot. Par.*
For,	Riches,	life	and	even,	for another's-sake	the wise	should give-up;

सन्निमित्ते वरं त्यागो विनाशे नियते सति ॥ ४३ ॥

sat-nimitte	varam	tyâgas,	vi-nâśe	ni-yate	sati.	(43)
Ttp. -tta, L. sg.	*-ra, N. sg. Adv.*	*-ga, N. sg.*	*-śa, L. sg.*	*yam with ni, L. sg. m. past Ptc. Pass.*	*as, L. sg. m. Ptc. Pres. Par.*	
for good's sake	preferable	the sacrifice,	destruction	destined	being.	

अयमपरश्चासाधारणो हेतुः ।

ayam	aparas	cha	a-sâdhâraṇas	hetus:
idam, N. sg. m.	*-ra, N. sg. m.*	*Ind.*	*Bahuv. -ṇa, N. sg. m.*	*-tu, N. sg.*
This	another	and	un-paralleled	argument:

जातिद्रव्यगुणानां च साम्यमेषां मया सह ।

jâti-dravya-guṇânâm	cha	sâmyam	eshâm	mayâ	saha,
Dvandva. -ṇa, G. pl.	*Ind.*	*-ya, N. sg. n.*	*etad, G. pl. m.*	*asmad, I. sg.*	*Ind.*
of kind-substance-quality	and	equality	of these	me	with,

मत्प्रभुत्वफलं ब्रूहि कदा किं तद्भविष्यति ॥ ४४ ॥

mad-prabhutva-phalam	brûhi	kadâ	kim	tad	bhavishyati?	(44)
Ttp. -la, Ac. sg. (cf. asmad)	*brû, 2 sg. Imp. Par.*	*Ind.*	*kim, N. sg. n.*	*tad, N. sg. n.*	*bhû, 3 sg. Fut. ii. Par.*	
of me-the superiority-fruit,	say,	when	what	that	will be?	

अन्यच्च । विना वर्तनमेवैते न त्यजंति ममांतिकं ।

anyad	cha,	vinâ	vartanam	eva	ete	na	tyajanti	mama	antikam,
-ya, *N. sg. n.*	*Ind.*	*Ind.*	-na, *Ac. sg.*	*Ind.*	etad, *N. pl. m.*	*Ind.*	tyaj, 3. *pl. Pres. Par.*	asmad, *G. sg.*	-ka, *Ac. sg.*
Again	and,	Without	wages	even,	these	not	abandon	of me	the proximity,

तन्मे प्राणव्ययेनापि जीवयैतान्ममाश्रितान् ॥ ४५ ॥

tad	me	prâṇa-vyayena	api	jîvaya	etân	mama	â-śritân.	(45)
Ind.	asmad, *G. sg.*	*Ttp.* -ya, *I. sg.*	*Ind.*	jîv, 2 *sg. Imp. Par. Caus.*	etad, *Ac. pl. m.*	asmad, *G. sg.*	śri with â, *Ac. pl. m. past Ptc. Pass.*	
therefore	of me	with the life-loss	even	cause to live	these	of me	the dependants.	

किंच । मांसमूत्रपुरीषास्थिनिर्मिते ऽस्मिन्कलेवरे ।

kim-cha,	mâṁsa-mûtra-purîsha-asthi-nirmite	asmin	kalevare
Ind. Ind.	*Ttp.* -ta, *L. sg. n.* (*rt.* mâ *with* nis)	idam, *L. sg. n.*	-ra, *L. sg.*
Moreover,	On the flesh-urine-excrement-bone-composed	this	body

विनश्वरे विहायास्थां यशः पालय मित्र मे ॥ ४६ ॥

vi-naśvare	vi-hâya	â-sthâm	yaśas	pâlaya	mitra	me.	(46)
-ra, *L. sg. n.*	hâ *with* vi, *Ger.*	-sthâ, *Ac. sg.*	-śas, *Ac. sg.*	pâ, 2 *sg. Imp. Par. Caus.*	-ra, *V. sg.*	asmad, *G. sg.*	
the perishable	having given up	consideration,	the fame	preserve,	O friend,	of me.	

अपरं च पश्य । यदि नित्यमनित्येन निर्मलं मलवाहिना ।

aparam	cha	paśya,	yadi	nityam	a-nityena	nis-malam	mala-vâhinâ
-ra, *Ac. sg. n.*	*Ind.*	dṛiś, 2 *sg. Imp. Par.*	*Ind.*	-ya, *N. sg. n.*	*Karm.* -ya, *I. sg. n.*	*Bahuv.* -la, *N. sg. n.*	*Ttp.* -hin, *I. sg. n.*
Another	and	behold,	If	the eternal	through the non-eternal,	the stain-less	through the stain-bringing,

यशः कायेन लभ्येत तन्न लब्धं भवेन्नु किं ॥ ४७ ॥

yaśas	kâyena	labhyeta,	tad	na	labdham	bhavet	nu	kim?	(47)
-śas, *N. sg.*	-ya, *I. sg.*	labh, 3 *sg. Pot. Pass.*	tad, *N. sg. n.*	*Ind.*	labh, *N. sg. n. past Ptc. Pass.*	bhû, 3 *sg. Pot. Par.*	*Ind.*	*Ind.*	
fame	through the body	might be obtained,	that	not	obtained	should be	well	why?	

यतः । शरीरस्य गुणानां च दूरमत्यंतमंतरं ।

yatas,	śarîrasya	guṇânâm	cha	dûram	ati-antam	antaram,
Ind.	-ra, *G. sg.*	-ṇa, *G. pl.*	*Ind.*	-ra, *N. sg. n.*	*Ttp.* -ta, *N. sg. n.*	-ra, *N. sg. n.*
For,	Of the body	of virtues	and,	a wide	exceeding	difference,

शरीरं क्षणविध्वंसि कल्पांतस्थायिनो गुणाः ॥ ४८ ॥

śarîram	kshaṇa-vidhvaṁsi,	kalpa-anta-sthâyinas	guṇâs.	(48)
-ra, *N. sg.*	*Ttp.* -sin, *N. sg. n.*	*Ttp.* -yin, *N. pl. m.*	-ṇa, *N. pl.*	
the body	in a moment-falling asunder,	to a kalpa's-end-lasting	virtues.	

इत्याकर्ण्य हिरण्यकः प्रहृष्टमनाः पुलकितः सन्नब्रवीत् ।

iti	â-karṇya	hiraṇyakas	prahṛishṭa-manâs	pulakitas	san	abravît:
Ind.	karṇ *with* â, *Ger.*	-ka, *N. sg.*	*Bahuv.* -nas, *N. sg. m.*	-ta, *N. sg. m.*	as, *N. sg. m. Ptc. Pres. Par.*	brû, 3 *sg. Impf. Par.*
Thus	having heard	Hiraṇyaka	of delighted-mind	thrilled	being	said:

साधु मित्र साधु । अनेनाश्रितवात्सल्येन त्रैलोक्यस्यापि

sâdhu,	mitra,	sâdhu;	anena	âśrita-vâtsalyena	trailokyasya	api
-dhu, *N. sg. n. Adv.*	-ra, *V. sg.*	-dhu, *N. sg. n. Adv.*	idam, *I. sg. n.*	*Ttp.* -ya, *I. sg.*	-ya, *G. sg.*	*Ind.*
Nobly,	friend,	nobly;	through this	towards the dependants-tenderness	of the three-worlds	even

प्रभुत्वं त्वयि युज्यते। एवमुक्त्वा तेन सर्वेषां

prabhutvam tvayi yujyate. evam uktvâ tena sarveshâm
-tva, *N. sg.* yashmad, *L.sg.* yuj, 3 *sg.Pres. Pass.* *Ind.* vach, *Ger.* tad, *I.sg.m.* -va, *G.pl.m.*
the sovereignty in thee is proper. Thus having spoken by him of all

बंधनानि छिन्नानि। ततो हिरण्यकः सर्वान्सादरं संपूज्याह।

bandhanâni chhinnâni. tatas hiraṇyakas sarvân sa-âdaram sam-pûjya âha:
-na, *N.pl.* chhid, *N.pl.n.past Ptc.Pass.* *Ind.* -ka, *N. sg.* -va, *Ac.pl.m.* *Avyay.* pûj *with* sam, *Ger.* ah, 3 *sg. Perf.Par.*
the bonds cut. Then Hiraṇyaka all respectfully having saluted said:

सखे चित्रग्रीव सर्वथात्र जालबंधनविधौ सति दोषमा-

sakhe chitra-grîva, sarvathâ atra jâla-bandhana-vidhau sati dosham
-khi, *V.sg.* *Bahuv.* -va, *V.sg.* *Ind.* *Ind.* *Ttp.* -dhi, *L. sg.* as, *L.sg.m.Ptc. Pres.Par.* -sha, *Ac.sg.*
Friend Chitragrîva, wholly here the net-confinement-destiny being, a fault

शंक्यात्मन्यवज्ञा न कर्तव्या।

â-śaṅkya âtmani ava-jñâ na kartavyâ.
śaṅk *with* â, *Ger.* -man, *L. sg.* -jñâ, *N. sg.* *Ind.* kṛi, *N.sg.f.Ptc.Fut.Pass.*
suspecting, of one's self disdain not to be made.

यतः। यो ऽधिकाद्योजनशतात्पश्यतीहामिषं खगः।

yatas, yas adhikât yojana-śatât paśyati iha âmisham kha-gas
Ind. yad, *N. sg. m.* -ka, *Ab. sg. n.* *Ttp.* -ta, *Ab. sg.* dṛiś, 3 *sg. Pres. Par.* *Ind.* -sha, *Ac. sg.* *Ttp.* -ga, *N. sg.*
For, Who from a great yojana-hundred espies here the prey, a bird,

स एव प्राप्तकालस्तु पाशबंधं न पश्यति ॥४९॥

sas eva prâpta-kâlas tu pâśa-bandham na paśyati. (49)
tad, *N. sg.m.* *Ind.* *Bahuv.* -la, *N. sg. m.* *Ind.* *Ttp.* -dha, *Ac. sg.* *Ind.* dṛiś, 3 *sg. Pres.Par.*
he even having reached-the time on the other hand the snare-knot not sees.

अपरं च। शशिदिवाकरयोर्ग्रहपीडनं

aparam cha, śaśin-divâkarayos graha-pîḍanam,
-ra, *N. sg. n.* *Ind.* *Dvandva.* -ra, *G. du.* *Ttp.* -na, *Ac. sg.*
Another and, Of moon-(and)-sun through eclipse-the distress,

गजभुजंगमयोरपि बंधनं।

gaja-bhujaṅgamayos api bandhanam,
Dvandva. -ma, *G. du.* *Ind.* -na, *Ac. sg.*
of elephant-(and)-serpent also the binding,

मतिमतां च विलोक्य दरिद्रतां

matimatâm cha vi-lokya daridratâm,
-mat, *G. pl.m.* *Ind.* lok *with* vi, *Ger.* -tâ, *Ac. sg.*
of the wise and having perceived the indigence,

विधिरहो बलवानिति मे मतिः ॥५०॥

vidhis aho balavân iti me matis. (50)
-dhi, *N. sg.* *Ind.* -vat, *N. sg. m.* *Ind.* asmad, *G. sg.* -ti, *N. sg.*
'destiny, Oh, powerful,' thus of me the thought.

अन्यच्च । व्योमैकांतविहारिणो ऽपि विहगाः संप्राप्नुवंत्यापदं ।

anyad	cha,	vyoman-ekânta-vihâriṇas	api	vihagâs	sam-pra-âpnuvanti	â-padam,
-ya, *N. sg.n.*	*Ind.*	*Tip.* -rin, *N. pl. m.*	*Ind.*	-ga, *N. pl.*	âp, *with* sam *and* pra, *3 pl. Pres.Par.*	-pad, *Ac. sg.*
Again	and,	In the air-exclusively-roaming	even	birds	meet	misfortune,

बध्यंते निपुणैरगाधसलिलान्मत्स्याः समुद्रादपि ।

badhyante	nipuṇais	agâdha-salilât	matsyâs	samudrât	api;
bandh, *3 pl. Pres.Pass.*	-ṇa, *I. pl. m.*	*Bahuv.* -la, *Ab. sg. m.*	-ya, *N. pl.*	-ra, *Ab. sg.*	*Ind.*
captured are	by artful men	out of the deep-water containing	fishes	ocean	even;

दुर्नीतं किमिहास्ति किं सुचरितं कः स्थानलाभे गुणः

dus-nîtam	kim	iha	asti,	kim	su-charitam?	kas	sthâna-lâbhe	guṇas?
Karm. -ta, *N. sg. n.*	kim, *N. sg. n.*	*Ind.*	as, *3 sg. Pres.Par.*	kim, *N. sg. n.*	*Karm.* -ta, *N. sg. n.*	kim, *N. sg. m.*	*Tip.* -bha, *L. sg.*	-ṇa, *N. sg.*
Badly-conducted	what	here	is,	what	well-performed?	what	in position-obtainment	merit?

कालो हि व्यसनप्रसारितकरो गृह्णाति दूरादपि ॥ ५१ ॥

kâlas	hi	vyasana-prasârita-karas	gṛihṇâti	dûrât	api.	(51)
-la, *N. sg.*	*Ind.*	*Bahuv.* -ra, *N. sg. m.*	grah, *3 sg. Pres. Par.*	-ra, *Ab. sg. n.*	*Ind.*	
time	for	to destruction-having forth stretched-the hands	seizes	from afar	even.	

इति प्रबोध्यातिथ्यं कृत्वालिंग्य च चित्रग्रीवस्तेन

iti	pra-bodhya	âtithyam	kṛitvâ	â-liṅgya	cha	chitra-grîvas	tena
Ind.	budh *with* pra, *Ger. Caus.*	-ya, *Ac. sg.*	kṛi, *Ger.*	liṅg *with* â, *Ger.*	*Ind.*	*Bahuv.* -va, *N. sg.*	tad, *I. sg. m.*
Thus	having instructed,	hospitality	having made,	having embraced	and,	Chitragrîva	by him

संप्रेषितो यथेष्टदेशान्सपरिवारो ययौ । हिरण्यको

sam-pra-eshitas	yathâ-ishṭa-deśân	sa-parivâras	yayau;	hiraṇyakas
ish *with* sam *and* pra, *N. sg. m. past Ptc. Pass. Caus.*	*Karm.* -śa, *Ac. pl.*	*Bahuv.* -ra, *N. sg. m.*	yâ, *3 sg. Perf. Par.*	-ka, *N. sg.*
dismissed	to ad libitum-places	with-attendants	went;	Hiraṇyaka

ऽपि स्वविवरं प्रविष्टः ।

api	sva-vivaram	pra-vishṭas.
Ind.	*Karm.* -ra, *Ac. sg.*	viś *with* pra, *N. sg. m. past Ptc. Pass.*
also	his-hole	entered.

यानि कानि च मित्राणि कर्तव्यानि शतानि च ।

yâni	kâni	cha	mitrâṇi	kartavyâni	śatâni	cha;
yad, *N. pl. n.*	kim, *N. pl. n.*	*Ind.*	-ra, *N. pl.*	kṛi, *N. pl. n. Ptc. Fut. Pass.*	-ta, *N. pl.*	*Ind.*
Whosoever			friends	are to be made	hundreds	and;

पश्य मूषिकमित्रेण कपोता मुक्तबंधनाः ॥ ५२ ॥

paśya	mûshika-mitreṇa	kapotâs	mukta-bandhanâs.	(52)
dṛiś, *2 sg. Imp. Par.*	*Karm.* -ra, *I. sg.*	-ta, *N. pl.*	*Bahuv.* -na, *N. pl. m.*	
Behold,	through the mouse-friend	the pigeons	bond-delivered,	

अथ लघुपतनकनामा काकः सर्ववृत्तांतदर्शी साश्चर्यमि-

atha	laghupatanaka-nâmâ	kâkas	sarva-vṛittânta-darśî	sa-âścharyam
Ind.	*Bahuv.* -man, *N. sg. m.*	-ka, *N. sg.*	*Tip.* -śin, *N. sg. m.*	*Avyay.*
Now	Laghupatanaka-named	the crow	the whole-event-seeing	with astonishment

दमाह। अहो हिरण्यक श्लाघ्योऽसि। अतोऽहम-
idam âha: aho hiraṇyaka ślâghyas asi; atas aham
idam, *Ac. sg. n.* ah, 3 *sg. Perf. Par.* *Ind.* -ka, *V. sg.* ślâgh, *N. sg. m. Ptc. Fut. Pass.* as, 2 *sg. Pres. Par.* *Ind.* asmad, *N. sg.*
this said: Oh Hiraṇyaka, to be praised thou art; hence I

पि त्वया सह मैत्रीमिच्छामि। अतो मां मैत्र्येणानुग्रहीतु-
api tvayâ saha maitrîm ichchhâmi; atas mâm maitryeṇa anu-grahitum
Ind. yushmad, *I. sg.* *Ind.* -ri, *Ac. sg.* ish, 1 *sg. Pres. Par.* *Ind.* asmad, *Ac. sg.* -ya, *I. sg.* grah *with* anu, *Inf.*
also thee with friendship wish; therefore me with friendship to favour

मर्हसि। एतच्छ्रुत्वा हिरण्यकोऽपि विवराभ्यंतरादाह।
arhasi. etad śrutvâ hiraṇyakas api vivara-abhyantarât âha:
arh, 2 *sg. Pres. Par.* etad, *Ac. sg. n.* śru, *Ger.* -ka, *N. sg.* *Ind.* *Tip.* -ra, *Ab. sg.* ah, 3 *sg.*
deign. This having heard Hiraṇyaka also from the hole's-inside said:

कस्त्वं। स ब्रूते। लघुपतनकनामा वायसोऽहं।
kas tvam? sas brûte: laghupatanaka-nâmâ vâyasas aham.
kim, *N. sg. m.* yushmad, *N. sg.* tad, *N. sg. m.* brû, 3 *sg. Pres. Âtm.* *Bahuv.* -man, *N. sg. m.* -sa, *N. sg.* asmad, *N. sg.*
Who thou? He says: Laghupatanaka-named a crow I.

हिरण्यको विहस्याह। का त्वया सह मैत्री।
hiraṇyakas vi-hasya âha: kâ tvayâ saha maitrî?
-ka, *N. sg.* has *with* vi *Ger.* ah, 3 *sg. Perf. Par.* kim, *N. sg. f.* yushmad, *I. sg.* *Ind.* -ri, *N. sg.*
Hiraṇyaka, laughing, says: What thee with friendship?

यतः। यद्येन युज्यते लोके बुधस्तत्तेन योजयेत्।
yatas, yad yena yujyate loke budhas tad tena yojayet;
Ind. yad, *N. sg. n.* yad, *I. sg. n.* yuj, 3 *sg. Pres. Pass.* -ka, *L. sg.* -dha, *N. sg. m.* tad, *Ac. sg. n.* tad, *I. sg. n.* yuj, 3 *sg. Pot. Par. Caus.*
For, What with what is fitting in the world, a wise man that with that should unite;

अहमन्नं भवान्भोक्ता कथं प्रीतिर्भविष्यति ॥ ५३ ॥
aham annam bhavân bhoktâ; katham prîtis bhavishyati? (53)
asmad, *N. sg.* -na, *N. sg.* -vat, *N. sg. m.* -tri, *N. sg. m.* *Ind.* -ti, *N. sg.* bhû, 3 *sg. Fut.* ii. *Par.*
I the food, you the eater; how love will be?

अपरं च। भक्ष्यभक्षकयोः प्रीतिः विपत्तेरेव कारणं।
aparam cha, bhakshya-bhakshakayos prîtis vi-pattes eva kâraṇam;
-ra, *N. sg. n.* *Ind.* *Dvandva.* -ka, *G. du. m.* -ti, *N. sg.* -tti, *G. sg.* *Ind.* -ṇa, *N. sg.*
Another and, Of the food- (and)- the feeder love, of misfortune alone the cause;

शृगालात्पाशबद्धोऽसौ मृगः काकेन रक्षितः ॥ ५४ ॥
śṛigâlât pâśa-baddhas asau mṛigas kâkena rakshitas. (54)
-la, *Ab. sg.* *Tip.* -dha, *N. sg. m.* adas, *N. sg. m.* -ga, *N. sg.* -ka, *I. sg.* raksh, *N. sg. m. past Ptc. Pass.*
through a jackal snare-bound that deer by the crow saved.

वायसोऽब्रवीत्। कथमेतत्। हिरण्यकः कथयति। अस्ति मगधदेशे
vâyasas abravît: katham etad? hiraṇyakas kathayati: asti magadha-deśe
-sa, *N. sg.* brû, 3 *sg. Impf. Par.* *Ind.* etad, *N. sg. n.* -ka, *N. sg.* kath, 3 *sg. Pres. Par.* as, 3 *sg. Pres. Par.* *Karm.* -śa, *L. sg.*
The crow said: How that? Hiraṇyaka relates: There is in the Magadha-country

चंपकवती नामारण्यानी। तस्यां चिरान्महता स्नेहेन
champakavatî nâma araṇyânî; tasyâm chirât mahatâ snehena
-tî, N. sg. -man, Ac. sg. Adv. -nî, N. sg. tad, L. sg. f. -ra, Ab. sg. n. Adv. -hat, I. sg. m. -ha, I. sg.
Champakavatî by name a large wood; therein since long with great affection

मृगकाकौ निवसतः। स च मृगः स्वेच्छया भ्राम्यन्
mṛiga-kâkau ni-vasatas. sas cha mṛigas sva-ichchhayâ bhrâmyan
Dvandva. -ka, N. du. vas with ni, 3 du. Pres. Par. tad, N. sg. m. Ind. -ga, N. sg. Karm. -châ, I. sg. bhram, N. sg. m. Ptc. Pres. Par
a deer- (and) a crow dwell. That and deer at his-pleasure roaming

हृष्टपुष्टांगः केनचिच्छृगालेनावलोकितः। तं दृष्ट्वा शृगालो
hṛishṭa-pushṭa-aṅgas kena - chid śṛigâlena ava-lokitas. tam dṛishṭvâ śṛigâlas
Bahuv. -ga, N. sg. m. kim, I. sg. m. Ind. -la, I. sg. lok with ava, N. sg. m. past Ptc. Pass. tad, Ac. sg. m. dṛiś, Ger. -la, N. sg.
frisky-fat-limbed by some jackal (was) espied. Him having seen the jackal

ऽचिंतयत्। आः कथमेतन्मांसं सुललितं भक्षयामि। भवतु
achintayat: âḥ katham etad-mâṁsam su-lalitam bhakshayâmi? bhavatu,
chint, 3 sg. Impf. Par. Ind. Ind. Ttp. -sa, Ac. sg. Karm. -ta, Ac. sg. n. bhaksh, 1 sg. Pres. Par. bhû, 3 sg. Imp. Par.
thought: Ah, how of him-the meat the very-delicate I eat? Be it,

विश्वासं तावदुत्पादयामि। इत्यालोच्योपसृत्याब्रवीत्।
vi-śvâsam tâvat ud-pâdayâmi. iti â-lochya upa-sṛitya abravît:
-sa, Ac. sg. Ind. pad with ud, 1 sg. Pres. Par. Caus. Ind. loch with â, Ger. sṛi with upa, Ger. brû, 3 sg. Impf. Par.
confidence first I produce. Thus having thought having approached he said:

मित्र कुशलं ते। मृगेणोक्तं। कस्त्वं। स
mitra kuśalam te. mṛigeṇa uktam: kas tvam? sas
-ra, V. sg. -la, N. sg. n. yushmad, D. sg. -ga, I. sg. vach, N. sg. n. past Ptc. Pass. kim, N. sg. m. yushmad, N. sg. tad, N. sg. m.
Friend, hail to thee. By the deer said: Who thou? He

ब्रूते। क्षुद्रबुद्धिनामा जंबुको ऽहं। अत्रारण्ये बंधुहीनो
brûte: kshudrabuddhi-nâmâ jambukas aham; atra araṇye bandhu-hînas
brû, 3 sg. Pres. Âtm. Bahuv. -man, N. sg. m. -ka, N. sg. asmad, N. sg. Ind. -ya, L. sg. Ttp. -na, N. sg. m. (hâ)
says: Kshudrabuddhi-named a jackal I; here in the wood relation-deprived

मृतवन्निवसामि। इदानीं त्वां मित्रमासाद्य पुनः सबंधु-
mṛita-vat ni-vasâmi; idânîm tvâm mitram â-sâdya punar sa-bandhus
Ind. vas with ni, 1 sg. Pres. Par. Ind. yushmad, Ac. sg. -ra, Ac. sg. sad with â, Ger. Caus. Ind. Bahuv. -dhu, N. sg. m.
dead-like I dwell; now thee a friend having found again relation-possessed

र्जीवलोकं प्रविष्टो ऽस्मि। अधुना तवानुचरेण मया सर्वथा
jîva-lokam pra-vishṭas asmi; adhunâ tava anu-chareṇa mayâ sarvathâ
Ttp. -ka, Ac. sg. viś with pra, N. sg. m. past Ptc. Pass. as, 1 sg. Pres. Par. Ind. yushmad, G. sg. -ra, I. sg. m. asmad, I. sg. Ind.
into of the living-the world entered I am; now of thee the attendant by me wholly

भवितव्यं। मृगेणोक्तं। एवमस्तु। ततः पश्चादस्तंगते
bhavitavyam. mṛigeṇa uktam: evam astu. tatas paśchât astam-gate
bhû, N. sg. n. Ptc. Fut. Pass. -ga, I. sg. vach, N. sg. n. past Ptc. Pass. Ind. as, 3 sg. Imp. Par. Ind. Ind. gam with astam, L. s. m. past Ptc. Pass.
to be. By the deer said: Thus it be. There-after, having gone-home

सवितरि भगवति मरीचिमालिनि तौ मृगस्य वासभूमिं गतौ।

savitari	bhagavati	marîchi-mâlini	tau	mṛigasya	vâsa-bhûmim	gatau.
-tṛi, L. sg.	*-vat, L. sg. m.*	*Bahuv.* -lin, *L. sg. m.*	tad, *N. du. m.*	*-ga, G. sg.*	*Ttp.* -mi, *Ac. sg.*	gam, *N. du. m. past Ptc. Pass*
the sun,	the venerable,	the ray-garlanded,	those two	of the deer	to the dwelling-place	proceeded

तत्र चंपकवृक्षशाखायां सुबुद्धिनामा काको मृगस्य चिरमित्रं

tatra	champaka-vṛiksha-śâkhâyâm	subuddhi-nâmâ	kâkas	mṛigasya	chira-mitram
Ind.	*Ttp.* -khâ, *L. sg.*	*Bahuv.* -man, *N. sg. m.*	-ka, *N. sg.*	-ga, *G. sg.*	*Karm.* -ra, *N. sg*
There	on a Champaka-tree-branch	Subuddhi-named	a crow,	of the deer	an old-friend,

निवसति। तौ दृष्ट्वा काको ऽवदत्। सखे चित्रांग को

ni-vasati.	tau	dṛishṭvâ	kâkas	avadat:	sakhe	chitra-aṅga,	kas
vas *with* ni, 3 *sg. Pres. Par.*	tad, *Ac. du. m.*	dṛiś, *Ger.*	-ka, *N. sg.*	vad, 3 *sg. Impf. Par.*	-khi, *V. sg.*	*Bahuv.* -ga, *V. sg.*	kim, *N. sg. m.*
dwells.	Those two	having seen	the crow	said:	Friend	Chitrâṅga,	who

ऽयं द्वितीयः। मृगो ब्रूते। जंबुको ऽयमस्मत्सख्यमिच्छन्ना-

ayam	dvitîyas?	mṛigas	brûte:	jambukas	ayam	asmad-sakhyam	ichchhan
idam, *N. sg. m.*	-ya, *N. sg. m.*	-ga, *N. sg.*	brû, 3 *sg. Pres. Âtm.*	-ka, *N. sg.*	idam, *N. sg. m.*	*Ttp.* -ya, *Ac. sg.*	ish, *N. sg. m. Ptc. Pres. Par.*
this	second?	The deer	says:	A jackal	this	of us-the friendship	wishing

गतः। काको ब्रूते। मित्र अकस्मादागंतुना सह मैत्री

â-gatas.	kâkas	brûte:	mitra	a-kasmât	â-gantunâ	saha	maitrî
gam *with* â, *N. sg. m. past Ptc. Pass.*	-ka, *N. sg.*	brû, 3 *sg. Pres. Âtm.*	-ra, *V. sg.*	*Ind.* (kim)	-tu, *I. sg.*	*Ind.*	-rî, *N. sg.*
approached.	The crow	says:	Friend,	from no-where	a comer	with,	friendship

न युक्ता। तथा चोक्तं।

na	yuktâ;	tathâ	cha	uktam:
Ind.	yuj, *N. sg. f. past Ptc. Pass.*	*Ind.*	*Ind.*	vach, *N. sg. n. past Ptc. Pass.*
not	proper;	thus	and	said:

अज्ञातकुलशीलस्य वासो देयो न कस्यचित्।

a-jñâta-kula-śîlasya	vâsas	deyas	na	kasya-chid,
Bahuv. -la, *G. sg. m.*	-sa, *N. sg.*	dâ, *N. sg. m. Ptc. Fut Pass.*	*Ind.*	kim, *G. sg. m. Ind.*
Of one of unknown-family-(and)character	residence	to be given	not	of any one;

मार्जारस्य हि दोषेण हतो गृध्रो जरद्गवः ॥ ५५ ॥

mârjârasya	hi	doshena	hatas	gṛidhras	jaradgavas. (55)
-ra, *G. sg.*	*Ind.*	-sha, *I. sg.*	han, *N. sg. m. past Ptc. Pass.*	-ra, *N. sg.*	-va, *N. sg.*
of a cat	for	through the offence	slain	the vulture	Jaradgava.

तावाहतुः। कथमेतत्। काकः कथयति।

tau	âhatus:	katham	etad?	kâkas	kathayati.
tad, *N. du. m.*	ah, 3 *du. Perf. Par.*	*Ind.*	etad, *N. sg. n.*	-ka, *N. sg.*	kath, 3 *sg. Pres. Par.*
They both	say:	How	that?	The crow	relates:

अस्ति भागीरथीतीरे गृध्रकूटनाम्नि पर्वते महान्पर्कटीवृक्षः।

as, 3 *sg. Pres. Par.*	*Ttp.* -ra, *L. sg.*	*Bahuv.* -man, *L. sg. m.*	-ta, *L. sg.*	-hat, *N. sg. m.*	*Karm.* -ksha, *N. sg.*
There is	on the Ganges-bank,	upon a Gṛidhra-kûṭa-named	mountain	a large	fig-tree.

तस्य कोटरे दैवदुर्विपाकाद्गलितनखनयनो जरद्गवनामा गृध्रः प्रतिवसति ।

tad, *G. sg. m.*	-ra, *L. sg.*	*Ttp.* -ka, *Ab. sg.*	*Bahuv.* -na, *N. sg. m.*	*Bahuv.* -man, *N. sg. m.*	-ra, *N. sg.*	vas *with* prati, *3 sg. Pres. Par*
Of it	in the hollow	through fate's-hard doom	having lost-claws-(and) eyes	Jaradgava-named	a vulture	dwells.

अथ कृपया तज्जीवनाय तद्वृक्षवासिनः पक्षिणः स्वाहारात्किंचित्किंचिदुद्धृत्य

Ind.	-pā, *I. sg.*	*Ttp.* -na, *D. sg.*	*Ttp.* -sin, *N. pl. m.*	-kshin, *N. pl. m.*	*Karm.* -ra, *Ab. sg.*	kim-chid, *Ac. sg. n.*		hṛi *with* ud, *Ger.*
Now	through pity	of him-for the support	on that-tree-roosting	birds	from their own-food	a little	a little	having taken

ददति । तेनासौ जीवति । अथ कदाचिद्दीर्घकर्णनामा मार्जारः

dā, *3 pl. Pres. Par.*	tad, *I. sg. n.*	adas, *N. sg. m.*	jīv, *3 sg. Pres. Par.*	*Ind.*	*Ind*	*Bahuv.* -man, *N. sg. m.*	-ra, *N. sg.*
give.	By that	he	lives.	Now	one day	Dīrghakarṇa-named	a cat

पक्षिशावकान्भक्षितुं तत्रागतः । ततस्तमा-

Ttp. -ka, *Ac. pl. m.*	bhaksh, *Inf.*	*Ind.*	gam *with* ā, *N. sg. m. past Ptc. Pass.*	*Ind.*	tad, *Ac. sg. m.*
of the birds-the young ones	to eat	there	arrived.	Then	him

यान्तं दृष्ट्वा पक्षिशावकैर्भयार्तैः कोलाहलः कृतः ।

yā *with* ā, *Ac. sg. m. Ptc. Pres. Par.*	dṛiś, *Ger.*	*Ttp.* -ka, *I. pl. m.*	*Ttp.* -ta, *I. pl. m.*	-la, *N. sg.*	kṛi, *N. sg. m. past Ptc. Pass.*
approaching	having seen	of the birds-by the young ones,	fear-stricken,	clamour	made.

तच्छ्रुत्वा जरद्गवेनोक्तं । कोऽयमायाति । दीर्घकर्णो

tad, *Ac. sg. n.*	śru, *Ger.*	-va, *I. sg.*	vach, *N. sg. n. past Ptc. Pass.*	kim, *N. sg. m.*	idam, *N. sg. m.*	yā *with* ā, *3 sg. Pres. Par.*	*Bahuv.* -ṇa, *N. sg.*
That	having heard	by Jaradgava	said:	Who	this	approaches?	Dīrghakarṇa,

गृध्रमवलोक्य सभयमाह । हा हतोऽस्मि ।

-ra, *Ac. sg.*	lok *with* ava, *Ger.*	*Avyay.*	ah, *3 sg. Perf. Par.*	*Ind.*	han, *N. sg. m. past Ptc. Pass.*	as, *1 sg. Pres. Par.*
the vulture	having perceived,	with fear	said:	Oh,	lost	I am.

यतः । तावद्भयस्य भेतव्यं यावद्भयमनागतं ।

Ind.	-vat, *Ac. sg. n. Adv.*	-ya, *G. sg.*	bhī, *N. sg. n. Ptc. Fut. Pass.*	-vat, *Ac. sg. n. Adv.*	-ya, *N. sg. n.*	*Karm.* -ta, *N. sg. n.* (*rt.* gam *with* ā)
Since,	So long	of danger	one must be afraid,	as	danger	not-approached,

आगतं तु भयं वीक्ष्य नरः कुर्याद्यथोचितं ॥ ५६ ॥

gam *with* ā, *Ac. sg. n. past Ptc. Pass.*	*Ind.*	-ya, *Ac. sg.*	īksh *with* vi, *Ger.*	-ra, *N. sg.*	kṛi, *3 sg. Pot. Par.*	*Ind.*	-ta, *N. sg. n.*
approached	but	danger	having seen	a man	should act	as	proper. (56)

अधुनास्य संनिधाने पलायितुमक्षमः । तद्यथा भवितव्यं

Ind.	idam, *G. sg. m.*	-na, *L. sg.*	ay *with* palā, *Inf.*	*Karm.* -ma, *N. sg. m.*	*Ind.*	*Ind.*	bhū, *N. sg. n. Ptc. Fut. Pass.*
Now	of him	in the presence	to escape	unable,	therefore	as	it is to be,

तद्भवतु तावद्विश्वासमुत्पाद्यास्य समीप-

tad, *N. sg. n.* bhû, 3 *sg. Imp. Par.* *Ind.* -sa, *Ac. sg.* pad *with* ud, *Ger. Caus.* idam, *G. sg. m.* -pa, *Ac. sg. n.*

that let be; first confidence having produced of him to the proximit

मुपगच्छामि। इत्यालोच्योपसृत्याब्रवीत्।

gam *with* upa, 1 *sg. Pres. Par.* *Ind.* loch *with* â, *Ger.* sṛi *with* upa, *Ger.* brû, 3 *sg. Impf. Pa*

I approach. Thus having reflected, having near-gone, he said:

आर्य त्वामभिवंदे। गृध्रो ऽवदत्। कस्त्वं।

-ya, *V. sg.* yushmad, *Ac. sg.* vand *with* abhi, 1 *sg. Pres. Âtm.* -ra, *N. sg.* vad, 3 *sg. Impf. Par.* kim, *N. sg. m.* yushmad, *N. sg*

Reverend Sir, thee I salute. The vulture said: Who thou?

सो ऽवदत्। मार्जारो ऽहं। गृध्रो ब्रूते।

tad, *N. sg. m.* vad, 3 *sg. Impf. Par.* -ra, *N. sg.* asmad, *N. sg.* -ra, *N. sg.* brû, 3 *sg. Pres. Âtm.*

He said: A cat I. The vulture says:

दूरमपसर नो चेद्धंतव्यो ऽसि मया। मार्जारो ऽवदत्।

-ra, *Ac. sg. n. Adv.* sṛi *with* apa, 2 *sg. Imp. Par.* *Ind.* *Ind.* han, *N. sg. m. Ptc. Fut. Pass.* as, 2 *sg. Pres. Par.* asmad, *I. sg.* -ra, *N. sg.* vad, 3 *sg Impf. Pa*

Far away-go; not if, to be killed thou art by me. The cat said:

श्रूयतां तावदस्मद्वचनं ततो यद्यहं वध्यस्तदा हंतव्यः।

śru, 3 *sg. Imp. Pass.* *Ind.* *Ttp.* -na, *N. sg.* *Ind.* *Ind.* asmad, *N. sg.* -ya, *N. sg. m.* (*rt.* han) *Ind.* han, *N. sg. m Ptc. Fut. Pas*

It may be heard first of me-the speech; thereafter if I to be punished, then to be killed

यतः। जातिमात्रेण किं कश्चिद्धन्यते पूज्यते क्वचित्।

Ind. *Ttp.* -ra, *I. sg.* *Ind.* kim-chid, *N. sg. m.* han, 3 *sg. Pres. Pass.* pûj, 3 *sg. Pres. Pass.* *Ind.*

For, Through birth-merely any one is punished, is honoured anywhere

व्यवहारं परिज्ञाय वध्यः पूज्यो ऽथवा भवेत्॥ ५७॥

-ra, *Ac. sg.* jñâ, *with* pari, *Ger.* -ya, *N. sg. m.* (*rt.* han) pûj, *N. sg. m. Ptc. Fut. Pass.* *Ind.* bhû, 3 *sg. Pot. Par.*

the conduct having scrutinised to be punished to be honoured or he should be. (57)

गृध्रो ब्रूते। ब्रूहि किमर्थमागतो ऽसि। सो ऽवदत्।

-ra, *N. sg.* brû, 3 *sg. Pres. Âtm.* 2 *sg. Imp. Par.* *Ind.* gam *with* â, *N. sg. m. past. Ptc. Pass.* as, 2 *sg. Pres. Par.* tad, *N. sg. m.* vad, 3 *sg. Imp Par.*

The vulture says: Say, wherefore approached thou art? He said:

अहमत्र गंगातीरे नित्यस्नायी ब्रह्मचारी चांद्रायणव्रत-

asmad, *N. sg.* *Ind.* *Ttp.* -ra, *L. sg.* *Karm.* -yin, *N. sg. m.* *Ttp.* -rin, *N. sg. m.* *Karm.* -ta, *Ac. sg.*

I here on the Ganges-bank, constantly-bathing, religious study-observing the Chândrâyaṇa-vo

माचरंस्तिष्ठामि । युष्मान्धर्मज्ञानरतान्विश्वासभूमयः

char *with* â, *N. sg. m. Ptc. Pres. Par.* sthâ, 1 *sg. Pres. Par.* yushmad, *Ac. pl.* *Ttp.* -ta, *Ac. pl. m.* *Ttp.* -mi, *N. pl.*

performing, stay. You of duty-the knowledge-enjoying of confidence-objects

पक्षिणः सर्वे सर्वदा ममाग्रे प्रस्तुवंति । अतो भवद्भ्यो

-kshin, *N. pl. m.* -va, *N. pl. m.* *Ind.* asmad, *G. sg.* -ra, *L. sg. Adv.* stu *with* pra, 3 *pl. Pres. Par.* *Ind.* -vat, *Ab. pl. m.*

birds all always of me in the presence praise ; therefore from you,

विद्यावयोवृद्धेभ्यो धर्मं श्रोतुमिहागतः । भवंतश्चैतादृशा

Ttp. -dha, *Ab. pl. m.* -ma, *Ac. sg.* śru, *Inf.* *Ind.* gam *with* â, *N. sg. m. past Ptc. Pass.* -vat, *N. pl. m.* *Ind.* -śa *N. pl. m.*

in wisdom-(and) age-old, the duty of religion to hear hither approached. You and such

धर्मज्ञा यन्मामतिथिं हंतुमुद्यताः । गृहस्थधर्मश्चैषः ।

Ttp. -jña, *N. pl. m.* *Ind.* asmad, *Ac. sg.* -thi, *Ac. sg.* han, *Inf.* yam *with* ud, *N. pl. m. past Ptc. Pass.* *Ttp.* -ma, *N. sg.* *Ind.* etad, *N. sg. m.*

of religion-knowers, that me a guest to kill ready. A householder's-duty and this :

अरावप्युचितं कार्यमातिथ्यं गृहमागते ।

-ri, *L. sg.* *Ind.* -ta, *N. sg. n.* kṛi, *N. sg. n. Ptc. Fut. Pass.* -ya, *N. sg.* -ha, *Ac. sg.* gam *with* â, *L. sg. m. past Ptc. Pass.*

To an enemy even proper to be exercised hospitality, to the house approached,

छेत्तुः पार्श्वगतां छायां नोपसंहरते द्रुमः ॥ ५८ ॥

-tṛi, *Ab. sg.* *Ttp.* -ta, *Ab. sg. m.* -yâ, *Ac. sg.* *Ind.* hṛi, *with* upa-sam, 3 *sg. Pres. Âtm.* -ma, *N. sg.*

from the cutter to its side-come the shade not withdraws a tree. (58)

यदि वा धनं नास्ति तदा प्रीतिवचसाप्यतिथिः

Ind. *Ind.* -na, *N. sg.* *Ind.* as 3 *sg. Pres. Par.* *Ind.* *Ttp.* -chas, *I. sg.* *Ind.* -thi, *N. sg.*

If or property not there is, then with affection-speech at least a guest

पूज्य एव ।

pûj, *N. sg. m. Ptc. Fut. Pass.* *Ind.*

to be honoured certainly.

यतः । तृणानि भूमिरुदकं वाक् चतुर्थी च सूनृता ।

Ind. -ṇa, *N. pl.* -mi, *N. sg.* -ka, *N. sg.* -ch, *N. sg.* -thâ, *N. sg. f.* *Ind.* -tâ, *N. sg. f.*

For, Straw, room, water, speech as fourth and gentle,

एतान्यपि सतां गेहे नोच्छिद्यंते कदाचन ॥ ५९ ॥

etad, *N. pl. n.* *Ind.* -t, *G. pl. m.* -ha, *L. sg.* *Ind.* chhid *with* ud, 3 *pl. Pres. Pass.* *Ind.*

these together of the good in the house not are wanting at any time. (59)

अपरं च। निर्गुणेष्वपि सत्त्वेषु दयां कुर्वंति साधवः।

-ra, N. sg. n. Ind. Bahuv. -ṇa, L. pl. n. Ind. -tva, L. pl. -yâ, Ac. sg. kṛi, 3 pl. Pres. Par. -dhu, N. pl. m.

Another and, Unto worthless even beings mercy show the good;

न हि संहरते ज्योत्स्नां चंद्रश्चांडालवेश्मनि ॥ ६० ॥

Ind. Ind. hṛi with sam, 3 sg. Pres. Âtm. -nâ, Ac. sg. -dra, N. sg. Tâp. -man, L. sg.

not for withholds (her) light the moon at the Chânḍâla-dwelling. (60)

अन्यच्च। अतिथिर्यस्य भग्नाशो गृहात्प्रतिनिवर्तते।

-ya, N. sg. n. Ind. -thi, N. sg. yad, G. sg. m. Bahuv. -śa, N. sg. m. -ha, Ab. sg. vṛit with prati-ni, 3 sg. Pres. Âtm.

Again and, A guest of whom broken-hoped from the house turns away,

स तस्मै दुष्कृतं दत्त्वा पुण्यमादाय गच्छति ॥ ६१ ॥

tad, N. sg. m. D. sg. m. Karm. -ta, Ac. sg. n. dâ, Ger. -ya, Ac. sg. dâ with â, Ger. gam, 3 sg. Pres. Par.

He to him the guilt having given, the merit having taken, goes. (61)

अन्यच्च। उत्तमस्यापि वर्णस्य नीचो ऽपि गृहमागतः।

-ya, N. sg. n. Ind. -ma, G. sg. m. Ind. -ṇa, G. sg. -cha, N. sg. m. Ind. -ha, Ac. sg. gam with â, N. sg. m. past Ptc. Pass.

Again and, Of the highest even caste a low person even to the house come

पूजनीयो यथा योग्यं सर्वदेवमयो ऽतिथिः ॥ ६२ ॥

pûj, N. sg. m. Ptc. Fut. Pass. Ind. -ya, N. sg. n. -ya, N. sg. m. -thi, N. sg.

to be honoured as proper, all-gods representing a guest. (62)

गृध्रो ऽवदत्। मार्जारो हि मांसरुचिः पक्षिशावकाश्चात्र

-ra, N. sg. vad, 3 sg. Impf. Par. -ra, N. sg. Ind. Bahuv. -chi, N. sg. m. Tâp. -ka, N. pl. m. Ind. Ind.

The vulture said: Cat certainly meat-liking, of birds-the young ones and here

निवसंति तेनाहमेवं ब्रवीमि। तच्छ्रुत्वा मार्जारो

vas with ni, 3 pl. Pres. Par. tad, I. sg. n. Adv. asmad, N. sg. Ind. brû, 1 sg. Pres. Par. tad, Ac. sg. n. śru, Ger. -ra, N. sg.

dwell, therefore I thus speak. This having heard the cat

भूमिं स्पृष्ट्वा कर्णौ स्पृशति ब्रूते च। मया धर्मशास्त्रं

-mi, Ac. sg. spṛiś, Ger. -ṇa, Ac. du. spṛiś, 3 sg. Pres. Par. brû, 3 sg. Pres. Âtm. Ind. asmad, I. sg. Tâp. -ra, Ac. sg.

the ground having touched, the ears touches, says and: By me the law-book

श्रुत्वा वीतरागेणेदं दुष्करं व्रतं चांद्रायणमध्यवसितं।

śru, Ger. Bahuv. -ga, I. sg. m. idam, N. sg. n. -ra. N. sg. n. -ta, N. sg. -ṇa, N. sg. n. so with adhi-ava N. sg. n. past. Ptc. Pass.

having heard, with gone-passions, this difficult vow Chândrâyaṇa undertaken.

परस्परं विवदमानानामपि धर्मशास्त्राणामहिंसा परमो

Ind. vad *with* vi, *G. pl. n. Ptc. Pres. Âtm.* *Ind.* *Tp.* -ra, *G. pl.* *Karm.* -sâ, *N. sg.* -ma, *N. sg. m.*

With-one-another of the disputing even law-books 'not-injuring the highest

धर्म इत्यत्रैकमत्यं । यतः ।

-ma, *N. sg.* *Ind.* *Ind.* -ya, *N. sg.* *Ind.*

duty' thus here unanimity. For,

सर्वहिंसानिवृत्ता ये नराः सर्वसहाश्च ये ।

Tp. -ta, *N. pl. m.* (*rt.* vṛit *with* ni). yad, *N. pl. m.* -ra, *N. pl.* *Tp.* -ha, *N. pl. m.* *Ind.* yad, *N. pl. m.*

From all-injury-abstaining which men, all-enduring and who,

सर्वस्याश्रयभूताश्च ते नराः स्वर्गगामिनः ॥ ६३ ॥

-va, *G. sg. n.* *Karm.* -ta, *N. pl. m.* *Ind.* tad, *N. pl. m.* -ra, *N. pl.* *Tp.* -min, *N. pl. m.*

of everything support-being and, those men to heaven-going. (63)

एक एव सुहृद्धर्मो निधनेऽप्यनुयाति यः ।

-ka, *N. sg. m.* *Ind.* -d, *N. sg.* -ma, *N. sg.* -na, *L. sg.* *Ind.* yâ *with* anu, 3 *sg. Pres. Par.* yad, *N. sg. m.*

One only friend, virtue, in death even follows who,

शरीरेण समं नाशं सर्वमन्यत्तु गच्छति ॥ ६४ ॥

-ra, *I. sg.* -ma, *Ac. sg. n. Adv.* -śa, *Ac. sg.* -va, *N. sg. n.* -ya, *N. sg. n.* *Ind.* gam, 3 *sg. Pres. Par.*

with the body together to destruction everything else but goes. (64)

योऽत्ति यस्य यदा मांसमुभयोः पश्यतांतरं ।

yad, *N. sg. m.* ad, 3 *sg. Pres. Par.* yad, *G. sg. m.* *Ind.* -sa, *Ac. sg.* -bha, *G. du. m.* dṛiś, 2 *pl. Imp. Par.* -ra, *Ac. sg.*

Who eats of whom when the flesh, of both behold the difference,

एकस्य क्षणिका प्रीतिरन्यः प्राणैर्विमुच्यते ॥ ६५ ॥

-ka, *G. sg. m.* -ka, *N. sg. f.* -ti, *N. sg.* -ya, *N. sg.* -ṇa, *I. pl.* much *with* vi, 3 *sg. Pres. Pass.*

of the one momentary enjoyment, the other of life deprived. (65)

मर्तव्यमिति यद्दुःखं पुरुषस्योपजायते ।

mṛi, *N. sg. n. Ptc. Fut. Pass.* *Ind.* yad, *N. sg. n.* -kha, *N. sg.* -sha, *G. sg.* jan *with* upa, 3 *sg. Pres. Âtm.*

'It must be died,' thus what pain of a man is produced,

शक्यस्तेनानुमानेन परोऽपि परिरक्षितुं ॥ ६६ ॥

-ya, *N. sg. m.* tad, *I. sg. n.* -na, *I. sg.* -ra, *N. sg. m.* *Ind.* raksh *with* pari, *Inf.*

possible by that analogy an enemy even to save. (66)

शृणु पुनः। स्वच्छंदवनजातेन शाकेनापि प्रपूर्यते।

śru, 2 sg. Imp. Par. Ind. Ttp. -ta, I. sg. m. or n. -ka, I. sg. Ind. prī with pra, 3 sg. Pres. Pass.

Listen again; By the spontaneously-in the wood-growing herb even it is filled,

अस्य दग्धोदरस्यार्थे कः कुर्यात्पातकं महत्॥ ६७॥

idam, G. sg. n. Karm. -ra, G. sg. -tha, L. sg. Adv. kim, N. sg. m. kṛi, 3 sg. Pot. Par. -ka, Ac. sg. -hat, Ac. sg. n.

of this burnt-stomach on account of who would commit a crime great? (67)

एवं विश्वास्य स मार्जारस्तरुकोटरे स्थितः। ततो

Ind. śvas, with vi, Ger. Caus. tad, N. sg. m. -ra, N. sg. Ttp. -ra, L. sg. sthâ, N. sg. m. past Ptc. Pass. Ind.

Thus having made to confide, that cat in the tree-hollow remained. Then,

दिनेषु गच्छत्सु पक्षिशावकानाक्रम्य कोटर-

-na, L. pl. gam, L. pl. m. or n. Ptc. Pres. Par. Ttp. -ka, Ac. pl. m. kram with â, Ger. -ra, Ac. sg.

the days passing on, of the birds-the young ones having approached, to the hollow

मानीय प्रत्यहं खादति। येषामपत्यानि खादितानि

nî with â, Ger. Avyay. khâd, 3 sg. Pres. Par. yad, G. pl. m. -ya, N. pl. khâd, N. pl. n. past Ptc. Pass.

having brought, daily he eats. Of whom the young ones eaten,

तैः शोकार्तैर्विलपद्भिरितस्ततो जिज्ञासा समारब्धा।

tad, I. pl. m. Ttp. -ta, I. pl. m. lap with vi, I. pl. m. Ptc. Pres. Par. Ind. Ind. -sâ, N. sg. rabh with sam-â N. sg. f. past Ptc. Pass.

by those, sorrow-pained, wailing, here (and) there enquiry begun.

तत्परिज्ञाय मार्जारः कोटरान्निःसृत्य बहिः

tad, Ac. sg. n. jñâ, with pari, Ger. -ra, N. sg. -ra, Ab. sg. sṛi with nis, Ger. Ind.

That having perceived, the cat from the hollow having slipped out

पलायितः। पश्चात्पक्षिभिरितस्ततो निरूपयद्भिस्तत्र

ay with palâ, N. sg. m. past Ptc. Pass. Ind. -kshin, I. pl. Ind. Ind. rûp with ni, I. pl. m. Ptc. Pres. Par. Ind.

away-gone. Afterwards by the birds here (and) there searching, there

तरुकोटरे शावकास्थीनि प्राप्तानि। अनंतरं त ऊचुः।

Ttp. -ra, L. sg. Ttp. -thi, N. pl. âp with pra, N. pl. n. past Ptc. Pass. Ind. tad, N. pl. m. vach, 3 pl. Perf. Par.

in the tree-hollow of the young ones-the bones discovered. Thereupon they said:

अनेनैव जरद्गवेनास्माकं शावकाः खादिता इति सर्वैः

idam, I. sg. m. Ind. -va, I. sg. asmad, G. pl. -ka, N. pl. m. khâd, N. pl. m. past Ptc. Pass. Ind. -va, I. pl. m.

'By this very Jaradgava of us the young ones eaten.' Thus by all

पक्षिभिर्निश्चित्य गृध्रो व्यापादितः। अतो ऽहं

-kshin, *N. pl. m.* chi, *with* nis, *Ger.* -ra, *N. sg.* pad *with* vi-â, *N. sg. m. past Ptc. Pass. Caus.* *Ind.* asmad, *N. sg.*

the birds having ascertained the vulture killed. Therefore I

ब्रवीमि। अज्ञातकुलशीलस्येत्यादि। इत्याकर्ण्य स

brû, 1 *sg. Pres. Par.* *Bahuv.* -la, *G. sg. m.* *Bahuv.* -di, *Ac. sg. n.* *Ind.* karṇ, *with* â, *Ger.* tad, *N. sg. m.*

say: of one of unknown-family-(and) character, etc. Thus having heard that

जंबुकः सकोपमाह। मृगस्य प्रथमदर्शनदिने भवानप्य-

-ka, *N. sg.* *Avyay.* ah, 3 *sg. Perf. Par.* -ga, *G. sg.* *Ttp.* -na, *L. sg.* -vat, *N. sg. m.* *Ind.*

jackal with anger says: Of the deer on the first-seeing-day you also

ज्ञातकुलशील एव। तत्कथं भवता सहैतस्य

Bahuv. -la, *N. sg. m.* *Ind.* *Ind. Ind.* -vat, *I. sg. m.* *Ind.* etad, *G. sg. m.*

one of unknown-family-(and) character just; then how you with of him

स्नेहानुवृत्तिरुत्तरोत्तरं वर्धते।

Ttp. -ti, *N. sg.* *Ind.* vṛidh, 3 *sg. Pres. Âtm.*

the affection-continuance higher-higher grows?

यत्र विद्वज्जनो नास्ति श्लाघ्यस्तत्राल्पधीरपि।

Ind. *Karm.* -na, *N. sg.* *Ind.* as, 3 *sg. Pres. Par.* ślâgh, *N. sg. m. Ptc. Fut. Pass.* *Ind.* *Bahuv.* -dhî, *N. sg. m.* *Ind.*

Where a learned-man not is, to be praised there one of little-intellect even,

निरस्तपादपे देशे एरंडो ऽपि द्रुमायते ॥ ६८ ॥

Bahuv. -pa, *L. sg. m.* -śa, *L. sg.* -ḍa, *N. sg.* *Ind.* drumâya, 3 *sg. Pres. Âtm.*

in an of trees-deprived place the Eraṇḍa plant even is considered a tree. (68)

अन्यच्च। अयं निजः परो वेति गणना लघुचेतसां।

-ya, *N. sg. n.* *Ind.* idam, *N. sg. m.* -ja, *N. sg. m.* -ra, *N. sg. m.* *Ind.* *Ind.* -nâ, *N. sg.* *Bahuv.* -tas, *G. pl. m.*

Again and, 'This one of us, a stranger or' thus calculation of the narrow-minded,

उदारचरितानां तु वसुधैव कुटुंबकं ॥ ६९ ॥

Bahuv. -ta, *G. pl. m.* *Ind.* *Ttp.* -dhâ, *N sg.* *Ind.* -ka, *N. sg.*

of persons of generous-conduct on the contrary the earth even a family. (69)

यथायं मृगो मम बंधुस्तथा भवानपि। मृगो

Ind. idam, *N. sg. m.* -ga, *N. sg.* asmad, *G. sg.* -dhu, *N sg.* *Ind.* -vat, *N. sg. m.* *Ind.* -ga, *N. sg.*

As this deer of me a friend, thus you also. The deer

ऽब्रवीत्। किमनेनोत्तरोत्तरेण। सर्वैरेकत्र विश्रंभालापैः

brû, 3 *sg. Impf. Par.* kim, *N. sg. n.* idam, *I. sg. n.* -ra, *I. sg.* -va, *I. pl. m.* *Ind.* *Ttp.* -pa, *I. pl.*

said : What with this discussion? by all in one place, with confidence-talks,

सुखिभिः स्थीयतां।

-khin, *I. pl. m.* sthâ, 3 *sg. Imp. Pass.*

happy let be remained.

यतः। न कश्चित्कस्यचिन्मित्रं न कश्चित्कस्यचिद्रिपुः।

Ind. *Ind.* kim-chit, *N. sg. m.* *G. sg. m.* -ra, *N. sg.* *Ind.* kim-chit, *N. sg. m.* *G. sg. m.* -pu, *N. sg.*

For, Not any body of any body the friend, not any body of any body the enemy,

व्यवहारेण मित्राणि जायंते रिपवस्तथा ॥ ७० ॥

-ra, *I. sg.* -ra, *N. pl.* jan, 3. *pl. Pres. Âtm.* -pu, *N. pl.* *Ind.*

through intercourse friends are made, enemies likewise. (70)

काकेनोक्तं। एवमस्तु। अथ प्रातः सर्वे यथाभिमतदेशं गताः।

-ka, *I. sg.* vach, *N. sg. n. past Ptc. Pass.* *Ind.* as, 3 *sg. Imp. Par.* *Ind.* *Ind.* -va, *N. pl. m.* *Karm.* -śa, *Ac. sg.* gam, *N. pl. m. past Ptc. Pass.*

By the crow said : Thus it be. Now in the morning all to ad libitum-place gone.

एकदा निभृतं शृगालो ब्रूते। सखे ऽस्मिन्वनैकदेशे शस्यपूर्णक्षेत्रम-

Ind. -ta, *Ac. sg. n. Adv.* -la, *N. sg.* brû, 3 *sg. Pres. Âtm.* -khi, *V. sg.* idam, *L. sg. m.* *Ttp.* -śa, *L. sg.* *Karm.* -ra, *N. sg.*

One day secretly the jackal says : Friend, in this of the wood-one part a corn-filled-field

स्ति। तदहं त्वां नीत्वा दर्शयामि। तथा कृते

as, 3 *sg. Pres. Par.* tad, *Ac. sg. n.* asmad, *N. sg.* yushmad, *Ac. sg.* nî, *Ger.* driś, 1 *sg. Pres. Par. Caus.* *Ind.* kṛi, *L. sg. n. past Ptc. Pass.*

is, that I, thee having conducted, show. Thus done

सति मृगः प्रत्यहं तत्र गत्वा शस्यं खादति। अथ क्षेत्रपतिना

as, *L. sg. n. Ptc. Pres. Par.* -ga, *N. sg.* *Avyay.* *Ind.* gam, *Ger.* -ya, *Ac. sg.* khâd, 3 *sg. Pres. Par.* *Ind.* *Ttp.* -ti, *I. sg.*

being, the deer daily there having gone the corn eats. Now by the field-owner

तद्दृष्ट्वा पाशो योजितः। अनंतरं पुनरागतो

tad, *Ac. sg. n.* driś, *Ger.* -śa, *N. sg.* yuj, *N. sg. m. past Ptc. Pass. Caus.* *Ind.* *Ind.* gam *with* â, *N. sg. m. past Ptc. Pass.*

that having perceived a snare fixed. Thereupon again approached

मृगः पाशैर्बद्धो ऽचिंतयत्। को मामितः कालपाशा-

-ga, *N. sg.* -śa, *I. pl.* bandh, *N. sg. m. past Ptc. Pass.* chint, 3 *sg. Impf. Par.* kim, *N. sg. m.* asmad, *Ac. sg.* *Ind.* *Ttp.* -śa, *Ab. sg.*

the deer by the snares caught thought: Who me from here from the death-snare,

दिव व्याधपाशात्त्रातुं मित्रादन्यः समर्थः । तत्रां-
Ind. Ttp. -ša, Ab. sg. trai, Inf. -ra, Ab. sg. -ya, N. sg. m. -tha, N. sg. m. Ind.
as it were, from the hunter's-snare to save, from the friend different, able? There

तरे जंबुकस्तत्रागत्योपस्थितो ऽचिंतयत् ।
-ra, L. sg. n. Adv. -ka, N. sg. m. Ind. gam with â, Ger. sthâ with upa, N. sg. m. past Ptc. Pass. chint, 3 sg. Impf. Par.
meantime the jackal there having gone, near-stepped thought:

फलिता तावदस्माकं कपटप्रबंधेन मनोरथसिद्धिः । एतस्यो-
-ta, N. sg. f. Ind. asmad, G. pl. Ttp. -dha, I. sg. Ttp. -dhi, N. sg. etad, G. sg. m.
Fruit-bearing then of us through the deceit-plot the wish-accomplishment; of him,

त्कृत्यमानस्य मांसासृग्लिप्तान्यस्थीनि मयावश्यं प्राप्तव्यानि ।
kṛit with ud, G. sg. m. Ptc. Pres. Pass. Ttp. -ta, N. pl. n. -thi, N. pl. asmad, I. sg. Ind. âp with pra, N. pl. n. Ptc. Fut. Pass.
being cut up, the flesh-blood-smeared bones by me surely to be got.

तानि बाहुल्येन भोजनानि भविष्यंति । मृगस्तं दृष्ट्वो-
tad, N. pl. n. -ya, I. sg. -na, N. pl. bhû, 3 pl. Fut. ii. Par. -ga, N. sg. tad, Ac. sg. m. dṛiś, Ger.
They in abundance food will be. The deer him having seen

ल्लासितो ब्रूते । सखे छिंधि तावन्मम बंधनं । सत्वरं त्रायस्व
las with ud, N. sg. m. past Ptc. Pass. Caus. brû, 3 sg. Pres. Âtm. -khi, V. sg. chhid, 2 sg. Imp. Par. Ind. asmad, G. sg. -na, Ac. sg. Avyay. trai, 2 sg Imp. Âtm.
delighted says: Friend, cut now of me the fetter; quickly deliver

मां । यतः ।
asmad, Ac. sg. Ind.
me. For,

आपत्सु मित्रं जानीयाद्युद्धे शूरमृणे शुचिं ।
-d, L. pl. -ra, Ac. sg. jñâ, 3 sg. Pot. Par. -dha, L. sg. -ra, Ac. sg. -na, L. sg. -chi, Ac. sg. m.
In misfortunes a friend one may know, in battle a hero, in debt an honest man,

भार्यां क्षीणेषु वित्तेषु व्यसनेषु च बांधवान् ॥ ७१ ॥
-yâ, Ac. sg. kshi, L. pl. n. past Ptc. Pass. -ta, L. pl. -na, L. pl. Ind. -va, Ac. pl.
a wife in lost riches, in troubles and relations. (71)

अपरं च । उत्सवे व्यसने चैव दुर्भिक्षे राष्ट्रविप्लवे ।
-ra, N. sg. n. Ind. -va, L. sg. -na, L. sg. Ind. Ind. -sha, L. sg. Ttp. -va, L. sg.
Another and, At a festival, in affliction and even, in dearth, in reign-revolution,

राजद्वारे श्मशाने च यस्तिष्ठति स बांधवः ॥ ७२ ॥
Ttp. -ra, L. sg. -na, L. sg. Ind. yad, N. sg. m. sthâ, 3 sg. Pres. Par. tad, N. sg. m. -va, N. sg.
at the king's door, on the cemetery and who stands, he a friend. (72)

जंबुको मुहुर्मुहुः पाशं विलोक्याचिंतयत्। दृढस्तावदयं
-ka, N. sg. Ind. Ind. -śa, Ac. sg. lok with vi, Ger. chint, 3 sg. Impf. Par. -ḍha, N. sg. m. Ind. idam, N. sg. m.
The jackal again-again the snare having eyed thought: Strong so far this

बंधः। ब्रूते च। सखे स्नायुनिर्मिता एते
-dha, N. sg. brû, 3 sg. Pres. Âtm. Ind. -khi, V. sg. Ttp. -ta, N. pl. m. etad, N. pl. m.
fetter; says and: Friend, of sinews-made these

पाशास्तदद्य भट्टारकवारे कथमेतान्दंतैः स्पृशामि।
-śa, N. pl. Ind. Ind. -ra, L. sg. Ind. etad, Ac. pl. m. -ta, I. pl. spriś, 1 sg. Pres. Par.
snares, therefore to-day on a Sun-day how these with the teeth I touch?

मित्र यदि चित्ते नान्यथा मन्यसे तदा प्रभाते
-ra, V. sg. Ind. -ta, L. sg. Ind. Ind. man, 2 sg. Pres. Âtm. Ind. -ta, L. sg.
Friend, if in thy mind not otherwise thou thinkest, then in the morning

यत्त्वया वक्तव्यं तत्कर्तव्यं।
yad, N. sg. n. yushmad, I. sg. m. vach, N. sg. n. Ptc. Fut. Pass. tad, N. sg. n. kṛi, N. sg. n. Ptc. Fut. Pass.
what by thee to be said, that to be done.

इत्युक्त्वा तत्समीप आत्मानमाच्छाद्य स्थितः
Ind. vach, Ger. Ttp. -pa, L. sg. -man, Ac. sg. chhad with â, Ger. sthâ, N. sg. m. past Ptc. Pass.
Thus having said, of him-in the neighbourhood himself having concealed stood

सः। अनंतरं स काकः प्रदोषकाले मृगमनागतम-
tad, N. sg. m. Ind. tad, N. sg. m. -ka, N. sg. Ttp. -la. L. sg. -ga, Ac. sg. Karm. -ta, Ac. sg. m.
he. Thereupon that crow at evening-time the deer not-returned

वलोक्येतस्ततोऽन्विष्य तथाविधं दृष्ट्वो-
lok with ava, Ger. Ind. Ind. ish with anu, Ger. -dha, Ac. sg. m. dṛiś, Ger.
having seen, here (and) there having searched, the so-conditioned having seen,

वाच। सखे किमेतत्। मृगेणोक्तं।
vach, 3 sg. Perf. Par. -khi, V. sg. kim, N. sg. n. etad, N. sg. n. -ga, I. sg. vach, N. sg. n. past Ptc. Pass.
said: Friend, what this? By the deer said:

अवधीरितसुहृद्वाक्यस्य फलमेतत्। तथा चोक्तं।
Karm. -ya, G. sg. -la, N. sg. etad, N. sg. n. Ind. Ind. vach, N. sg. n. past Ptc. Pass.
Of the slighted-friend's-word the fruit this. Thus and said:

सुहृदां हितकामानां यः शृणोति न भाषितं।
-d, *G. pl.* *Bahuv.* -ma, *G. pl. m.* yad, *N. sg. m.* śru, 3 *sg. Pres. Par.* *Ind.* -ta, *Ac. sg.*
Of friends well-wishing who hears not the word,

विपत्संनिहिता तस्य स नरः शत्रुनंदनः ॥ ७३ ॥
-pad, *N. sg.* dhâ *with* sam-ni, *N. sg. f.* *past Ptc. Pass.* tad, *G. sg. m.* *N. sg. m.* -ra, *N. sg.* *Ttp.* -na, *N. sg. m.*
adversity near of him; that man an enemy-delighter. (73)

काको ब्रूते। स वंचकः क्वास्ते। मृगे-
-ka, *N. sg.* brû, 3 *sg. Pres. Âtm.* tad, *N. sg. m.* -ka, *N. sg.* *Ind.* âs, 3 *sg. Pres. Âtm.* -ga, *I. sg.*
The crow says: that rogue (jackal) where does he sit? By the deer

णोक्तं। मन्मांसार्थी तिष्ठत्यत्रैव। काको ब्रूते।
vach, *N. sg. n.* *past Ptc. Pass.* *Ttp.* -thin, *N. sg. m.* sthâ, 3 *sg. Pres. Par.* *Ind.* *Ind.* -ka, *N. sg.* brû, 3 *sg. Pres. Âtm.*
said: For my-flesh-longing he stands there just. The crow says:

उक्तमेव मया पूर्वं।
vach, *N. sg. n.* *past Ptc. Pass.* *Ind.* asmad, *I. sg.* -va, *Ac. sg. n. Adv.*
Said indeed by me before.

अपराधो न मेऽस्तीति नैतद्विश्वासकारणं।
-dha, *N. sg.* *Ind.* asmad, *G. sg.* as, 3 *sg. Pres. Par.* *Ind.* *Ind.* etad, *N. sg. n.* *Ttp.* -ṇa, *N. sg.*
'An offence not of me is,' thus not this for confidence-a reason,

विद्यते हि नृशंसेभ्यो भयं गुणवतामपि ॥ ७४ ॥
vid, 3 *sg. Pres. Pass.* *Ind.* -sa, *Ab. pl. m.* -ya, *N. sg.* -vat, *G. pl. m.* *Ind.*
it is known for from the mischievous danger of the virtuous even. (74)

दीपनिर्वाणगंधं च सुहृद्वाक्यमरुंधतीं।
Ttp. -dha, *Ac. sg.* *Ind.* *Ttp.* -ya, *Ac. sg.* -ti, *Ac. sg.*
Of a lamp-extinction-the smell and, a friend's-word, the star Arundhatî,

न जिघ्रंति न शृण्वंति न पश्यंति गतायुषः ॥ ७५ ॥
Ind. ghrâ, 3 *pl. Pres. Par.* *Ind.* śru, 3 *pl. Pres. Par.* *Ind.* driś, 3 *pl. Pres. Par.* *Bahuv.* -yus, *N. pl. m.*
not smell, not hear, not see those whose life-is gone. (75)

परोक्षे कार्यहंतारं प्रत्यक्षे प्रियवादिनं।
-ksha, *L. sg. n.* *Ttp.* -tṛi, *Ac. sg. m.* -ksha, *L. sg. n.* *Ttp.* -din, *Ac. sg. m.*
Away from-the eye design-destroying, before-the eye kind words-speaking,

वर्जयेत्तादृशं मित्रं विषकुंभं पयोमुखं ॥ ७६ ॥
vṛij, 3 *sg. Pot. Par.* -śa, *Ac. sg. n.* -ra, *Ac. sg.* *Ttp.* -bha, *Ac. sg.* *Bahuv.* -kha, *Ac. sg. m.*
one should avoid such a friend, a poison-pot having a milk-surface. (76)

ततः काको दीर्घं निःश्वस्य। अरे वंचक किं

ततः	काको	दीर्घं	निःश्वस्य।	अरे	वंचक	किं
Ind.	-ka, *N. sg.*	-gha, *Ac. sg. n. Adv.*	śvas *with* nis, *Ger.*	*Ind.*	-ka, *V. sg.*	kim, *N. sg. n.*
Then	the crow	deeply	having sighed:	Alas,	rogue,	what

त्वया पापकर्मणा कृतं। यतः।

त्वया	पापकर्मणा	कृतं।	यतः।
yushmad, *I. sg.*	*Bahuv.* -man, *I. sg. m.*	kṛi, *N. sg. n. past Ptc. Pass.*	*Ind.*
by thee	wicked-deeds performing	done?	For,

संलापितानां मधुरैर्वचोभिर्मिथ्योपचारैश्च वशीकृतानां।

संलापितानां	मधुरैः	वचोभिः	मिथ्योपचारैः	च	वशीकृतानां।
lap *with* sam, *G. pl. m. past Ptc. Pass. Caus.*	-ra, *I. pl. n.*	-chas, *I. pl.*	*Karm.* -ra, *I. pl.*	*Ind.*	vaśi-kṛi, *G. pl. m. past. Ptc. Pass.*
Of those addressed	with sweet	words,	with pretended-services	and	enchanted,

आशावतां श्रद्दधतां च लोके किमर्थिनां वंचयितव्यमस्ति ॥ ७७ ॥

आशावतां	श्रद्दधतां	च	लोके	किम्	अर्थिनां	वंचयितव्यमस्ति ॥ ७७ ॥
-vat, *G. pl. m.*	śrad-dhâ, *G. pl. m. Ptc. Pres. Par.*	*Ind.*	-ka, *L. sg.*	*Ind.*	-thin, *G. pl. m.*	vañch, *N. sg. n. Ptc. Fut. Pass. Caus.*
of the hopeful,	of the confiding	and	in the world,	why	of supplicants	cheating to be done is? (77)

उपकारिणि विश्रब्धे शुद्धमतौ यः समाचरति पापं।

उपकारिणि	विश्रब्धे	शुद्धमतौ	यः	समाचरति	पापं।
-rin, *L. sg. m.*	śrambh *with* vi, *L. sg. m. past Ptc. Pass.*	*Bahuv.* -ti, *L. sg. m.*	yad, *N. sg. m.*	char *with* sam-â, *3 sg. Pres. Par.*	-pa, *Ac. sg. n.*
Upon the beneficent,	the confident,	the pure-minded,	who	practices	wickedness,

तं जनमसत्यसंधं भगवति वसुधे कथं वहसि ॥ ७८ ॥

तं	जनम्	असत्यसंधं	भगवति	वसुधे	कथं	वहसि ॥ ७८ ॥
tad, *Ac. sg. m.*	-na, *Ac. sg.*	*Bahuv.* -dha, *Ac. sg. m.*	-vat, *V. sg. f.*	*Ttp.* -dhâ, *V. sg.*	*Ind.*	vah, *2 sg. Pres. Par.*
that	man	treacherous,	O venerable	earth,	how	dost thou bear? (78)

दुर्जनेन समं सख्यं प्रीतिं चापि न कारयेत्।

दुर्जनेन	समं	सख्यं	प्रीतिं	च	अपि	न	कारयेत्।
Karm. -na, *I. sg.*	-ma, *Ac. sg. n. Adv.*	-ya, *Ac. sg.*	-ti, *Ac. sg.*	*Ind.*	*Ind.*	*Ind.*	kṛi, *3 sg. Pot. Par. Caus.*
The wicked man	with	friendship,	affection	and	also	not	one should make,

उष्णो दहति चांगारः शीतः कृष्णायते करं ॥ ७९ ॥

उष्णो	दहति	च	अंगारः	शीतः	कृष्णायते	करं ॥ ७९ ॥
-ṇa, *N. sg. m.*	dah, *3 sg. Pres. Par.*	*Ind.*	-ra, *N. sg.*	-ta, *N. sg. m.*	kṛishṇâya, *3 sg. Pres. Âtm.*	-ra, *Ac. sg.*
hot	burns	and	the coal,	cold	it blackens	the hand. (79)

अथवा स्थितिरियं दुर्जनानां।

अथवा	स्थितिः	इयं	दुर्जनानां।
Ind.	-ti, *N. sg.*	idam, *N. sg. f.*	*Karm.* -na, *G. pl.*
Or else	the maxim	this	of the wicked:

प्राक्पादयोः पतति खादति पृष्ठमांसं

प्राक्	पादयोः	पतति	खादति	पृष्ठमांसं
prâch, *Ac. sg. n. Adv.*	-da, *L. du.*	pat, *3 sg. Pres. Par.*	khâd, *3 sg. Pres. Par.*	*Ttp.* -sa, *Ac. sg.*
In front	at the feet	he falls,	he eats	of the back-the flesh;

कर्णे कलं किमपि रौति शनैर्विचित्रं।
-ṇa *L. sg.* -la, *Ac. sg. n.* kim, *Ac. sg. n. Ind.* ru, 3 *sg. Pres. Par.* *Ind.* -ra, *Ac. sg. n.*
in the ear tune some he hums softly a wondrous one ;

छिद्रं निरूप्य सहसा प्रविशत्यशंकः
-ra *Ac. sg.* rûp *with* ni, *Ger.* -has, *I. sg.* viś, *with* pra, 3 *sg. Pres. Par.* *Bahuv.* -ka, *N. sg. m.*
a hole having espied with haste he enters fearless ;

सर्वं खलस्य चरितं मशकः करोति ॥ ८० ॥
-va, *Ac. sg. n.* -la, *G. sg. m.* -ta, *Ac. sg. n.* -ka, *N. sg.* kṛi, 3 *sg. Pres. Par.*
the whole of the wicked conduct the gnat practises. (80)

दुर्जनः प्रियवादी च नैतद्विश्वासकारणं।
Karm. -na, *N. sg.* *Ttp.* -din, *N. sg. m.* *Ind.* *Ind.* etad, *N. sg. n.* *Ttp.* -ṇa, *N. sg.*
A wicked a kind words-speaking and, not this a confidence-reason,

मधु तिष्ठति जिह्वाग्रे हृदि हालाहलं विषं ॥ ८१ ॥
-dhu, *N. sg. n.* sthâ, 3 *sg. Pres. Par.* *Ttp.* -ra, *L. sg.* -d, *L. sg.* -la, *N. sg. n.* -sha, *N. sg.*
honey stands on the tongue-tip, in the heart Hâlâhala poison. (81)

अथ प्रभाते क्षेत्रपतिर्लगुडहस्तस्तं प्रदेशमागच्छन्का-
Ind. -ta, *L. sg.* *Ttp.* -ti, *N. sg.* *Bahuv.* -ta, *N. sg. m.* tad, *Ac. sg. m.* -śa, *Ac. sg.* gam *with* â, *N. sg. m Ptc. Pres. Par.*
Now in the morning the field-owner staff-in hand that place approaching

केनावलोकितः। तमालोक्य काकेनोक्तं। सखे
-ka, *I. sg.* lok *with* ava, *N. sg. m. past Ptc. Pass.* tad, *Ac. sg. m.* lok *with* â, *Ger.* -ka, *I. sg.* vach, *N. sg. n. past Ptc. Pass.* -khi, *V. sg.*
by the crow espied. Him having seen by the crow said : Friend

मृग त्वमात्मानं मृतवत्संदर्श्य वातेनोदरं पूरयित्वा
-ga, *V. sg* yushmad, *N. sg.* -man, *Ac. sg.* *Ind.* dṛiś *with* sam, *Ger. Caus.* -ta, *I. sg.* -ra, *Ac. sg.* pṛi, *Ger.*
deer, thou thyself dead-like having shown, with wind the stomach having filled,

पादान्स्तब्धीकृत्य तिष्ठ। यदाहं शब्दं करोमि तदा त्वमु-
-da, *Ac. pl.* stabdhi-kṛi, *Ger.* sthâ, 2 *sg. Imp. Par.* *Ind.* asmad, *N. sg.* -da, *Ac. sg.* kṛi, 1 *sg. Pres. Par.* *Ind.* yushmad, *N. sg.*
the feet having stiffened, remain. When I a noise make, then thou

त्थाय सत्वरं पलायिष्यसि। मृगस्तथैव काकवचनेन
sthâ *with* ud, *Ger.* *Avyay.* ay *with* palâ, 2 *sg. Fut. II. Par.* -ga, *N. sg.* *Ind.* *Ind.* *Ttp.* -na, *I. sg.*
having got up with-haste wilt run away. The deer thus just by the crow's-word

स्थितः। ततः क्षेत्रपतिना हर्षोत्फुल्ललोचनेन तथाविधो
sthâ, *N. sg. m. past Ptc. Pass.* *Ind.* *Ttp.* -ti, *I. sg.* *Bahuv.* -na, *I. sg. m.* -dha, *N. sg. m.*
remained. Then by the field-owner, whose eyes-(were) expanded-with joy, the so-conditioned

मृग आलोकितः। आः स्वयं मृतो ऽसि। इत्युक्त्वा मृगं

-ga, *N. sg.* lok *with* â, *N. sg. m. past Ptc. Pass.* *Ind.* *Ind.* mṛi, *N. sg. m. past Ptc. Pass.* as, *2 sg. Pres. Par.* *Ind.* vach, *Ger.* -ga, *Ac. sg.*

deer perceived. 'Ha! of thyself dead thou art.' Thus having said the deer

बंधनान्मोचयित्वा पाशान्ग्रहीतुं सयत्नो बभूव। ततः

-na, *Ab. sg.* much, *Ger.* -śa, *Ac. pl.* grah, *Inf.* *Bahuv.* -na, *N. sg. m.* bhû, *3 sg. Perf. Par.* *Ind.*

from the fetter having delivered, the snare to take up busy he was. Then

काकशब्दं श्रुत्वा मृगः सत्वरमुत्थाय पलायितः।

Ttp. -da, *Ac. sg.* śru, *Ger.* -ga, *N. sg.* *Avyay.* sthâ *with* ud, *Ger.* ay *with* palâ, *N. sg. m. past Ptc. Pass.*

the crow's-voice having heard, the deer with-haste having risen, escaped.

तमुद्दिश्य तेन क्षेत्रपतिना क्षिप्तेन लगुडेन शृगालो हतः।

tad, *Ac. sg. m.* diś *with* ud, *Ger.* tad, *I. sg. m.* *Ttp.* -ti, *I. sg.* kship, *I. sg. m. past Ptc. Pass.* -ḍa, *I. sg.* -la, *N. sg.* han, *N. sg. m. past Ptc. Pass.*

Him aiming-at by that field-owner with a thrown stick the jackal killed.

तथा चोक्तं। त्रिभिर्वर्षैस्त्रिभिर्मासैस्त्रिभिः पक्षैस्त्रिभिर्दिनैः।

Ind. *Ind.* vach, *N. sg. n. past Ptc. Pass.* tri, *I. pl.* -sha, *I. pl.* tri, *I. pl.* -sa, *I. pl.* tri, *I. pl.* -sha, *I. pl.* tri, *I. pl.* -na, *I. pl.*

Thus and said: In three years, in three months, in three fortnights, in three days,

अत्युत्कटैः पापपुण्यैरिहैव फलमश्नुते ॥ ८२ ॥

Karm. -ṭa, *I. pl. n.* *Dvandva.* -ya, *I. pl. n.* *Ind.* *Ind.* -la, *Ac. sg.* aś, *3 sg. Pres. Âtm.*

through extraordinary good (and)-bad (actions) here even the fruit one reaps. (82)

अतो ऽहं ब्रवीमि भक्ष्यभक्षकयोः प्रीतिरित्यादि। काकः पुनराह।

Ind. asmad, *N. sg.* brû, *1 sg. Pres. Par.* *Dvandva.* -ka, *G. du.* -ti, *N. sg.* *Bahuv.* -di, *Ac. sg. n.* -ka, *N. sg.* *Ind.* ah, *3 sg. Perf. Par.*

Therefore I say: Of the food-(and) the eater the affection, etc. The crow again says:

भक्षितेनापि भवता नाहारो मम पुष्कलः।

bhaksh, *I sg. m. past Ptc. Pass.* *Ind.* -vat, *I. sg. m.* *Ind.* -ra, *N. sg.* asmad, *G. sg. m.* -la, *N. sg. m.*

Eaten even by you not the food of me plenteous,

त्वयि जीवति जीवामि चित्रग्रीव इवानघ ॥ ८३ ॥

yushmad, *L. sg.* jîv, *L. sg. m. Ptc. Pres. Par.* *1 sg. Pres. Par.* *Bahuv.* -va, *N. sg.* *Ind.* *Bahuv.* -gha, *V. sg.*

in thee living I live, Chitragrîva like, oh harmless! (83)

अन्यच्च। तिरश्चामपि विश्वासो दृष्टः पुण्यैककर्मणां।

-ya, *N. sg. n.* *Ind.* tiryach, *G. pl. m.* *Ind.* -sa, *N. sg.* dṛiś, *N. sg. m. past Ptc. Pass.* *Bahuv.* -man, *G. pl. m.*

Again and, Of brutes even confidence is seen (performing) pure-only-actions,

सतां हि साधुशीलत्वात्स्वभावो न निवर्तते ॥ ८४ ॥

-t, G. pl. m. — *Ind.* — -tva, *Ab. sg.* — *Karm.* -va, *N. sg.* — *Ind.* — vṛit *with* ni, *3 sg. Pres. Âtm.*

of the good for from good-character the natural-disposition not turns away. (84)

किंच । साधोः प्रकोपितस्यापि मनो नायाति विक्रियां ।

Ind. — -dhu, *G. sg. m.* — kup *with* pra, *G. sg. m. past Ptc. Pass. Caus.* — *Ind.* — -nas, *N. sg.* — *Ind.* — yâ *with* â, *3 sg. Pres. Par.* — -yâ, *Ac. sg.*

Moreover, of the good irritated even the mind not goes-to change,

न हि तापयितुं शक्यं सागराम्भस्तृणोल्कया ॥ ८५ ॥

Ind. — *Ind.* — tap, *Inf. Caus.* — -ya, *N. sg. n.* — *Ttp.* -bhas, *N. sg.* — *Ttp.* -kâ, *I. sg.*

Not for to heat possible the ocean-water with a straw-fire. (85)

हिरण्यको ब्रूते । चपलस्त्वं चपलेन सह स्नेहः सर्वथा

-ka, *N. sg.* — brû, *3 sg. Pres. Âtm.* — -la, *N. sg. m.* — yushmad, *N. sg.* — -la, *I. sg.* — *Ind.* — -ha, *N. sg.* — *Ind.*

Hiraṇyaka says: Unsteady thou, an unsteady one with friendship by any means

न कर्तव्यः ।

Ind. — kṛi, *N. sg. m. Ptc. Fut. Pass.*

not to be made.

तथा चोक्तं । मार्जारो महिषो मेषः काकः कापुरुषस्तथा ।

Ind. — *Ind.* — vach, *N. sg. n. past Ptc. Pass.* — -ra, *N. sg.* — -sha, *N. sg.* — -sha, *N. sg.* — -ka, *N. sg.* — *Karm.* -sha, *N. sg.* — *Ind.*

Thus and said: A cat, a buffalo, a ram, a crow, a bad man likewise,

विश्वासात्प्रभवंत्येते विश्वासस्तत्र नोचितः ॥ ८६ ॥

-sa, *Ab. sg.* — bhû *with* pra, *3 pl. Pres. Par.* — etad, *N. pl. m.* — -sa, *N. sg.* — *Ind.* — *Ind.* — -ta, *N. sg. m.*

from confidence become strong these; confidence there not proper. (86)

किंचान्यत् । शत्रुपक्षो भवानस्माकं । उक्तं चैतत् ।

Ind. — -ya, *N. sg. n.* — *Bahuv.* -sha, *N. sg. m.* — -vat, *N. sg. m.* — asmad, *G. pl.* — vach, *N. sg. n. past Ptc. Pass.* — *Ind.* — etad, *N. sg. n.*

Besides another; with the enemies-siding you of us; said and this:

शत्रुणा न हि संदध्यात्सुश्लिष्टेनापि संधिना ।

-ru, *I. sg.* — *Ind.* — *Ind.* — dhâ *with* sam, *3 sg. Pot. Par.* — *Karm.* -ta, *I. sg. m.* — *Ind.* — -dhi, *I. sg.*

With an enemy not surely one should unite oneself through a well-fastened even union,

सुतप्तमपि पानीयं शमयत्येव पावकं ॥ ८७ ॥

Karm. -ta, *N. sg. n.* — *Ind.* — -ya, *N. sg.* — śam, *3 sg. Pres. Par. Caus.* — *Ind.* — -ka, *Ac. sg.*

well-heated also water quenches yet the fire. (87)

दुर्जनः परिहर्तव्यो विद्ययालंकृतोऽपि सन् ।

Karm. -na, *N. sg.* hṛi *with* pari, *N. sg. m. Ptc. Fut. Pass.* -yâ, *I. sg.* kṛi *with* alam, *N. sg. m. past Ptc. Pass.* *Ind.* as, *N. sg. m. Ptc. Pres. Par.*
A wicked man to be avoided with knowledge decorated even being,

मणिना भूषितः सर्पः किमसौ न भयंकरः ॥ ८८ ॥

-ṇi, *I. sg.* bhûsh, *N. sg. m. past Ptc. Pass.* -pa, *N. sg.* *Ind.* adas, *N. sg. m.* *Ind.* *Tip.* -ra, *N. sg. m.*
with the jewel decorated the serpent, (is) he not terrific? (88)

यदशक्यं न तच्छक्यं यच्छक्यं शक्यमेव तत् ।

yad, *N. sg. n.* *Karm.* -ya, *N. sg. n.* *Ind.* tad, *N. sg. n.* -ya, *N. sg. n.* yad, *N. sg. n.* -ya, *N. sg. n.* *id.* *Ind.* tad, *N. sg. n.*
What impossible, not that possible; what possible, possible certainly that;

नोदके शकटं याति न च नौर्गच्छति स्थले ॥ ८९ ॥

Ind. -ka, *L. sg.* -ṭa, *N. sg.* yâ, 3 *sg. Pres. Par.* *Ind.* *Ind.* nau, *N. sg.* gam, 3 *sg. Pres. Par.* -la, *L. sg.*
not in water a cart goes, not and a ship goes on dry land. (89)

अपरं च । महताप्यर्थसारेण यो विश्वसिति शत्रुषु ।

-ra, *N. sg. n.* *Ind.* -hat, *I. sg. m.* *Ind.* *Tip.* -ra, *I. sg.* yad, *N. sg. m.* śvas *with* vi, 3 *sg. Pres. Par.* -ru, *L. pl.*
Another and, With great even wealth-affluence who confides in enemies,

भार्यासु च विरक्तासु तदन्तं तस्य जीवनं ॥ ९० ॥

-yâ, *L. pl.* *Ind.* rañj *with* vi, *L. pl. f. past Ptc. Pass.* *Bahuv.* -ta, *N. sg. n.* tad, *G. sg. m.* -na, *N. sg.*
in wives and disaffectionate, there-ending of him the sustenance. (90)

लघुपतनको ब्रूते । श्रुतं मया सर्वं । तथापि मम

-ka, *N. sg.* brû, 3 *sg. Pres. Atm.* śru, *N. sg. n. past Ptc. Pass.* asmad, *I. sg.* -va, *N. sg. n.* *Ind.* *Ind.* asmad, *G. sg.*
Laghupatanaka says: Heard by me all. Thus even of me

चैतावान्संकल्पस्त्वया सह सौहृद्यमवश्यं करणीयमिति ।

Ind. -vat, *N. sg. m.* -pa, *N. sg.* yushmad, *I. sg.* *Ind.* -ya, *N. sg.* -ya, *Ac. sg. n. Adv.* kṛi, *N. sg. n. Ptc. Fut. Pass.* *Ind.*
and such the resolution: 'Thee with friendship necessarily to be made,' thus;

नो चेदनाहारेणात्मानं व्यापादयिष्यामि । तथा हि ।

Ind. *Ind.* *Karm.* -ra, *I. sg.* -man, *Ac. sg.* pad *with* vi-â, 1 *sg. Fut.* ii. *Par. Caus.* *Ind.* *Ind.*
not if, through want of food myself I shall kill. Thus for:

मृद्घटवत्सुखभेद्यो दुःसंधानश्च दुर्जनो भवति ।

Ind. -ya, *N. sg. m.* (*rt.* bhid) -na, *N. sg. m.* *Ind.* *Karm.* -na. *N. sg.* bhû, 3 *sg. Pres. Par.*
Earthen-pot-like easy-to be broken, difficult-to be united and, the wicked man is;

सुजनस्तु कनकघटवद्दुर्भेद्यश्चाशुसंधेयः ॥ ९१ ॥

Karm. -na, *N. sg.* | *Ind.* | *Ind.* | -ya, *N. sg. m.* | *Ind.* | -ya, *N. sg. m.* (*rt.* dhā *with* sam) *Ptc. Fut. Pass.*

the good man, | on the contrary | golden-pot-like | difficult-to be broken | and | easily to be united. (91)

किंच। द्रवत्वात्सर्वलोहानां निमित्तान्मृगपक्षिणां।

Ind. | -tva, *Ab. sg.* | *Karm.* -ha, *G. pl.* | -ta, *Ab. sg.* | *Dvandva.* -kshin, *G. pl.*

Moreover, | From fluxibility | of all-metals, | from a motive | of beasts-(and) birds,

भयाल्लोभाच्च मूर्खाणां संगतं दर्शनात्सतां ॥ ९२ ॥

-ya, *Ab. sg.* | -bha, *Ab. sg.* | *Ind.* | -kha, *G. pl.* | -ta, *N. sg. n.* | -na, *Ab. sg.* | -t, *G. pl. m.*

from fear, | cupidity | and, | of the fools | the union, | from sight | of the good. (92)

किंच। नारिकेलसमाकारा दृश्यंते ऽपि हि सज्जनाः।

Ind. | *Bahuv.* -ra, *N. pl. m.* | dṛiś, 3 *pl. Pres. Pass.* | *Ind.* | *Ind.* | *Karm.* -na, *N. pl.*

Moreover, | Cocoanut-like-formed | are seen | also | indeed | the good-men,

अन्ये बदरिकाकारा बहिरेव मनोहराः ॥ ९३ ॥

-ya, *N. pl. m.* | *Bahuv.* -ra, *N. pl. m.* | *Ind.* | *Ind.* | *Ttp.* -ra, *N. pl. m.*

others | jujube-shaped | externally | merely | charming. (93)

स्नेहच्छेदे ऽपि साधूनां गुणा नायांति विक्रियां।

Ttp. -da, *L. sg.* | *Ind.* | -dhu, *G. pl. m.* | -na, *N. pl.* | *Ind.* | yā *with* ā, 3 *pl. Pres. Par.* | -yā, *Ac. sg.*

In love-interruption | even | of the good | the virtues | not | go-to | change,

भग्ने ऽपि हि मृणालानामनुबध्नंति तंतवः ॥ ९४ ॥

-ga, *L. sg.* | *Ind.* | *Ind.* | -la, *G. pl.* | bandh *with* anu, 3 *pl. Pres. Par.* | -tu, *N. pl.*

in the fracture | even | for | of lotus stalks | remain connected | the fibres. (94)

अन्यच्च। शुचित्वं त्यागिता शौर्यं सामान्यं सुखदुःखयोः।

-ya, *N. sg. n.* *Ind.* | -tva, *N. sg. n.* | -tā, *N. sg.* | -ya, *N. sg.* | -ya, *N. sg.* | *Dvandva.* -kha, *L. du.*

Again and, | Purity, | generosity, | bravery, | constancy | in happiness (and)-misfortune,

दाक्षिण्यं चानुरक्तिश्च सत्यता च सुहृद्गुणाः ॥ ९५ ॥

-ya, *N. sg.* | *Ind.* | -ti, *N. sg.* | *Ind.* | -tā, *N. sg.* | *Ind.* | *Ttp.* -ṇa, *N. pl.*

rectitude | and, | attachment | and, | veracity | and, | a friend's-qualities. (95)

एतैर्गुणैरुपेतो भवदन्यो मया कः सुहृत्प्रा-

etad, *I. pl. m.* | -ṇa, *I. pl.* | i *with* upa, *N. sg. m.* *past Ptc. Pass.* | *Ttp.* -ya, *N. sg. m.* | asmad, *I. sg.* | kim, *N. sg. m.* | -d, *N. sg.*

With these | qualities | endowed | but you-another | by me | who | as a friend

प्यः। इत्यादि तद्वचनमाकर्ण्य हिरण्यको

āp *with* pra, *N. sg. m.* *Ptc. Fut. Pass.* | *Bahuv.* -di, *Ac. sg. n.* | *Ttp.* -na, *Ac. sg.* | karṇ *with* ā, *Ger.* | -ka, *N. sg.*

to be found? | Thus-beginning | of him-the speech | having heard, | Hiraṇyaka

वहिर्निःसृत्याह। आप्यायितोऽहं भवतामनेन
Ind. sri with nis, Ger. | ah, 3 sg. Perf. Par. | pyai with â, N. sg. m. past Ptc. Pass. Caus. | asmad, N. sg. | -vat, G. pl. m. | idam, I. sg. n.
forth out-slipping says: Regaled I of you by this

वचनामृतेन। तथा चोक्तं।
Tip. -ta, I. sg. | Ind. | Ind. | vach, N. sg. n. past Ptc. Pass.
word-nectar. Thus and said:

घर्मार्तं न तथा सुशीतलजलैः स्नानं न मुक्तावली
Tip. -ta, Ac. sg. m. | Ind. | Ind. | Karm. -la, I. pl. | -na, N. sg. | Ind. | Tip. -lî, N. sg.
The heat-oppressed not thus with cool-waters bathing, not a pearl-necklace,

न श्रीखंडविलेपनं सुखयति प्रत्यंगमप्यर्पितं।
Ind. | Tip. -na, N. sg. | sukhaya, 3 sg. Pres. Par. | Avyay. | Ind. | ṛi, N. sg. n. past Ptc. Pass. Caus.
not sandal-ointment comforts, limb by limb even applied,

प्रीत्यै सज्जनभाषितं प्रभवति प्रायो यथा चेतसः
-ti, D. sg. | Tip. -ta, N. sg. | bhû with pra, 3 sg. Pres. Par. | Ind. | Ind. | -tas, G. sg.
to the gratification of good-men-the speech serves commonly as of the mind,

सद्युक्त्या च पुरस्कृतं सुकृतिनामाकृष्टिमंत्रोपमं ॥ ९६ ॥
Karm. -ti, I. sg. | Ind. | kṛi with puras, N. sg. n. past Ptc. Pass. | -tin, G. pl. m. | Bahuv. -ma, N. sg. n.
with good-argument and put-forth of the good, attraction-charm-equal. (96)

अन्यच्च। रहस्यभेदो याच्ञा च नैष्ठुर्यं चलचित्तता।
-ya, N. sg. n. | Ind. | Tip. -da, N. sg. | -ñâ, N. sg. | Ind. | -ya, N. sg. | -tâ, N. sg.
Again and, Secret-betrayal, begging and, severity, fickle-mindedness,

क्रोधो निःसत्यता द्यूतमेतन्मित्रस्य दूषणं ॥ ९७ ॥
-dha, N. sg. | -tâ, N. sg. | -ta, N. sg. | etad, N. sg. n. | -ra, G. sg. | -ṇa, N. sg.
anger want-of truth, gambling,— this a friend's fault. (97)

अनेन वचनक्रमेण तदेकदूषणमपि त्वयि न लक्ष्यते॥
idam, I. sg. m. | Tip. -ma, I. sg. | Tip. -ṇa, N. sg. | Ind. | yushmad, L. sg. | Ind. | laksh, 3 sg. Pres. Pass.
Through this speech-course of them-one-fault even in thee not is perceived:

यतः। पटुत्वं सत्यवादित्वं कथायोगेन बुध्यते।
Ind. | -tva, N. sg. | -tva, N. sg. | Tip. -ga, I. sg. | budh, 3 sg. Pres. Pass.
For, Eloquence, veracity, through the speech-course is known,

अस्तब्धत्वमचापल्यं प्रत्यक्षेणावगम्यते ॥ ९८ ॥
-tva, N. sg. | -ya, N. sg. | -ksha, I. sg. n. Adv. | gam with ava, 3 sg. Pres. Pass.
unsteadiness, fickleness, at sight is discovered. (98)

अपरं च। अन्यथैव हि सौहार्दं भवेत्स्वच्छांतरात्मनः।
-ra, *N. sg. n.* *Ind.* *Ind.* *Ind.* *Ind.* -da, *N. sg.* bhû, 3 *sg. Pot. Par.* *Bahuv.* -man, *G. sg. m.*
Another and, Otherwise truly for the friendship will be of the pure-minded,

प्रवर्तते ऽन्यथा वाणी शाठ्योपहतचेतसः ॥ ९९ ॥
vṛit *with* pra, 3 *sg. Pres. Âtm.* *Ind.* -ṇî, *N. sg.* *Bahuv.* -tas, *G. sg. m.*
proceeds otherwise the language of one whose heart-is affected-by deceit. (99)

मनस्यन्यद्वचस्यन्यत्कार्यमन्यद्दुरात्मनां।
-nas, *L. sg.* -ya, *N. sg. n.* -chas, *L. sg.* -ya, *N. sg. n.* -ya, *N. sg. n.* -ya, *N. sg. n.* *Bahuv.* -man, *G. pl. m.*
In the mind another thing, in the speech another, the action another of the wicked,

मनस्येकं वचस्येकं कर्मण्येकं महात्मनां ॥ १०० ॥
-nas, *L. sg.* -ka, *N. sg. n.* -chas, *L. sg.* -ka, *N. sg. n.* -man, *L. sg.* -ka, *N. sg. n.* *Bahuv.* -man, *G. pl. m.*
in the mind one thing, in the speech one, in the action one of the noble-minded. (100)

तद्भवतु भवतो ऽभिमतमेव। इत्युक्त्वा हिरण्यको
Ind. bhû, 3 *sg. Imp. Par.* -vat, *G. sg. m.* man *with* abhi, *N. sg. n. past. Ptc. Pass.* *Ind.* *Ind.* vach, *Ger.* -ka, *N. sg.*
Therefore be of you the wished even. Thus having said Hiraṇyaka

मैत्र्यं विधाय भोजनविशेषैर्वायसं संतोष्य विवरं
-ya, *Ac. sg.* dhâ *with* vi, *Ger.* *Ttp.* -sha, *I. pl.* -sa, *Ac. sg.* tush+sam, *Ger. Caus.* -ra, *Ac. sg.*
friendship having made, with food-dainties the crow having regaled, the hole

प्रविष्टः। वायसो ऽपि स्वस्थानं गतः। ततः प्रभृति तयो-
viś *with* pra, *N. sg. m. past. Ptc. Pass.* -sa, *N. sg.* *Ind.* *Karm.* -na, *Ac. sg.* gam *N. sg. m. past Ptc. Pass.* *Ind.* *Ind.* tad, *G. du. m.*
entered. The crow also to his-place gone. Thence-forward of those two

रन्योन्याहारप्रदानेन कुशलप्रश्नैर्विश्रंभालापैश्च कालो ऽतिवर्तते।
Ttp. -na, *I. sg.* *Ttp.* -na, *I. pl.* *Ttp.* -pa, *I. pl.* *Ind.* -la, *N. sg.* vṛit *with* ati, 3 *sg. Pres. Âtm.*
with mutual-food-presenting, with health-enquiries, with confidential-conversations and, the time passes by.

एकदा लघुपतनको हिरण्यकमाह। सखे कष्टतरलभ्याहार-
Ind. -ka, *N. sg.* -ka, *Ac. sg.* ah, 3 *sg. Perf. Par.* -khi, *V. sg.* *Bahuv.* -ra, *Ac. sg. n.*
One day Laghupatanaka to Hiraṇyaka says: Friend, with very difficult-to be procured-food

मिदं स्थानं परित्यज्य स्थानांतरं गंतुमिच्छामि।
idam, *Ac. sg. n.* -na, *Ac. sg.* tyaj *with* pari, *Ger.* *Ttp.* -ra, *Ac. sg.* gam, *Inf.* ish, 1 *sg. Pres. Par.*
this place having left to another place to go I wish.

हिरण्यको ब्रूते। मित्र क गंतव्यं। तथा चोक्तं।

-ka, *N. sg.* brû, 3 *sg. Pres. Âtm.* -ra, *V. sg.* *Ind.* gam, *N. sg. n. Ptc. Fut. Pass.* *Ind.* *Ind.* vach, *N. sg. n. past Ptc. Pass.*

Hiraṇyaka says: Friend, where to be gone? Thus and said:

चलत्येकेन पादेन तिष्ठत्येकेन बुद्धिमान्।

chal, 3 *sg. Pres. Par.* -ka, *I. sg. m.* -da, *I. sg.* sthâ, 3 *sg. Pres. Par.* -ka, *I. sg. m.* -mat, *N. sg. m.*

He goes with one foot, he stands with one, the wise man,

नासमीक्ष्य परं स्थानं पूर्वमायतनं त्यजेत् ॥ १०१ ॥

Ind. îksh *with* sam, *Ger. with* a -ra, *Ac. sg. n.* -na, *Ac. sg.* -va, *Ac. sg. n.* -na, *Ac. sg.* tyaj, 3 *sg. Pot. Par.*

not, without-having seen another place, the former abode one should leave. (101)

वायसो ब्रूते। अस्ति सुनिरूपितस्थानं। हिरण्यको ऽवदत्।

-sa, *N. sg.* brû, 3 *sg. Pres. Âtm.* as, 3 *sg. Pres. Par*, *Karm.* -na, *N. sg.* -ka, *N. sg.* vad, 3 *sg. Impf. Par.*

The crow says: There is a well-investigated-place. Hiraṇyaka said:

किं तत्। वायसो ब्रूते। अस्ति दंडकारण्ये

kim, *N. sg. n.* tad, *N. sg. n.* -sa, *N. sg.* brû, 3 *sg. Pres. Âtm.* as, 3 *sg. Pres. Par.* *Karm.* -ya, *L. sg.*

What that? The crow says: There is in the Daṇḍaka-wood

कर्पूरगौराभिधानं सरः। तत्र चिरकालोपार्जितः प्रियसुहृन्मे

Bahuv. -na, *N. sg. n.* -ras, *N. sg.* *Ind.* *Ttp.* -ta, *N. sg. m.* *Karm.* -d, *N. sg.* asmad, *G. sg.*

Karpûragaura-named a lake; there since a long-time-acquired a dear-friend of me

मंथराभिधानः कच्छपो धार्मिकः प्रतिवसति।

Bahuv. -na, *N. sg. m.* -pa, *N. sg.* -ka, *N. sg. m.* vas *with* prati, 3 *sg. Pres. Par.*

Manthara-named a tortoise, virtuous, dwells.

यतः। परोपदेशे पांडित्यं सर्वेषां सुकरं नृणां।

Ind. *Ttp.* -śa, *L. sg.* -ya, *N. sg.* -va, *G. pl. m.* -ra, *N. sg. n.* nṛi, *G. pl.*

For, In to others-advice skill of all easy of men,

धर्मे स्वीयमनुष्ठानं कस्यचित्तु महात्मनः ॥ १०२ ॥

-ma, *L. sg.* -ya, *N. sg. n.* -na, *N. sg.* kim-chid, *G. sg. m.* *Ind.* *Bahuv.* -man, *G. sg. m.*

in virtue one's own practice of some one, indeed, highminded. (102)

स च भोजनविशेषैर्मां संवर्धयिष्यति। हिरण्यको

tad, *N. sg. m.* *Ind.* *Ttp.* -sha, *I. pl.* asmad, *Ac. sg.* vṛidh *with* sam, 3 *sg. Fut.* ii. *Par. Caus.* -ka, *N. sg.*

He and with food-dainties me will treat. Hiraṇyaka

ऽप्याह । तत्किमत्रावस्थाय मया कर्तव्यं ।

Ind. ah, 3 *sg. Perf.*, *Ind.* kim, *N. sg. n.* *Ind.* sthâ *with* ava. *Ger.* asmad, *I. sg.* kṛi, *N. sg. n. Ptc. Fut. Pass.*

also says: Then, what, here staying, by me to be done?

यतः । यस्मिन्देशे न संमानो न वृत्तिर्न च बांधवः ।

Ind. yad, *L. sg. m.* -śa, *L. sg.* *Ind.* -na, *N. sg.* *Ind.* -ti, *N. sg.* *Ind.* *Ind.* -va, *N. sg.*

For, In which place not honour, not employment, not and a friend,

न च विद्यागमः कश्चित्तं देशं परिवर्जयेत् ॥ १०३ ॥

Ind. *Ind.* *Ttp.* -ma, *N. sg.* kim-chid, *N. sg. m.* tad, *Ac. sg. m.* -śa, *Ac. sg.* vṛij *with* pari, 3 *sg. Pot. Par.*

not and knowledge-advancement some, that place one should abandon. (103)

अपरं च । लोकयात्राभयं लज्जा दाक्षिण्यं त्यागशीलता ।

-ra, *N. sg. n.* *Ind.* *Ttp.* -râ, *N. sg.* *Karm.* -ya, *N. sg.* -jâ, *N. sg.* -ya, *N. sg.* -tâ, *N. sg.*

Another and, Traffic, safety, shame, rectitude, generosity,

पंच यत्र न विद्यंते न कुर्यात्तत्र संस्थितिं ॥ १०४ ॥

-chan, *N.* *Ind.* *Ind.* vid, 3 *pl. Pres. Pass.* *Ind.* kṛi, 3 *sg. Pot. Par.* *Ind.* -ti, *Ac. sg.*

the five where not are found, not should one make there a residence. (104)

तत्र मित्र न वस्तव्यं यत्र नास्ति चतुष्टयं ।

Ind. -ra, *V. sg.* *Ind.* vas, *Ptc. Fut. Pass.* *Ind.* *Ind.* as, 3 *sg.* -ya, *N. sg.*

There, O friend, not to be dwelt where not is a collection of the four,

ऋणदाता च वैद्यश्च श्रोत्रियः सजला नदी ॥ १०५ ॥

Ttp. -tṛi, *N. sg. m.* *Ind.* -ya, *N. sg.* *Ind.* -ya, *N. sg.* -la, *N. sg. f.* -dî, *N. sg.*

a creditor and, a physician and, a Brahman learned in the Vedas, full of water a river. (105)

ततो मामपि तत्र नय । अथ वायसस्तत्र

Ind. asmad, *Ac. sg.* *Ind.* *Ind.* nî, 2 *sg. Imp. Par.* *Ind.* -sa, *N. sg.* *Ind.*

Therefore me also there conduct. Then the crow there

तेन मित्रेण सह विचित्रालापैः सुखेन तस्य सरसः समीपं

tad, *I. sg. n.* -ra, *I. sg.* *Ind.* *Karm.* -pa, *I. pl.* -kha, *I. sg. n.* tad, *G. sg. n.* -ras, *G. sg.* -pa, *Ac. sg. n.*

that friend with, under various-conversations pleasantly of that lake into the proximity

ययौ । ततो मंथरो दूरादवलोक्य लघुपतनकस्य यथोचित-

yâ, 3 *sg. Perf. Par.* *Ind.* -ra, *N. sg.* -ra, *Ab. sg. n. Adv.* lok *with* ava, *Ger.* -ka, *G. sg.* *Avyay.*

went. Then Manthara from afar having seen, of Laghupatanaka as-proper

मातिथ्यं विधाय मूषिकस्यातिथिसत्कारं चकार ।

-ya, Ac. sg. dhâ, *with* vi, *Ger.* -ka, *G. sg.* *Ttp.* -ra, *Ac. sg.* kṛi, 3 *sg. Perf. Par.*

hospitality having performed, of the mouse hospitable-reception made.

यतः । बालो वा यदि वा वृद्धो युवा वा गृहमागतः ।

Ind. -la, *N. sg.* *Ind.* *Ind.* *Ind.* -dha, *N. sg. m.* -van, *N. sg. m.* *Ind.* -ha, *Ac. sg.* gam *with* â, *N. sg. m. past Ptc. Pass.*

For, A child either, or an old man, a youth or to the house come,

तस्य पूजा विधातव्या सर्वत्राभ्यागतो गुरुः ॥ १०६ ॥

tad, *G. sg. m.* -jâ, *N. sg.* dhâ *with* vi, *N. sg. f. Ptc. Fut. Pass.* *Ind.* gam *with* abhi-â, *N. sg. m. past Ptc. Pass.* -ru, *N. sg. m.*

of him honour to be made; everywhere the arrived (guest) (is) an object of respect. (106)

गुरुरग्निर्द्विजातीनां वर्णानां ब्राह्मणो गुरुः ।

-ru, *N. sg. m.* -ni, *N. sg.* *Bahuv.* -ti, *G. pl.* -ṇa, *G. pl.* -ṇa, *N. sg.* -ru, *N. sg. m.*

An object of respect (is) fire for the twice-born, for the castes the Bráhman an object of respect;

पतिरेको गुरुः स्त्रीणां सर्वत्राभ्यागतो गुरुः ॥ १०७ ॥

-ti, *N. sg.* -ka, *N. sg. m.* -ru, *N. sg. m.* -rî, *G. pl.* *Ind.* gam *with* abhi-â, *N. sg. m. past. Ptc. Pass.* -ru, *N. sg. m.*

the husband alone an object of respect for women; everywhere the arrived (guest) (is) an object of respect. (107)

वायसोऽवदत् । सखे मंथर सविशेषपूजामस्मै विधेहि

-sa, *N. sg.* vad, 3 *sg. Impf. Par.* -khi, *V. sg.* -ra, *V. sg.* *Karm.* -jâ, *Ac. sg.* idam, *D. sg. m.* dhâ *with* vi, 2 *sg. Imp. Par.*

The crow said: Friend Manthara, extraordinary-attention to him pay;

यतोऽयं पुण्यकर्मणां धुरीणः कारुण्यरत्नाकरो हिरण्यकनामा

Ind. idam, *N. sg. m.* *Bahuv.* -man, *G. pl. m.* -ṇa, *N. sg. m.* *Ttp.* -ra, *N. sg.* *Bahuv.* -man, *N. sg. m.*

for he of the pure-actions performing the leader, of gentleness-jewels-a mine, Hiraṇyaka-named,

मूषिकराजः । एतस्य गुणस्तुतिं जिह्वासहस्रद्वयेनापि सर्पराजो न

Ttp. -ja, *N. sg.* etad, *G. sg. m.* *Ttp.* -ti, *Ac. sg.* *Ttp.* -ya, *I. sg.* *Ind.* *Ttp.* -ja, *N. sg.* *Ind.*

the mouse-king. Of him the virtue-praise with of tongues-two thousands even the serpent-king not

कदाचित्कथयितुं समर्थः स्यात् । इत्युक्त्वा चित्रग्रीवोपाख्यानं

Ind. kath, *Inf.* -tha, *N. sg. m.* as, 3 *sg. Pot.* *Ind.* vach, *Ger.* *Ttp.* -na, *Ac. sg.*

ever to relate able would be. Thus having said, of Chitragrîva-the tale

वर्णितवान् । मंथरः सादरं हिरण्यकं संपूज्याह । भद्र-

varṇ, *N. sg. m. Ptc. Perf. Par.* -ra, *N. sg.* *Avyay.* -ka, *Ac. sg.* pûj *with* sam, *Ger.* ah, 3 *sg. Perf Par.* -ra, *V. sg.*

(he) related. Manthara with-respect Hiraṇyaka having saluted says: My dear,

त्मनो निर्जनवनागमनकारणमाख्यातुमर्हसि। हिरण्यको ऽवदत्। कथयामि।

-man, G. sg. — *Ttp. -ṇa, Ac. sg.* — khyâ *with* â, *Inf.* — arh, *2 sg. Pres. Par.* — *-ka, N. sg.* — vad, *3 sg. Impf. Par,* — kath, *1 sg. Pres. Par.*

of yourself — the desert-wood-approaching-reason — to tell — deign. — Hiraṇyaka — said: — I tell;

श्रूयतां। अस्ति चंपकाभिधानायां नगर्यां परिव्राजकावसथः।

śru, *3 sg. Imp. Pass.* — as, *3 sg. Pres. Par.* — *Bahuv. -na, L. sg. f.* — *-ri, L. sg.* — *Ttp. -tha, N. sg.*

it may be heard: — There is — in the Champaka-named — town — a mendicant-dwelling.

तत्र चूडाकर्णो नाम परिव्राट् प्रतिवसति। स च

Ind. — *Bahuv. -ṇa, N. sg.* — *-man, Ac. sg. Adv.* — *-vrâj, N. sg.* — vas *with* prati, *3 sg. Pres. Par.* — tad, *N. sg. m.* — *Ind.*

Therein — Chûḍâkarṇa — by name — a mendicant — dwells. — He — and

भोजनावशिष्टभिक्षान्नसहितं भिक्षापात्रं नागदंतके ऽवस्थाप्य

Ttp. -ta, Ac. sg. n. — *Ttp. -ra, Ac. sg.* — *Ttp. -ka, L. sg.* — sthâ *with* ava, *Ger. Caus.*

with-the of the meals remaining-alms-food — the alms-dish — on a pin in the wall — having placed

स्वपिति। अहं च तदन्नमुत्प्लुत्य प्रत्यहं भक्षयामि। अनंतरं

svap, *3 sg. Pres. Par.* — asmad *N. sg.* — *Ind.* — *Ttp. -na, Ac. sg.* — plu *with* ud, *Ger.* — *Avyay.* — bhaksh *1 sg. Pres. Par.* — *Ind.*

sleeps. — I — and — his-food, — having leaped up, — daily — eat. — Thereupon

तस्य प्रियसुहृद्वीणाकर्णो नाम परिव्राजकः समायातः।

tad, *G. sg. m.* — *Karm. -d, N. sg.* — *Bahuv. -ṇa, N. sg.* — *-man, Ac. sg. Adv.* — *-ka, N. sg.* — yâ *with* sam-â, *N. sg. m. past Ptc. Pass.*

of him — the dear-friend — Vîṇâkarṇa — by name — a mendicant — came.

तेन सह कथाप्रसंगावस्थितो मम त्रासार्थं जर्जरवंशखंडेन

tad, *I. sg. m.* — *Ind.* — *Ttp. -ta, N. sg. m.* (*rt.* sthâ). — asmad, *G. sg.* — *Avyay.* — *Ttp. -ḍa, I. sg.*

Him — with — in conversation-engaged — of me — for frightening's sake — with a split-bamboo-piece

चूडाकर्णो भूमिमताडयत्। वीणाकर्ण उवाच। सखे किमिति मम

Bahuv. -ṇa, N. sg. — *-mi, Ac. sg.* — tad, *3 sg. Impf. Par.* — *Bahuv. -ṇa, N. sg.* — vach, *3 sg. Perf Par.* — *-khi, V. sg.* — *Ind.* — *Ind.* — asmad, *G. sg.*

Chûḍâkarṇa — the ground — struck. — Vîṇâkarṇa — said: — Friend, — why — thus — of me

कथाविरक्तो ऽन्यासक्तो भवान्। चूडाकर्णेनोक्तं।

Ttp. -ta, N. sg. m. — *Ttp. -ta, N. sg. m.* — *-vat, N. sg. m.* — *Bahuv. -ṇa, I. sg.* — vach. *N. sg. n. past Pass. Ptc.*

the speech-neglecting — on something else-intent — you? — By Chûḍâkarṇa — said:

मित्र नाहं विरक्तः किंतु पश्यायं मूषिको ममा-

-ra, V. sg. — *Ind.* — asmad, *N. sg.* — rañj *with* vi, *N. sg. m. past Ptc. Pass.* — *Ind.* — dris, *2 sg. Imp. Par.* — idam, *N. sg. m.* — *-ka, N. sg.* — asmad, *G. sg.*

Friend, — not — I — absent; — but — look, — this — mouse — of me

पकारी सदा पात्रस्थं भिक्षान्नमुत्प्लुत्य

-rin, *N. sg. m.* | *Ind.* | *Ttp.* -stha, *Ac. sg. n.* | *Ttp.* -na, *Ac. sg.* | plu *with* ud, *Ger.*

the plunderer | always | the in the dish-staying | alms-food, | leaping up,

भक्षयति । वीणाकर्णो नागदंतकं विलोक्याह । कथं

bhaksh, 3 *sg. Pres. Par.* | *Bahuv.* -ṇa, *N. sg.* | *Ttp.* -ka, *Ac. sg.* | lok *with* vi, *Ger.* | ah, 3 *sg. Perf. Par.* | *Ind.*

eats. | Viṇâkarṇa | the pin in the wall | having examined, | says : | How

मूषिकः स्वल्पबलो ऽप्येतावद्दूरमुत्पतति ।

-ka, *N. sg.* | *Bahuv.* -la, *N. sg. m.* | *Ind.* | -vat, *Ac. sg. n.* | -ra, *Ac. sg. n. Adv.* | pat *with* ud, 3 *sg. Pres. Par.*

a mouse, | of very-little-strength | though, | so | far | jumps up?

तदत्र केनापि कारणेन भवितव्यं । तथा चोक्तं ।

Ind. | *Ind.* | kim, *I. sg. n. Ind.* | -ṇa, *I. sg.* | bhû, *N. sg. n. Ptc. Fut. Pass.* | *Ind.* | *Ind.* | vach, *N. sg. n. past. Ptc. Pass.*

Therefore | here | something | the reason | must be. | Thus | and | said :

अकस्माद्युवती वृद्धं केशेष्वाकृष्य चुंबति ।

Ind. (kim, *Ab. sg. n.*) | -van, *N. sg. f.* | vṛidh, *Ac. sg. m. past Ptc. Pass.* | -śa, *L. pl.* | kṛish *with* â, *Ger.* | chumb, 3 *sg. Pres. Par.*

Without-a why | the young wife | the old man | by the hairs | having drawn near | kisses,

पतिं निर्दयमालिंग्य हेतुरत्र भविष्यति ॥ १०८ ॥

-ti, *Ac. sg.* | *Avyay.* | liṅg *with* â, *Ger.* | -tu, *N. sg.* | *Ind.* | bhû, 3 *sg. Fut.* ii. *Par.*

the husband | unmercifully | having embraced, | a reason | here | must be. (108)

चूडाकर्णः पृच्छति । कथमेतत् । वीणाकर्णः कथयति ।

Bahuv. -ṇa, *N. sg.* | prachh, 3 *sg. Pres. Par.* | *Ind.* | etad, *N. sg. n.* | *Bahuv.* -ṇa, *N. sg.* | kath, 3 *sg. Pres. Par.*

Chûḍâkarṇa | asks : | How | that? | Viṇâkarṇa | relates :

अस्ति गौडीये कौशांबी नाम नगरी । तस्यां चंदनदासनामा

as, 3 *sg. Pres. Par.* | -ya, *L. sg.* | -bî, *N. sg.* | -man, *Ac. sg. Adv.* | -rî, *N. sg.* | tad, *L. sg. f.* | *Bahuv.* -man, *N. sg. m*

There is | in Gaur Kauśâmbî | by name | a town. | Therein | Chandanadâsa-named

वणिग्महाधनो निवसति । तेन पश्चिमे वयसि वर्तमानेन

-ṇij, *N. sg.* | *Bahuv.* -na, *N. sg. m.* | vas *with* ni, 3 *sg. Pres. Par.* | tad, *I. sg. m.* | -ma, *L. sg. n.* | -yas, *L. sg.* | vṛit, *I. sg. Ptc. Pres. Âtm.*

a merchant of great-wealth | lives. | By him, | in the last stage of life | being,

कामाधिष्ठितचेतसा धनदर्पाल्लीलावती नाम

Bahuv. -tas, *I. sg. m.* | *Ttp.* -pa, *Ab. sg.* | -tî, *N. sg.* | -man, *Ac. sg. Adv.*

having the mind-possessed-by love, | from wealth-pride | Lîlâvatî | by name

वणिक्पुत्री परिणीता । सा च मकरकेतोर्विजयवैजयं-

Ttp. -ri, *N. sg.* — ṇī *with* pari, *N. sg. f. past Ptc. Pass.* — tad, *N. sg. f.* — *Ind.* — *Bahuv.* -tu, *G. sg. m.* — *Ttp.* -ti, *N. sg.*

a merchant's-daughter — wedded. — She — and — of the God of Love — the victory-banner

तीव यौवनवती बभूव । स च वृद्धपतिस्तस्याः संतोषाय

Ind. — -vat, *N. sg. f.* — bhû, 3 *sg. Perf. Par.* — tad, *N. sg. m.* — *Ind.* — *Karm.* -ti, *N. sg.* — tad, *G. sg. f.* — -sha, *D. sg.*

like — youthful — was. — That — and — old-husband — of her — to the satisfaction

नाभवत् ।

Ind. — bhû, 3 *sg. Impf. Par.*

not — was.

यतः । शशिनीव हिमार्तानां घर्मार्तानां रवाविव ।

Ind. — -śin, *L. sg. m.* — *Ind.* — *Ttp.* -ta, *G. pl. m.* — *Ttp.* -ta, *G. pl. m.* — -vi, *L. sg.* — *Ind.*

For, — In the moon — as — of the cold-pained, — of the heat-oppressed — in the sun — as,

मनो न रमते स्त्रीणां जराजीर्णेन्द्रिये पतौ ॥ १०९ ॥

-nas, *N. sg.* — *Ind.* — ram, 3 *sg. Pres. Âtm.* — -ri, *G. pl.* — *Bahuv.* -ya, *L. sg. m.* — -ti, *L. sg.*

the mind — not — delights — of women — in a by old age-impaired-senses possessing — husband. — (109)

अन्यच्च । पलितेष्वपि दृष्टेषु पुंसः का नाम कामिता ।

-ya, *N. sg. n.* — *Ind.* — -ta, *L. pl. n.* — *Ind.* — dṛiś, *L. pl. n. past Ptc. Pass.* — -ṁs, *G. sg.* — kim, *N. sg. f.* — -man, *Ac. sg. Adv.* — -tâ, *N. sg.*

Again — and, Grey hairs — already — being seen, — of a man — what — ever — lovership?

भैषज्यमिव मन्यंते यदन्यमनसः स्त्रियः ॥ ११० ॥

-ya, *Ac. sg.* — *Ind.* — man, 3 *pl. Pres. Âtm.* — *Ind.* — *Bahuv.* -nas, *N. pl. f.* — -ri, *N. pl.*

a drug — like — they consider, — since — having others-in their hearts — women. (110)

स च वृद्धपतिस्तस्यामतीवानुरागवान् ।

tad, *N. sg. m.* — *Ind.* — *Karm.* -ti, *N. sg.* — tad, *L. sg. f.* — *Ind.* — -vat, *N. sg. m.*

That — and — old-husband — of her — exceedingly — fond;

यतः । धनाशा जीविताशा च गुर्वी प्राणभृतां सदा ।

Ind. — *Ttp.* -śâ, *N. sg.* — *Ttp.* -śâ, *N. sg.* — *Ind.* — -ru, *N. sg. f.* — *Ttp.* -t, *G. pl. m.* — *Ind.*

For, — Wealth-hope, — life-hope — and, — dear — of the living beings — always,

वृद्धस्य तरुणी भार्या प्राणेभ्योऽपि गरीयसी ॥ १११ ॥

vṛidh, *G. sg. m. past Ptc. Pass.* — -ṇa, *N. sg. f.* — -yâ, *N. sg.* — -ṇa, *Ab. pl.* — *Ind.* — -ru, *N. sg. f. Compar.*

of an old man — a youthful — wife — than life — even — dearer. — (111)

नोपभोक्तुं न च त्यक्तुं शक्नोति विषयाञ्जरी ।

Ind. — bhuj *with* upa, *Inf.* — *Ind.* — *Ind.* — tyaj, *Inf.* — śak, 3 *sg. Pres. Par.* — -ya, *Ac. pl.* — -rin, *N. sg. m.*

Not — enjoy, — not — and — give up — can — the objects of sense — an old man,

अस्थि निर्दशनः श्वेव जिह्वया लेढि केवलं ॥ ११२ ॥

thi, *Ac. sg.* *Bahuv.* -na, *N. sg. m.* śvan, *N. sg.* *Ind.* -vā, *I. sg.* lih, 3 *sg. Pres.P.* -la, *Ac. sg. n.*
the bone a toothless dog as with the tongue licks merely. (112)

अथ सा लीलावती यौवनदर्पादतिक्रांतकुलमर्यादा केनापि

Ind. tad, *N. sg. f.* -ti, *N. sg.* *Ttp.* -pa, *Ab. sg.* *Bahuv.* -da, *N. sg. f.* kim, *I. sg. m.* *Ind.*
Now that Lilâvati through youth-pride having transgressed-of her family-the bounds some

वणिक्पुत्रेण सहानुरागवती बभूव ॥

Ttp. -ra, *I. sg.* *Ind.* -vat, *N. sg. f.* bhû, 3 *sg. Perf. Par.*
merchant's-son with in love was.

यतः । स्वातंत्र्यं पितृमंदिरे निवसतिर्यात्रोत्सवे संगतिः

Ind. -ya, *N. sg.* *Ttp.* -ra, *L. sg.* -ti, *N. sg.* *Ttp.* -va, *L. sg.* -ti, *N. sg.*
For, Independence, in the father's-house residing, at a public-festival attendance,

गोष्ठीपुरुषसंनिधावनियमो वासो विदेशे तथा ।

Ttp. -dhi, *L. sg.* -ma, *N. sg.* -sa, *N. sg.* -śa, *L. sg.* *Ind.*
of a company-in the presence want of-restraint, living in a strange-place and,

संसर्गः सह पुंश्चलीभिरसकृद्वृत्तेर्निजायाः क्षतिः

-ga, *N. sg.* *Ind.* -li, *I. pl.* *Ind.* -ti, *G. sg.* -ja, *G. sg. f.* -ti, *N. sg.*
associating with wanton women, repeatedly of the livelihood, of her own, waste,

पत्युर्वार्धकमीर्षितं प्रवसनं नाशस्य हेतुः स्त्रियाः ॥ ११२ ॥

-ti, *G. sg.* -ka, *N. sg.* -ta, *N. sg.* -na, *N. sg.* -śa, *G. sg.* -tu, *N. sg.* -ri, *G. sg.*
of the husband old age, jealousy, sojourn abroad, of the ruin the cause of a woman. (113)

अपरं च । पानं दुर्जनसंसर्गः पत्या च विरहोऽटनं ।

-ra, *N. sg. n.* *Ind.* -na, *N. sg.* *Ttp.* -ga, *N. sg.* -ti, *I. sg.* *Ind.* -ha, *N. sg.* -na, *N. sg.*
Another and, Drinking, with wicked-associating, from the husband and separation, roaming about,

स्वप्नश्चान्यगृहे वासो नारीणां दूषणानि षट् ॥ ११४ ॥

-na, *N. sg.* *Ind.* *Ttp.* -ha, *L. sg.* -sa, *N. sg.* -ri, *G. pl.* -ṇa, *N. pl.* shash, *N.*
Sleeping and, in another's-house dwelling, of women injurious things six. (114)

स्थानं नास्ति क्षणं नास्ति नास्ति प्रार्थयिता नरः ।

-na, *N. sg.* *Ind.* as, 3 *sg. Pres. Par.* -ṇa, *N. sg.* *Ind.* as, 3 *sg. Pres. Par.* *Ind.* as, 3 *sg. Pres. Par.* -tṛi, *N. sg. m.* -ra, *N. sg.*
A place not there is, a moment not there is, not there is a soliciting man,

तेन नारद नारीणां सतीत्वमुपजायते ॥ ११५ ॥
tad, I. sg. n. Adv. -da, *V. sg.* -ri, *G. pl.* -tva, *N. sg.* jan *with* upa, *3 sg. Pres. Âtm.*
therefore, O Nârada, of women chastity is produced. (115)

न स्त्रीणामप्रियः कश्चित्प्रियो वापि न विद्यते ।
Ind. -ri, *G. pl.* *Karm.* -ya, *N. sg. m.* kim-chid, *N. sg. m.* -ya, *N. sg. m.* *Ind.* *Ind.* *Ind.* vid, *3 sg. Pres. Pass.*
Not of women disliked anyone, liked or also not is known,

गावस्तृणमिवारण्ये प्रार्थयंति नवं नवं ॥ ११६ ॥
go, *N. pl.* -ṇa, *Ac. sg.* *Ind.* -ya, *L. sg.* arth *with* pra, *3 pl. Pres. Par.* -va, *Ac. sg. m.*
cows grass as in a wood, they seek a new, a new one. (116)

अपरं च । घृतकुंभसमा नारी तप्तांगारसमः पुमान् ।
-ra, *N. sg. n.* *Ind.* *Tîp.* -ma, *N. sg. f.* -ri, *N. sg.* *Tîp.* -ma, *N. sg. m.* puṁs, *N. sg.*
Again and, Butter-pot-like the woman, burning-coal-like the man,

तस्माद्घृतं च वह्निं च नैकत्र स्थापयेद्बुधः ॥ ११७ ॥
tad, *Ab. sg. n. Adv.* -ta, *Ac. sg.* *Ind.* -ni, *Ac. sg.* *Ind.* *Ind.* *Ind.* sthâ, *3 sg. Pot. Par. Caus.* -dha, *N. sg. m.*
therefore butter and fire and not together should put a sage. (117)

न लज्जा न विनीतत्वं न दाक्षिण्यं न भीरुता ।
Ind. -jâ, *N. sg.* *Ind.* -tva, *N. sg.* *Ind.* -ya, *N. sg.* *Ind.* -tâ, *N. sg.*
Not shame, not modesty, not regard, not fear,

प्रार्थनाभाव एवैकं सतीत्वे कारणं स्त्रियाः ॥ ११८ ॥
Tîp. -va, *N. sg.* *Ind.* -ka, *N. sg. n.* -tva, *L. sg.* -ṇa, *N. sg.* -ri, *G. sg.*
of asking-the want merely the only for the chastity cause of a woman. (118)

पिता रक्षति कौमारे भर्ता रक्षति यौवने ।
-tṛi, *N. sg.* raksh, *3 sg. Pres. Par.* -ra, *L. sg.* -tṛi, *N. sg.* raksh, *3 sg. Pres. Par.* -na, *L. sg.*
The father guards in infancy, the husband guards in youth,

पुत्रस्तु स्थाविरे भावे न स्त्री स्वातंत्र्यमर्हति ॥ ११९ ॥
-ra, *N. sg.* *Ind.* -ra, *L. sg. m.* -va, *L. sg.* *Ind.* -ri, *N. sg.* -ya, *Ac. sg.* arh, *3 sg. Pres. Par.*
the son and in old state of life; not woman independence deserves. (119)

एकदा सा लीलावती रत्नावलीकिरणकर्बुरे पर्यंके तेन वणिक्पुत्रेण
Ind. tad, *N. sg. f.* -ti, *N. sg.* *Tîp.* -ra, *L. sg. m.* -ka, *L. sg.* tad, *I. sg. m.* *Tîp.* -ra, *I. sg.*
One day that Lîlâvatî on a with gem-string-lustre-variegated couch that merchant-son

सह विस्रंभालापैः सुखासीना तमलक्षितोपस्थितं
Ind. *Tîp.* -pa, *I. pl.* *Karm.* -na, *N. sg. f.* (*rt.* âs) tad, *Ac. sg. m.* *Karm.* -ta, *Ac. sg. m.*
with in confidence-talks pleasantly-seated that unobserved-approached

पतिमवलोक्य सहसोत्थाय केशेष्वाकृष्य

-ti, *Ac. sg.* lok *with* ava, *Ger.* -has, *I. sg.* sthâ *with* ud, *Ger.* -śa, *L. pl.* kṛish *with* â, *Ger.*

husband having perceived, suddenly having risen, by the hairs having drawn,

गाढमालिंग्य चुंबितवती। तेनावसरेण जारश्च पलायितः।

-ḍha, *Ac. sg. n. Adv.* liṅg *with* â, *Ger.* chumb, *N. sg. f. Ptc. Perf. Par.* tad, *I. sg. m.* -ra, *I. sg.* -ra, *N. sg. Ind.* ay *with* palâ.

ardently having embraced kissed. By that opportunity the lover and escaped.

उक्तं च। उशना वेद यच्छास्त्रं यच्च वेद बृहस्पतिः।

vach, *N. sg. n. past Ptc. Pass.* *Ind.* -nas, *N. sg.* vid, 3 *sg. Perf. Par.* yad, *Ac. sg. n.* -ra, *Ac. sg.* yad, *Ac. sg. n.* *Ind.* vid, 3 *sg. Perf. Par.* *Ttp.* -ti, *N. sg.*

Said and, Uśanas knows what science, what and knows Vṛihaspati,

स्वभावेनैव तच्छास्त्रं स्त्रीबुद्धौ सुप्रतिष्ठितं ॥ १२० ॥

Karm. -va, *I. sg.* *Ind.* tad, *N. sg. n.* -ra, *N. sg.* *Ttp.* -dhi, *L. sg.* *Karm.* -ta, *N. sg. n.*

by nature already that science in a woman's mind is well-implanted. (120)

तदालिंगनमवलोक्य समीपवर्तिनी कुट्टन्यचिंतयत्।

Ttp. -na, *Ac. sg.* lok *with* ava, *Ger.* *Ttp.* -tin, *N. sg. f.* -ni, *N. sg.* chint, 3 *sg. Impf. Par.*

Of him-the embracing having seen near-being a procuress thought:

अकस्मादियमेनमुपगूढवतीति। ततस्तया

Ind. (kim, *Ab. sg. n.*) idam, *N. sg. f.* etad, *Ac. sg. m.* guh *with* upa, *N. sg. f. Ptc. Perf. Par.* *Ind.* *Ind.* tad, *I. sg. f.*

'Without-a why this woman him embraced,' thus. Thereupon by that

कुट्टन्या तत्कारणं परिज्ञाय सा लीलावती गुप्तेन

-ni, *I. sg.* *Ttp.* -ṇa, *Ac. sg.* jñâ *with* pari, *Ger.* tad, *N. sg. f.* -ti, *N. sg.* gup, *I. sg. m. past Ptc. Pass.*

procuress of it-the reason having discovered that Lîlâvatî with a secret (fine)

दंडिता। अतोऽहं ब्रवीमि। अकस्माद्युवती वृद्धमि-

daṇḍ, *N. sg. f. past Ptc. Pass.* *Ind.* asmad, *N. sg.* brû, 1 *sg. Pres. Par.* *Ind.* (kim, *Ab. sg. n.*) -van, *N. sg. f.* -dha, *Ac. sg. m.*

punished. Therefore I say: without-a why the young woman the old man,

त्यादि। मूषिकबलोपस्तंभेन केनापि कारणेनात्र भवितव्यं।

Bahuv. -di, *Ac. sg. n.* *Ttp.* -bha, *I. sg.* kim, *I. sg. m. Ind.* -ṇa, *I. sg.* *Ind.* bhû, *N. sg. n. Ptc. Fut. Pass.*

etc. Mouse-strength-support some the cause here must be.

क्षणं विचिंत्य परिव्राजकेनोक्तं। कारणं चात्र

-ṇa, *Ac. sg.* chint *with* vi, *Ger.* -ka, *I. sg.* vach, *N. sg. n. past Ptc. Pass.* -ṇa, *N. sg.* *Ind.* *Ind.*

A moment having reflected, by the mendicant said: The reason and here

धनबाहुल्यमेव भविष्यति ।

Tŕp. -ya, *N. sg.* *Ind.* bhû, 3 *sg. Fut.* II. *Par.*
wealth-abundance only will be;

यतः । धनवान्बलवांल्लोके सर्वः सर्वत्र सर्वदा ।

Ind. -vat, *N. sg. m.* -vat, *N. sg. m.* -ka, *L. sg.* -va, *N. sg. m.* *Ind.* *Ind.*
For, The wealthy strong in the world every one, everywhere, at every time,

प्रभुत्वं धनमूलं हि राज्ञामप्युपजायते ॥ १२१ ॥

-tva, *N. sg.* *Bahuv.* -la, *N. sg. n.* *Ind.* -jan, *G. pl.* *Ind.* jan *with* upa, 3 *sg. Pres. Âtm.*
the superiority on riches-founded for of kings also is produced. (121)

ततः खनित्रमादाय तेन विवरं खनित्वा चिरसंचितं

Ind. -ra, *Ac. sg.* dâ *with* â, *Ger.* tad, *I. sg. m.* -ra, *Ac. sg.* khan, *Ger.* *Karm.* -ta, *N. sg. n.*
Then a spade having taken, by him the hole having dug open, long-amassed

मम धनं गृहीतं । ततः प्रभृति निजशक्तिहीनः सत्त्वोत्साहरहितः

asmad, *G. sg.* -na, *N. sg.* grah, *N. sg. n. past Ptc. Pass.* *Ind.* *Ind.* *Tŕp.* -na, *N. sg. m.* (*rt.* hâ) *Tŕp.* -ta, *N. sg. m.*
of me wealth was taken. Thence-forward of my-strength-forsaken, of vigour-energy-deprived,

स्वाहारमप्युत्पादयितुमक्षमः सत्रासं मंदं मंदमुपसर्पंश्चू-

Karm. -ra, *Ac. sg.* *Ind.* pad *with* ud, *Inf. Caus.* *Karm.* -ma, *N. sg. m.* *Avyay.* -da, *Ac. sg. n. Adv.* sŕip *with* upa, *N. sg. m. Ptc. Pres. Par.*
my own-food even to procure unable with-fear slowly slowly creeping-on

डाकर्णेनावलोकितः । ततस्तेनोक्तं ।

-ṇa, *I. sg.* lok *with* ava, *N. sg. m. past Ptc. Pass.* *Ind.* tad, *I. sg. m.* vach, *N. sg. n. past Ptc. Pass.*
by Chûḍâkarṇa (I was) perceived. Then by him said:

धनेन बलवांल्लोके धनाद्भवति पंडितः ।

-na, *I. sg.* -vat, *N. sg. m.* -ka, *I. sg.* -na, *Ab. sg.* bhû, 3 *sg. Pres. Par.* -ta, *N. sg. m.*
With wealth strong in the world, through wealth one is wise,

पश्यैतं मूषिकं पापं स्वजातिसमतां गतं ॥ १२२ ॥

dŕiś, 2 *sg. Imp. Par.* etad, *Ac. sg. m.* -ka, *Ac. sg.* -ra, *Ac. sg. m.* *Tŕp.* -tâ, *Ac. sg.* gam, *Ac. sg. m. past Ptc. Pass.*
Behold that mouse wretched of his own-species-to the level gone. (122)

किंच । अर्थेन तु विहीनस्य पुरुषस्याल्पमेधसः ।

Ind. -tha, *I. sg.* *Ind.* hâ *with* vi, *G. sg. m. past Ptc. Pass.* -sha, *G. sg.* *Bahuv.* -dhas, *G. sg. m.*
Moreover, By wealth but of a forsaken man, (as) of one with little-judgment,

क्रियाः सर्वा विनश्यंति ग्रीष्मे कुसरितो यथा ॥ १२३ ॥

-yā, *N. pl.* -va, *N. pl. f.* naś *with* vi, 3 *pl. Pres. Par.* -ma, *L. sg.* *Karm.* -t, *N. pl.* *Ind.*

the actions all disappear, in summer little-rivers as. (123)

अपरं च । यस्यार्थास्तस्य मित्राणि यस्यार्थास्तस्य बांधवाः ।

-ra, *N. sg. n.* *Ind.* yad, *G. sg. m.* -tha, *N. pl.* tad, *G. sg. m.* -ra, *N. pl.* yad, *G. sg. m.* -tha, *N. pl.* tad, *G. sg. m.* -va, *N. pl.*

Another and, Of whom wealth, of him friends, of whom wealth, of him relations,

यस्यार्थाः स पुमांल्लोके यस्यार्थाः स हि पंडितः ॥ १२४ ॥

yad, *G. sg. m.* -tha, *N. pl.* tad, *N. sg. m.* puṁs, *N. sg.* -ka, *L. sg.* yad, *G. sg. m.* -tha, *N. pl.* tad, *N. sg. m.* *Ind.* -ta, *N. sg. m.*

of whom wealth, he a man in the world, of whom wealth, he indeed wise. (124)

अन्यच्च । अपुत्रस्य गृहं शून्यं सन्मित्ररहितस्य च ।

-ya, *N. sg. n.* *Ind.* *Bahuv.* -ra, *G. sg. m.* -ha, *N. sg.* -ya, *N. sg. n.* *Ttp.* -ta, *G. sg. m.* *Ind.*

Again and, Of a son-less the house empty, of one of a good-friend-destitute and,

मूर्खस्य च दिशः शून्याः सर्वशून्या दरिद्रता ॥ १२५ ॥

-kha, *G. sg. m.* *Ind.* -ś, *N. pl.* -ya, *N. pl. f.* *Karm.* -ya, *N. sg. f.* -tā, *N. sg.*

of a fool and the regions empty, all-empty poverty. (125)

अपरं च । तानींद्रियाण्यविकलानि तदेव नाम

-ra, *N. sg. n.* *Ind.* tad, *N. pl. n.* -ya, *N. pl.* *Karm.* -la, *N. pl. n.* tad, *N. sg. n.* *Ind.* -man, *N. sg.*

Another and, ‘Those senses unimpaired, that same name,

सा बुद्धिरप्रतिहता वचनं तदेव ।

tad, *N. sg. f.* -dhi, *N. sg.* *Karm.* -ta, *N. sg. f.* -na, *N. sg.* tad, *N. sg. n.* *Ind.*

that intellect uninjured, language that same,

अर्थोष्मणा विरहितः पुरुषः स एव

Ttp. -man, *I. sg.* rah *with* vi, *N. sg. m. past Ptc. Pass.* -sha, *N. sg.* tad, *N. sg. m.* *Ind.*

by the wealth-heat forsaken man that same

अन्यः क्षणेन भवतीति विचित्रमेतत् ॥ १२६ ॥

-ya, *N. sg. m.* -ṇa, *I. sg.* bhū, 3 *sg. Pres Par.* *Ind.* -tra *N. sg. n.* etad, *N. sg. n.*

another in a moment is;’ thus strange this. (126)

एतत्सर्वमाकर्ण्य मयालोचितं । ममात्रावस्थानमयुक्तमिदानीं

This all having heard by me considered: Of me here staying improper now,

यच्चान्यस्मा एतद्वृत्तांतकथनं तदप्यनुचितं ।

what and to another of these-affairs-communication, that also improper.

यतः । अर्थनाशं मनस्तापं गृहे दुश्चरितानि च ।

For, Fortune-loss, of mind-distress, at home malpractices and,

वंचनं चापमानं च मतिमान्न प्रकाशयेत् ॥ १२७ ॥

the being cheated and, the being slighted and, the wise not should make public. (127)

अपि च । आयुर्वित्तं गृहच्छिद्रं मंत्रमैथुनभेषजं ।

Also and, Age, wealth, at home-trouble, design-love-medicine,

तपोदानापमानं च नव गोप्यानि यत्नतः ॥ १२८ ॥

penance-liberality-dishonour and, nine (things) to be concealed carefully. (128)

तथा चोक्तं । अत्यंतविमुखे दैवे व्यर्थे यत्ने च पौरुषे ।

Thus and said, Very-averse (being) fortune, in vain the exertion and human,

मनस्विनो दरिद्रस्य वनादन्यत्कुतः सुखं ॥ १२९ ॥

of the wise poor, (different) from the forest other whence comfort? (129)

अन्यच्च । मनस्वी म्रियते कामं कार्पण्यं न तु गच्छति ।

Again and, The wise dies rather, to misery not but he goes,

अपि निर्वाणमायाति नानलो याति शीततां ॥ १३० ॥

even to extinction goes, not fire goes to coldness. (130)

किंच । कुसुमस्तवकस्येव द्वे वृत्ती तु मनस्विनः ।

Moreover, Of a flower-cluster as, two conditions forsooth of the wise,

सर्वेषां मूर्ध्नि वा तिष्ठेद्विशीर्येदथवा वने ॥ १३१ ॥

of all at the head either he may stand, he may fade away or in a forest. (131)

यच्चात्रैव याच्ञया जीवनं तदतीव गर्हितं ।

What and here just through begging living, that exceedingly reprobated.

यतः । वरं विभवहीनेन प्राणैः संतर्पितो ऽनलः ।

For, Better by one of wealth-deprived with the life satiated a fire,

नोपचारपरिभ्रष्टः कृपणः प्रार्थितो जनः ॥ १३२ ॥

not an of civility-destitute miserly solicited person. (132)

दारिद्र्याद्ध्रियमेति ह्रीपरिगतः सत्त्वात्परिभ्रश्यते
From poverty to shame one goes, shame-laden of strength one is deprived,

निःसत्त्वः परिभूयते परिभवान्निर्वेदमापद्यते ।
strengthless one is oppressed, from oppression into despondency one falls,

निर्विण्णः शुचमेति शोकनिहतो बुद्ध्या परित्यज्यते
the despondent to sorrow goes, the sorrow-stricken by reason is forsaken,

निर्बुद्धिः क्षयमेत्यहो विधनता सर्वापदामास्पदं ॥ १३३ ॥
the reason-less to destruction goes, Oh, poverty of all-evils the foundation. (133)

किंच । वरं मौनं कार्यं न च वचनमुक्तं यदनृतं
Moreover, Better silence to be observed, not and a word spoken, which untrue,

वरं क्लैब्यं पुंसां न च परकलत्राभिगमनं ।
better impotence of men, not and with another's-wife-intercourse,

वरं प्राणत्यागो न च पिशुनवाक्येष्वभिरुचिः
better life-abandonment, not and in calumnious-words delight,

वरं भिक्षाशित्वं न च परधनास्वादनसुखं ॥ १३४ ॥
better alms-eating, not and another's-wealth-tasting-pleasure. (134)

वरं शून्या शाला न च खलु वरो दुष्टवृषभः
Better an empty stable, not and by any means better a vicious-bull,

वरं वेश्या पत्नी न पुनरविनीता कुलवधूः ।
better a wanton (as) wife, not but an ill-mannered noble-wife,

वरं वासो ऽरण्ये न पुनरविवेकाधिपपुरे
better dwelling in a wood, not but in an undiscriminating-ruler's-town,

वरं प्राणत्यागो न पुनरधमानामुपगमः ॥ १३५ ॥
better life-abandonment, not but of low persons society. (135)

अपि च । सेवेव मानमखिलं ज्योत्स्नेव तमो जरेव लावण्यं ।
Also and, Servitude as respect totally, moonlight as darkness, old age as loveliness,

हरिहरकथेव दुरितं गुणशतमप्यर्थिता हरति ॥ १३६ ॥
of Hari (and) -Hara- legend as sin, of virtues-a hundred even beggary takes away. (136)

इति विमृश्य तत्किमहं परपिंडेनात्मानं पोषयामि ।
Thus having reflected, then why I with another's-cake myself nourish?

कष्टं भोः । तदपि द्वितीयं मृत्युद्वारं ।
Oh, the misery! That even a second death-gate.

यतः । पल्लवग्राहि पांडित्यं क्रयक्रीतं च मैथुनं ।
For, Buds gathering (superficial) wisdom, with money-purchased and love,

भोजनं च पराधीनं तिस्रः पुंसां विडंबनाः ॥ १३७ ॥
subsistence and on another-depending, three of men afflictions. (137)

रोगी चिरप्रवासी परान्नभोजी परावसथशायी ।
The sick, the long-exiled, the another's-bread-eating, in another's-house-living,

यज्जीवति तन्मरणं यन्मरणं सो ऽस्य विश्रामः ॥ १३८ ॥
what he lives, that death; what death, that of him the deliverance. (138)

इत्यालोच्यापि लोभात्पुनरप्यर्थं ग्रहीतुं ग्रहमकरवं ।
Thus having considered also, from desire again even wealth to acquire taking away I made.

तथा चोक्तं । लोभेन बुद्धिश्चलति लोभो जनयते तृषां ।
Thus and said, Through desire reason departs, desire produces covetousness,

तृषार्तो दुःखमाप्नोति परत्रेह च मानवः ॥ १३९ ॥
by covetousness-tormented pain experiences hereafter here and a man. (139)

ततो ऽहं मंदं मंदमुपसर्पंस्तेन वीणाकर्णेन जर्जरवंशखंडेन
Then I slowly slowly creeping-on, by that Viṇâkarṇa with a split-bamboo-piece

ताडितश्चाचिंतयं ।
beaten and, reflected:

धनलुब्धो ह्यसंतुष्टो ऽनियतात्माजितेंद्रियः ।
The wealth-desirous indeed discontented, of unrestrained-mind, of unsubdued-senses;

सर्वा एवापदस्तस्य यस्य तुष्टं न मानसं ॥ १४० ॥

all verily misfortunes of him, whose content not mind. (140)

तथा च। सर्वाः संपत्तयस्तस्य संतुष्टं यस्य मानसं।

Thus and, All kinds of happiness of him, content of whom the mind;

उपानद्गूढपादस्य ननु चर्मावृतेव भूः ॥ १४१ ॥

of him whose foot-is covered-with a shoe is not with leather-covered as it were the earth? (141)

अपरं च। संतोषामृततृप्तानां यत्सुखं शांतचेतसां।

Another and, Of the with the contentment-nectar-satiated what happiness of the placid-minded,

कुतस्तद्धनलुब्धानामितश्चेतश्च धावतां ॥ १४२ ॥

whence that of the wealth-desirous hither and thither running? (142)

किंच। तेनाधीतं श्रुतं तेन तेन सर्वमनुष्ठितं।

Moreover, By him read, heard by him, by him everything accomplished,

येनाशाः पृष्ठतः कृत्वा नैराश्यमवलंबितं ॥ १४३ ॥

by whom, hopes behind the back having placed, hope-freedom depended upon. (143)

अपि च। असेवितेश्वरद्वारमदृष्टविरहव्यथं।

Also and, Not having served-a master's-door, not having perceived-separation-pain,

अनुक्तक्लीववचनं धन्यं कस्यापि जीवनं ॥ १४४ ॥

not having uttered-an unmanly-word, happy of any man the life. (144)

यतः। न योजनशतं दूरं बाध्यमानस्य तृष्णया।

For, Not a yojana-hundred far for one stricken with covetousness,

संतुष्टस्य करप्राप्तेऽप्यर्थे भवति नादरः ॥ १४५ ॥

of the contented for the to hand-come even treasure is not regard. (145)

तदत्रावस्थोचितकार्यपरिच्छेदः श्रेयान्।

Therefore here of (my) situation-suiting-action-discrimination better.

को धर्मो भूतदया किं सौख्यमरोगिता जगति जंतोः ।

What religion? for the living-compassion. What happiness? health in the world of man.

कः स्नेहः सद्भावः किं पांडित्यं परिच्छेदः ॥ १४६ ॥

What love? a noble-state of mind. What wisdom? discrimination. (146)

तथा च । परिच्छेदो हि पांडित्यं यदापन्ना विपत्तयः ।

Thus and, Discrimination indeed wisdom, when approached misfortunes

अपरिच्छेदकर्तॄणां विपदः स्युः पदे पदे ॥ १४७ ॥

of the without-discrimination-acting misfortunes will be at step at step. (147)

त्यजेदेकं कुलस्यार्थे ग्रामस्यार्थे कुलं त्यजेत् ।

One should give up one for a family's-sake, for a village's-sake a family one should give up;

ग्रामं जनपदस्यार्थे स्वात्मार्थे पृथिवीं त्यजेत् ॥ १४८ ॥

a village for the country's-sake, for one's self's-sake the earth one should give up. (148)

अपरं च । पानीयं वा निरायासं स्वाद्वन्नं वा भयोत्तरं ।

Again and, Water either without-exertion, sweet food or with danger-attended,

विचार्य खलु पश्यामि तत्सुखं यत्र निर्वृतिः ॥ १४९ ॥

having deliberated indeed I see, that happiness where ease. (149)

इत्यालोच्याहं निर्जनवनमागतः ।

Thus having considered I the lonely-wood approached.

यतः । वरं वनं व्याघ्रगजेंद्रसेवितं द्रुमालयः पक्वफलांबुभोजनं ।

For, Better a wood by tigers-(and) elephants-haunted, a tree-habitation on ripe-fruits-(and)water-living,

तृणानि शय्या परिधानवल्कलं न बंधुमध्ये धनहीनजीवनं ॥ १५० ॥

grass for a bed, a garment-(of) bark, not of friends-in the midst of one of wealth-deprived-the living. (150)

ततोऽस्मत्पुण्योदयादनेन मित्रेणाहं स्नेहानुवृत्त्या-

Afterwards, through my-fortune's-(i.e. good works) rise (i.e. reward) by this friend I with affection-continuity

नुगृहीतः । अधुना च पुण्यपरंपरया भवदाश्रयः स्वर्ग एव मया प्राप्तः ।

favoured. Now and by fortune-continuation of you-the company, a paradise verily, by me found.

यतः । संसारविषवृक्षस्य द्वे अत्र रसवत्फले ।
For, Of the world's-poison-tree two here delicious-fruits,

काव्यामृतरसास्वादः संगमः सुजनैः सह ॥ १५१ ॥
the poem-nectar-flavour-tasting, association good-men with. (151)

मंथर उवाच । अर्थाः पादरजोपमा गिरिनदीवेगोपमं यौवनं
Manthara said: Riches on the feet-the dust-resembling, mountain-rivers-fleetness-like youth,

आयुष्यं जलबिंदुलोलचपलं फेनोपमं जीवितं ।
vital strength as a water-drop-trembling-unsteady, froth-like life;

धर्मं यो न करोति निंदितमतिः स्वर्गार्गलोद्घाटनं
virtue who not practises base-minded, the heaven-bar-unbolting,

पश्चात्तापयुतो जरापरिगतः शोकाग्निना दह्यते ॥ १५२ ॥
afterwards repentance-seized, by old age-overpowered, with the sorrow-fire is burnt. (152)

युष्माभिरतिसंचयः कृतस्तस्यायं दोषः । शृणु ।
By you too much-accumulation made; of it this the fault (i.e. cause); Listen:

उपार्जितानां वित्तानां त्याग एव हि रक्षणं ।
Of accumulated riches giving away only indeed the preservation;

तडागोदरसंस्थानां परीवाह इवांभसां ॥ १५३ ॥
of the in a pond's-interior-standing a drain as of waters. (153)

अन्यच्च । यदधोऽधः क्षितौ वित्तं निचखान मितंपचः ।
Again and, When low low in the ground wealth has buried the miser,

तदधोनिलयं गंतुं चक्रे पंथानमग्रतः ॥ १५४ ॥
then to a mansion below to go he has made himself a path beforehand. (154)

अन्यच्च । निजसौख्यं निरुंधानो यो धनार्जनमिच्छति ।
Again and, His own-happiness opposing who wealth-acquisition wishes,

परार्थं भारवाहीव क्लेशस्यैव हि भाजनं ॥ १५५ ॥
for another's-sake a burthen-bearer as, of pain merely indeed a vessel. (155)

अपरं च । दानोपभोगहीनेन धनेन धनिनो यदि ।
Another and, Through of liberality-(and) enjoyment-deprived riches rich if (we are),

पृथ्वीखातनिखातेन धनेन धनिनो वयं ॥ १५६ ॥
through the in the earth-caverns-buried riches rich we. (156)

अन्यच्च । असंभोगेन सामान्यं कृपणस्य धनं परैः ।
Again and, Through non-enjoyment common of a miser the wealth with others,

अस्येदमिति संबंधो हानौ दुःखेन गम्यते ॥ १५७ ॥
'of him this' thus the connection at the loss by pain is ascertained. (157)

दानं प्रियवाक्सहितं ज्ञानमगर्वं क्षमान्वितं शौर्यं ।
Liberality by kind-words-accompanied, knowledge without-conceit, with clemency-endowed heroism,

वित्तं त्यागनियुक्तं दुर्लभमेतच्चतुर्भद्रं ॥ १५८ ॥
wealth with liberality-connected, difficult-to be found these four-good things. (158)

उक्तं च । कर्तव्यः संचयो नित्यं कर्तव्यो नातिसंचयः ।
Said and, To be made accumulation constantly, to be made not exceeding-accumulation,

पश्य संचयशीलो ऽसौ धनुषा जंबुको हतः ॥ १५९ ॥
behold, accumulation-practising that by a bow jackal slain. (159)

तावाहतुः । कथमेतत् । मंथरः कथयति । आसीत्कल्याणकटक-
Those two say: How that? Manthara relates: There was of Kalyāṇa-kaṭaka-

वास्तव्यो भैरवो नाम व्याधः । स चैकदा मृगमन्विष्यमाणो
an inhabitant, Bhairava by name, a hunter. He and one day a deer pursuing

विंध्याटवीं गतवान् । ततस्तेन व्यापादितं मृगमादाय
to the Vindhya-forest went. Afterwards by him the killed deer having taken up

गच्छता घोराकृतिः शूकरो दृष्टः । तेन व्याधेन मृगं भूमौ
going, of formidable-appearance a boar seen. By that hunter the deer upon the ground

निधाय शूकरः शरेणाहतः । शूकरेणापि घनघोरगर्जनं
having laid, the boar with an arrow hit. By the boar in turn as of clouds-a terrible-roar

कृत्वा स व्याधो मुष्कदेशे हतः संछिन्नद्रुम इव
having made that hunter in the groin wounded being a cut-tree like

भूमौ निपपात ।
on the ground fell-down.

यतः । जलमग्निं विषं शस्त्रं क्षुद्व्याधी पतनं गिरेः ।
For, Water, fire, poison, a weapon, hunger-illness, falling from a rock,

निमित्तं किंचिदासाद्य देही प्राणैर्विमुच्यते ॥ १६० ॥
a cause (i.e. accident) of some kind having encountered the corporeal being of life is deprived. (160)

अथ तयोः पादास्फालनेन सर्पोऽपि मृतः । अथानंतरं
Then of them through the feet-trampling a serpent also killed. Now thereupon

दीर्घरावो नाम जंबुकः परिभ्रमन्नाहारार्थी तान्मृतान्
Dîrgharâva by name, a jackal, roaming-about, food-seeking, those dead

मृगव्याधसर्पशूकरानपश्यदचिंतयच्च । अहो अद्य महद्भोज्यं मे
deer-hunter-serpent-boar saw, reflected and: Oh! to-day a great meal of me

समुपस्थितं । अथवा ।
fallen in the way. However,

अचिंतितानि दुःखानि यथैवायांति देहिनां ।
Unthought-of troubles as just happen to men,

सुखान्यपि तथा मन्ये दैवमत्रातिरिच्यते ॥ १६१ ॥
blessings also thus; I think; fate in this plays the chief part. (161)

तद्भवतु । एषां मांसैर्मासत्रयं मे सुखेन गमिष्यति ।
Then be it, Of these with the flesh a month-triad to me pleasantly will pass.

मासमेकं नरो याति द्वौ मासौ मृगशूकरौ ।
Month one the man goes, two months deer-(and) boar,

अहिरेकं दिनं याति अद्य भक्ष्यो धनुर्गुणः ॥ १६२ ॥
the serpent one day goes! to-day to be eaten the bow-string. (162)

ततः प्रथमबुभुक्षायामिदं निःस्वादु कोदंडलग्नं स्नायुबंधनं
Then in the first-desire of eating this unsweet to the bow-fastened sinew-string

खादामि। इत्युक्त्वा तथा कृते सति छिन्ने स्नायुबंधन
I eat. Thus having said, thus done being, being cut the sinew-string,

उत्पतितेन धनुषा हृदि निर्भिन्नः स दीर्घरावः पंचत्वमा-
by the up-springing bow in the heart pierced, that Dirgharâva to the dissolution into the five elements

गतः। अतोऽहं ब्रवीमि कर्तव्यः संचयो नित्यमित्यादि।
gone. Therefore I say: 'To be made accumulation constantly,' etc.

तथा च। यद्ददाति यदश्नाति तदेव धनिनो धनं।
Thus and, What he gives, what he eats, that alone of a rich man the wealth;

अन्ये मृतस्य क्रीडंति दारैरपि धनैरपि ॥ १६३ ॥
others of the dead sport with the wife also, with the riches also. (163)

किंच। यद्ददासि विशिष्टेभ्यो यच्चाश्नासि दिने दिने।
Moreover, What thou givest to the distinguished, what and thou eatest day by day,

तत्ते वित्तमहं मन्ये शेषं कस्यापि रक्षसि ॥ १६४ ॥
that of thee the wealth I consider; the rest for somebody else thou preservest. (164)

यातु। किमिदानीमतिक्रांतोपवर्णनेन।
Let it go. What at present with excessive-description?

यतः। नाप्राप्यमभिवांछंति नष्टं नेच्छंति शोचितुं।
For, Not the unattainable long after, the lost not wish to bewail,

आपत्स्वपि न मुह्यंति नराः पंडितबुद्धयः ॥ १६५ ॥
in misfortunes even not are perplexed men of wise-intellect. (165)

तत्सखे सर्वदा त्वया सोत्साहेन भवितव्यं।
Therefore, friend, always by thee full-of energy to be.

यतः। शास्त्राण्यधीत्यापि भवंति मूर्खाः
For, Books having read even they are fools.

यस्तु क्रियावान्पुरुषः स विद्वान् ।

who on the contrary an active man, he wise;

सुचिंतितं चौषधमातुराणां

a well-devised also medicine of the diseased

न नाममात्रेण करोत्यरोगं ॥ १६६ ॥

not by the name-merely effects freedom-from disease. (166)

अन्यच्च । न स्वल्पमप्यध्यवसायभीरोः

Again and, Not a very-small even of the of exertion-afraid

करोति विज्ञानविधिर्गुणं हि ।

produces a wisdom-precept benefit indeed,

अंधस्य किं हस्ततलस्थितो ऽपि

of a blind man (what?) on the palm-standing even

प्रकाशयत्यर्थमिह प्रदीपः ॥ १६७ ॥

does make visible an object here a lamp? (167)

तदत्र सखे दशाविशेषे शांतिः करणीया ।

Then here, O friend, in each special condition tranquillity to be observed.

एतदप्यतिकष्टं त्वया न मंतव्यं ।

This also too-hard by thee not to be considered.

यतः । राजा कुलवधूर्विप्रा मंत्रिणश्च पयोधराः ।

For, 'A king, a noble wife, the wise, ministers likewise, clouds,

स्थानभ्रष्टा न शोभंते दंताः केशा नखा नराः ॥ १६८ ॥

from (their) places-removed not shine, teeth, hairs, nails, men. (168)

इति विज्ञाय मतिमान्स्वस्थानं न परित्यजेत् । कापुरुषवचनमेतत् ।

Thus perceiving a wise man his-place not should abandon,' a weak man's-speech this.

यतः । स्थानमुत्सृज्य गच्छंति सिंहाः सत्पुरुषा गजाः ।

For, (Their) country quitting go lions, brave-men, elephants;

तत्रैव निधनं यांति काकाः कापुरुषा मृगाः ॥ १६८ ॥

there even to death go crows, weak-men, deer. (169)

को वीरस्य मनस्विनः स्वविषयः को वा विदेशस्तथा

What of a brave man, of a wise, his own-country, what or a strange-country likewise?

यं देशं श्रयते तमेव कुरुते बाहुप्रतापार्जितं ।

to what place he comes, that even does he make through his arms-majesty-acquired.

यद्दंष्ट्रानखलांगूलप्रहरणः सिंहो वनं गाहते

What teeth-claws-tail-(having as) weapons, a lion wood enters,

तस्मिन्नेव हतद्विपेंद्ररुधिरैस्तृष्णां छिनत्त्यात्मनः ॥ १७० ॥

in that verily with the slain-elephant's-blood the thirst he quenches of himself. (170)

अपरं च । निपानमिव मंडूकाः सरः पूर्णमिवांडजाः ।

Again and, A pool as frogs, a lake full as fishes,

सोद्योगं नरमायांति विवशाः सर्वसंपदः ॥ १७१ ॥

(so) the exerting man approach by themselves all-fortunes. (171)

अन्यच्च । सुखमापतितं सेवेद्दुःखमापतितं तथा ।

Again and, Happiness fallen to one's share one should cherish trouble fallen to one's share likewise,

चक्रवत्परिवर्तंते दुःखानि च सुखानि च ॥ १७२ ॥

wheel-like turn-round troubles and, joys and. (172)

अन्यच्च । उत्साहसंपन्नमदीर्घसूत्रं

Again and, To the exertion-endued, unprocrastinating,

क्रियाविधिज्ञं व्यसनेष्वसक्तं ।

of action-the rules-knowing, to vices not-attached,

शूरं कृतज्ञं दृढसौहृदं च

to a hero, benefits-remembering, one of steady-friendship and,

लक्ष्मीः स्वयं याति निवासहेतोः ॥ १७३ ॥

Lakshmi of her own accord goes for the sake of residing (with him). (173)

विशेषतश्च । विनाप्यर्थैर्वीरः स्पृशति बहुमानोन्नतिपदं

Especially and, Without even riches a hero touches of honour-elevation-a place,

समायुक्तो ऽप्यर्थैः परिभवपदं याति कृपणः ।

endowed even with riches to of disgrace-a place goes the miser;

स्वभावादुद्भूतां गुणसमुदयावाप्तिविषयां

the from the inborn-nature springing, for virtue-multitude-acquirement-fit

द्युतिं सैंहीं किं श्वा धृतकनकमालो ऽपि लभते ॥ १७४ ॥

splendour of a lion (what?) a dog bearing-a gold-necklace even obtains? (174)

धनवानिति हि मदो मे किं गतविभवो विषादमुपयामि ।

'Of riches possessed,' thus truly pride to me; why with departed-wealth sorrow I approach?

करनिहितकंदुकसमाः पातोत्पाता मनुष्याणां ॥ १७५ ॥

the in the hand-placed-ball-like (are) the sinkings- (and) risings of men. (175)

अपरं च । अभ्रच्छाया खलप्रीतिर्नवशस्यानि योषितः ।

Again and, A cloud's-shadow, of wicked-the friendship, new-corn, women,

किंचित्कालोपभोग्यानि यौवनानि धनानि च ॥ १७६ ॥

for some-time- (only) to be enjoyed, youth, riches and. (176)

वृत्त्यर्थं नातिचेष्टेत सा हि धात्रैव निर्मिता ।

For the sake of a-livelihood not too much one should strive, that for by the Creator already provided;

गर्भादुत्पतिते जंतौ मातुः प्रस्रवतः स्तनौ ॥ १७७ ॥

from the womb when comes forth a creature, of the mother stream the breasts. (177)

अपि च सखे । येन शुक्लीकृता हंसाः शुकाश्च हरितीकृताः ।

Also and, O friend, By whom white-made the geese, the parrots and green-made,

मयूराश्चित्रिता येन स ते वृत्तिं विधास्यति ॥ १७८ ॥

the peacocks variegated by whom, He for thee a livelihood will provide. (178)

अपरं च । सतां रहस्यं शृणु मित्र ।

Again and, Of the good the secret hear, O friend,

जनयंत्यर्जने दुःखं तापयंति विपत्तिषु ।

They produce in the acquisition trouble, they cause pain in failures,

मोहयंति च संपत्तौ कथमर्थाः सुखावहाः ॥ १७८ ॥

they infatuate and in success, how (are) riches happiness-conferring? (179)

अपरं च । धर्मार्थं यस्य वित्तेहा वरं तस्य निरीहता ।

Another and, For religion's-sake of whom wealth-desire, better of him freedom from-desire,

प्रक्षालनाद्धि पंकस्य दूरादस्पर्शनं वरं ॥ १८० ॥

than wiping off for of mud far not-touching better. (180)

यतः । यथा ह्यामिषमाकाशे पक्षिभिः श्वापदैर्भुवि ।

For, As truly prey in the air by birds, by beasts on earth

भक्ष्यते सलिले नक्रैस्तथा सर्वत्र वित्तवान् ॥ १८१ ॥

is eaten, in water by crocodiles, thus everywhere the rich man. (181)

राजतः सलिलादग्नेश्चौरतः स्वजनादपि ।

From a king, from water, from fire, from the robber, from their own-people likewise,

भयमर्थवतां नित्यं मृत्योः प्राणभृतामिव ॥ १८२ ॥

fear of the rich constantly, from death of the living as. (182)

तथा हि । जन्मनि क्लेशबहुले किं नु दुःखमतः परं ।

Thus for, In life with troubles-abounding what possibly pain than this greater?

इच्छासंपद्यतो नास्ति यच्चेच्छा न निवर्तते ॥ १८३ ॥

desire-fulfilment because not is, because and the desire not ceases? (183)

अन्यच्च भ्रातः शृणु ।

Another and, brother, hear:

धनं तावदसुलभं लब्धं कृच्छ्रेण रक्ष्यते ।

Wealth at first not-easy-to obtained, obtained with difficulty it is preserved,

लब्धनाशो यथा मृत्युस्तस्मादेतन्न चिंतयेत् ॥ १८४ ॥

of the obtained-the loss like death, therefore of this not one should think. (184)

M

तृष्णां चेह परित्यज्य को दरिद्रः क ईश्वरः ।

Covetousness and here having abandoned, who poor? who a lord?

तस्याश्चेत्प्रसरो दत्तो दास्यं च शिरसि स्थितं ॥ १८५ ॥

of it if way given, servitude and at the head placed. (185)

अपरं च । यद्यदेव हि वांछेत ततो वांछा प्रवर्तते ।

Again and, What what just indeed one may desire, thence the desire starts,

प्राप्त एवार्थतः सोऽर्थो यतो वांछा निवर्तते ॥ १८६ ॥

obtained verily in reality that object, from which the desire turns away. (186)

किं बहुना मम पक्षपातेन । मयैव सहात्र

What with so much of my side of the question? With me just together here

कालो नीयतां ।

the time may be spent.

यतः । आमरणांताः प्रणयाः कोपास्तत्क्षणभंगुराः ।

For, At-death-ending the affections, the anger at that-moment-vanishing,

परित्यागाश्च निःसंगा भवंति हि महात्मनां ॥ १८७ ॥

the gifts and free from-self-interest are truly of the noble-minded. (187)

इति श्रुत्वा लघुपतनको ब्रूते । धन्योऽसि मंथर

Thus having heard Laghupatanaka says: Happy art thou, O Manthara,

सर्वथा श्लाघ्यगुणोऽसि ।

in every way of praiseworthy-virtue thou art.

यतः । संत एव सतां नित्यमापदुद्धरणक्षमाः ।

For, The good only of the good constantly out of misfortune-to lift-able,

गजानां पंकमग्नानां गजा एव धुरंधराः ॥ १८८ ॥

of elephants into a mire-plunged elephants only the burthen-bearers (rescuers). (188)

श्लाघ्यः स एको भुवि मानवानां

To be praised that alone on earth of men,

स उत्तमः सत्पुरुषः स धन्यः ।
he the greatest, a good man, he happy,

यस्यार्थिनो वा शरणागता वा
of whom the needy either, the refuge-taking or,

नाशाविभंगा विमुखाः प्रयांति ॥ १८९ ॥
not broken-hoped with averted-faces go away. (189)

तदेवं ते स्वेच्छाहारविहारं कुर्वाणाः संतुष्टाः
Then thus those according to their-desire-feeding-(and) sporting making contented

सुखं निवसंति । अथ कदाचिच्चित्रांगनामा मृगः केनापि त्रासि-
happily dwell. Now one-day Chitrâṅga-named a deer by somebody frightened

तस्तत्रागत्य मिलितः । ततः पश्चादायांतं मृगमवलोक्य भयं
there having approached was met. Thence after approaching the deer having seen, danger

संचिंत्य मंथरो जलं प्रविष्टो मूषिकश्च विवरं गतः काको
suspecting, Manthara the water entered, the mouse and to the hole went, the crow

ऽप्युड्डीय वृक्षमारूढः । ततो लघुपतनकेन सुदूरं निरूप्य
also up-flying a tree ascended. Then by Laghupatanaka, very-far having looked,

भयहेतुर्न को ऽप्यायातीत्यालोचितं । पश्चात्तद्वचना-
'fear-cause not any approaches' thus was considered. Afterwards upon his word

दागत्य पुनः सर्वे मिलित्वा तत्रैवोपविष्टाः । मंथरेणोक्तं । भद्र
having arrived again all having met there just seated. By Manthara said: Hail!

मृग स्वागतं । स्वेच्छयोदकाद्याहारो ऽनुभूयतां ।
deer, welcome! According to your-wish, of water-etc. consisting-food may be enjoyed.

अत्रावस्थानेन वनमिदं सनाथीक्रियतां । चित्रांगो ब्रूते ।
By here residing forest this with a lord-may be endowed. Chitrâṅga says:

लुब्धकत्रासितो ऽहं भवतां शरणमागतः । भवद्भिः सह
By a hunter-frightened I of you the protection approached. You with

सख्यमिच्छामि । हिरण्यको ऽवदत् । मित्रत्वं तावदस्माभिः सह भवता-
friendship I wish. Hiranyaka said: Friendship truly us with by you

यत्नेन मिलितं ।
without-trouble met.

यतः । औरसं कृतसंबंधं तथा वंशक्रमागतं ।
For, One's own offspring, one formed by connection, likewise one in race-line-descended,

रक्षितं व्यसनेभ्यश्च मित्रं ज्ञेयं चतुर्विधं ॥ १९० ॥
one rescued from dangers and, a friend to be known of four-kinds. (190)

तदत्र भवता स्वगृहनिर्विशेषं स्थीयतां ।
Therefore here by you from your own-house-without a difference may be remained.

तच्छ्रुत्वा मृगः सानंदो भूत्वा स्वेच्छाहारं
That having heard the deer, full of-joy being, according to his-desire-feeding

कृत्वा पानीयं पीत्वा जलासन्नतरुच्छायायामुपविष्टः । अथ
making, water drinking, in a water-near standing-tree's-shade settled. Then,

मंथरेणोक्तं । सखे मृग एतस्मिन्निर्जने वने केन त्रासितो
by Manthara said: Friend deer, in this lonely forest by whom frightened

ऽसि । कदाचित्किं व्याधाः संचरंति । मृगेणोक्तं । अस्ति
art thou? Ever (do) hunters walk about? By the deer said: There is

कलिंगविषये रुक्मांगदो नाम नरपतिः । स च दिग्विज-
in the Kalinga-country Rukmângada by name a prince. He and by the world-

यव्यापारक्रमेणागत्य चंद्रभागानदीतीरे समावा-
conquest-business-course having approached, on the Chandrabhâgâ-bank having

सितकटको वर्तते । प्रातश्च तेनात्रागत्य
pitched-his camp resides. 'In the morning and he here having arrived

कर्पूरसरःसमीपे भवितव्यमिति व्याधानां मुखात्किंवदंती
in the Karpûra-lake-proximity will be,' thus of the hunters from the mouth a report

श्रूयते। तदत्रापि प्रातरवस्थानं भयहेतुकमित्या-
is heard. Therefore here also in the morning residing (is) fear-cause having, thus

लोच्य यथावसरकार्यमारभ्यतां। तच्छ्रुत्वा
considering according to-the occasion-action may be undertaken. That having heard

कूर्मः सभयमाह। जलाशयांतरं गच्छामि। काक-
the tortoise with-fear says: To another-water-reservoir I go. The crow-

मृगावप्युक्तवंतौ। एवमस्तु। ततो हिरण्यको विहस्याह।
(and)-mouse also said: So be it. Then Hiraṇyaka smiling said:

जलाशयांतरे प्राप्ते मंथरस्य कुशलं स्थले गच्छतः
Another-water-reservoir being reached, of Manthara welfare; on the land of the going

क: प्रतीकारः।
what help?

यतः। अंभांसि जलजंतूनां दुर्गं दुर्गनिवासिनां।
For, Water of water-animals, a fort of the in the fort-residing,

स्वभूमिः श्वापदादीनां राज्ञां मंत्री परं बलं ॥ १९१ ॥
their own-place of beasts, etc., of kings a minister the chief strength. (191)

सखे लघुपतनक अनेनोपदेशेन तथा भवितव्यं
Friend Laghupatanaka, through this advice thus to be fared:

स्वयं वीक्ष्य यथा वध्वाः पीडितं कुचकुड्मलं।
Himself having seen as of his wife pressed the bosom-bud,

वणिक्पुत्रो ऽभवद्दुःखी त्वं तथैव भविष्यसि ॥ १९२ ॥
the merchant's-son became sad; thou thus just wilt be. (192)

त ऊचुः। कथमेतत्। हिरण्यकः कथयति। अस्ति कान्यकुब्ज-
They said: How that? Hiraṇyaka relates: There is in the Kânyakubja-

विषये वीरसेनो नाम राजा। तेन वीरपुराख्ये नगरे
country Vîrasena by name a king. By him in the Vîrapura-named town

तुंगबलो नाम राजपुत्रो भोगपतिः कृतः । स च महाधनस्त-
Tuṅgabala by name a prince governor appointed. He and of great-wealth,

रुण एकदा स्वनगरे भ्राम्यन्नतिप्रौढयौवनां लावण्यवतीं
young, one-day in his-town perambulating in full-blown youth Lâvaṇyavatî

नाम वणिक्पुत्रवधूमालोकयामास । ततः स्वहर्म्यं गत्वा स्मरा-
by name a merchant's-son's-wife saw. Then to his-palace having gone by love-

कुलमतिस्तस्याः कृते दूतीं प्रेषितवान् ।
disturbed-in mind on her account a female messenger he dispatched.

यतः सन्मार्गे तावदास्ते प्रभवति पुरुषस्तावदेवेन्द्रियाणां
For, On the right-path so long he remains, master is a man so long only of the senses,

लज्जां तावद्विधत्ते विनयमपि समालंबते तावदेव ।
shame so long he has, decency also he maintains so long only,—

भ्रूचापाकृष्टमुक्ताः श्रवणपथगता नीलपक्ष्माण एते
by the eyebrows-bow-drawn back-(and) darted, to the ear-reaching, black-feathered those

यावल्लीलावतीनां न हृदि धृतिमुषो दृष्टिबाणाः पतंति ॥ १९३ ॥
as of fair-ones not into the heart the steadiness-stealing look-arrows fall. (193)

सापि लावण्यवती तदवलोकनक्षणात्प्रभृति स्मरशरप्रहारजर्ज-
She also Lâvaṇyavatî him-seeing-the moment from by the Love-arrow-stroke-

रितहृदया तदेकचित्ताभवत् ।
broken-hearted of him-alone-thinking was.

तथा चोक्तं । असत्यं साहसं माया मात्सर्यं चातिलुब्धता ।
Thus for said, Untruth, violence, fraud, envy and extreme-covetousness,

निर्गुणत्वमशौचत्वं स्त्रीणां दोषाः स्वभावजाः ॥ १९४ ॥
want-of virtue, impurity, of women the faults from their-nature-springing. (194)

अथ दूतीवचनं श्रुत्वा लावण्यवत्युवाच । अहं पतिव्रता
Now the messenger's-word having heard Lâvaṇyavatî said: I husband-devoted

कथमेतस्मिन्नधर्मे पतिलंघने प्रवर्ते ।
how in this unrighteousness, husband-imposition, I engage?

यतः । सा भार्या या गृहे दक्षा सा भार्या या प्रजावती ।
For, She a wife, who in the house clever; she a wife who prolific,

सा भार्या या पतिप्राणा सा भार्या या पतिव्रता ॥ १९५ ॥
she a wife whose husband-is her life, she a wife who husband-devoted. (195)

न सा भार्येति वक्तव्या यस्या भर्ता न तुष्यति ।
Not she 'a wife' thus to be called, with whose husband not is gratified,

तुष्टे भर्तरि नारीणां संतुष्टाः सर्वदेवताः ॥ १९६ ॥
being gratified the husband of women, gratified all-divinities. (196)

ततो यद्यदादिशति मे प्राणेश्वरस्तदेवाहमविचारितं
therefore whatever commands of me the life-lord, that only I without-examination

करोमि । दूत्योक्तं । सत्यतममेतत् । लावण्यवत्युवाच । ध्रुवं
do. By the messenger said: Quite true this? Lâvaṇyavatî said: Certainly,

सत्यमेतत् । ततो दूतिकया गत्वा तत्तत्सर्वं तुंगबलस्याग्रे
true this. Then by the messenger having gone that that all of Tuṅgabala in the presence

निवेदितं । तच्छ्रुत्वा तुंगबलो ऽब्रवीत् । स्वामिनानीय
reported. That having heard Tuṅgabala said: 'By the husband, having led (her) near,

समर्पयितव्येति कथमेतच्छक्यं । कुट्टन्याह । उपायः क्रियतां ।
she is to be surrendered,' how this possible? The procuress said: A stratagem be made.

तथा चोक्तं । उपायेन हि यच्छक्यं न तच्छक्यं पराक्रमैः ।
Thus and said, By a stratagem truly what possible, not that possible by valour,

शृगालेन हतो हस्ती गच्छता पंकवर्त्मना ॥ १९७ ॥
by a jackal slain an elephant, going on a swamp-way. (197)

राजपुत्रः पृच्छति । कथमेतत् । सा कथयति । अस्ति ब्रह्मारण्ये
The prince asks: How that? She relates: There is in the Brahma-wood

कर्पूरतिलको नाम हस्ती। तमवलोक्य सर्वे शृगालाश्चिंतयंति स्म।
Karpûratilaka by name an elephant. Him having seen all the jackals thought:

यद्ययं केनाप्युपायेन म्रियते तदास्माकमेतद्देहेन मासचतुष्टयस्य
If he by some stratagem dies, then of us through his-body of a month-tetrad

भोजनं भविष्यति। तत्रैकेन वृद्धशृगालेन प्रतिज्ञातं। मया बुद्धि-
food will be. There by one old-jackal promised: By me through-intellect-

प्रभावादस्य मरणं साधयितव्यं। अनंतरं स वंचकः
superiority of him the death to be accomplished: Thereupon that cheat

कर्पूरतिलकसमीपं गत्वा साष्टांगपातं प्रणम्यो-
Karpûratilaka-near having gone with-of the eight-limbs-prostration having saluted

वाच। देव दृष्टिप्रसादं कुरु। हस्ती ब्रूते। कस्त्वं कुतः
said: Sire, look-favour make. The elephant says: Who thou, whence

समायातः। सो ऽवदत्। जंबुको ऽहं सर्वैर्वनवासिभिः पशुभिर्मि-
approached? He said: A jackal I by all wood-inhabiting animals,

लित्वा भवत्सकाशं प्रस्थापितः। यद्विना राज्ञावस्थातुं
after having met, to your-presence despatched. Because without a king to remain

न युक्तं तदत्राटवीराज्ये ऽभिषेक्तुं भवान्
not proper, therefore here in the forest-sovereignty to be inaugurated you

सर्वस्वामिगुणोपेतो निरूपितः।
with all-lord's-virtues-endowed selected.

यतः। यः कुलाभिजनाचारैरतिशुद्धः प्रतापवान्।
For, Who by race-descent- (and) conduct very-pure, majestic,

धार्मिको नीतिकुशलः स स्वामी युज्यते भुवि ॥ १९८ ॥
just, behaviour-clever, he as a master is fit on earth. (198)

अपरं च पश्य। राजानं प्रथमं विंदेत्ततो भार्यां ततो धनं।
Another and see, A king first he should find, then a wife, then riches,

राजन्यसति लोके ऽस्मिन्कुतो भार्या कुतो धनं ॥ १९९ ॥
a king not-being in this world, whence a wife, whence riches? (199)

अन्यञ्च । पर्जन्य इव भूतानामाधारः पृथिवीपतिः ।
Again and, Cloud-like of the living a support an earth-lord,

विकले ऽपि हि पर्जन्ये जीव्यते न तु भूपतौ ॥ २०० ॥
failing also for a cloud it is lived, not but an earth-lord (failing). (200)

नियतविषयवर्ती प्रायशो दंडयोगात्
In the allotted-office-remaining generally through the rod-use

जगति परवशे ऽस्मिन्दुर्लभः साधुवृत्तः ।
in the world on another-dependent this; difficult-to be found one of good-character;

कृशमपि विकलं वा व्याधितं वाधनं वा
a meagre also, defective or, sick or, poor or

पतिमपि कुलनारी दंडभीत्याभ्युपैति ॥ २०१ ॥
husband also a noble woman through the rod-fear approaches. (201)

तद्यथा लग्नवेला न विचलति तथा कृत्वा सत्वरमा-
Therefore that the lucky-moment not passes away, thus acting, with-haste

गम्यतां देवेन । इत्युक्त्वोत्थाय चलितः । ततो
may be approached by your highness. Thus having spoken, rising (he) went. Then

ऽसौ राज्यलोभाकृष्टः कर्पूरतिलकः शृगालवर्त्मना
that by the sovereignty-desire-attracted Karpûratilaka on the jackal's-way

धावन्महापंके निमग्नः । ततस्तेन हस्तिनोक्तं । सखे शृगाल
running in a great-mire immersed. Then by that elephant said: Friend jackal,

किमधुना विधेयं । पंके निपतितो ऽहं । म्रिये । परावृत्य पश्य ।
what now to be done? in a mire fallen I; I die; turning back look!

शृगालेन विहस्योक्तं । देव मम पुच्छकावलंबनं कृत्वोत्तिष्ठ । यद्
By the jackal smiling said: Sire, of me tail-holding having made rise. Because

मद्विधस्य वचसि त्वया प्रत्ययः कृतस्तदनुभूयतामशरणं दुःखं ।
of me-like in word by thee confidence placed, therefore may be suffered helpless pain.

तथा चोक्तं । यदा सत्संगरहितो भविष्यसि भविष्यसि ।
Thus and said: If of the good-society-deprived thou wilt be, thou wilt be,

तदासज्जनगोष्ठीषु पतिष्यसि पतिष्यसि ॥ २०२ ॥
then into bad-men's-companies thou wilt fall, thou wilt fall. (202)

ततो महापंके निमग्नो हस्ती शृगालैर्भक्षितः । अतो
Then into the great-mire plunged the elephant by the jackals eaten. Therefore

ऽहं ब्रवीमि । उपायेन हि यच्छक्यमित्यादि । ततः कुट्टन्युपदे-
I say: By a stratagem truly what possible, etc. Then by the procuress'-

शेन तं चारुदत्तनामानं वणिक्पुत्रं स राजपुत्रः सेवकं
advice that Chârudatta-named merchant's-son that prince (his) attendant

चकार । ततोऽसौ तेन सर्वविश्वासकार्येषु नियोजितः । एकदा
made. Then he by him in all-confidence-affairs (was) employed. One day

तेन राजपुत्रेण स्नातानुलिप्तेन कनकरत्नालंकारधारिणा प्रोक्तं ।
by that prince bathed- (and) anointed gold-jewel-ornaments-bearing announced:

अद्यारभ्य मासमेकं गौरीव्रतं कर्तव्यं । तदत्र
To-day beginning for month one the Gaurî-vow to be performed. Therefore hither

प्रतिरात्रमेकां कुलीनां युवतीमानीय समर्पय । सा मया
every-night one noble virgin having led surrender (her). She by me

यथोचितेन विधिना पूजयितव्या । ततः स चारुदत्तस्तथाविधां
in the usual manner to be honoured. Then that Chârudatta such a one

नवयुवतीमानीय समर्पयति । पश्चात्प्रच्छन्नः सन्किमयं
quite-young having led near surrenders. Afterwards concealed being, 'what he

करोतीति निरूपयति । स च तुंगबलस्तां युवतीमस्पृशन्नेव
does?' thus espies. That and Tungabala that maiden not-touching even

दूराद्वस्त्रालंकारगंधचंदनैः संपूज्य रक्षकं
from afar with garments-ornaments-perfumes-sandal wood having honoured, a guardian

दत्त्वा प्रस्थापयति । अथ वणिक्पुत्रेण तद्दृष्टोपजातविश्वासेन
having given, sends away. Now by the merchant's-son, that having-seen, with increased-confidence,

लोभाकृष्टमनसा स्ववधूं लावण्यवतीं समानीय
with by covetousness-attracted-mind, his-wife Lâvaṇyavatî having led near

समर्पिता । स च तुंगबलस्तां हृदयप्रियां लावण्यवतीं
(she was) surrendered. He and Tuṅgabala that heart-beloved Lâvaṇyavatî

विज्ञाय ससंभ्रममुत्थाय निर्भरमालिंग्य निमीलिताक्षः
having recognised, with-haste up-jumping, ardently embracing, with half-closed-eyes,

पर्यंके तया सह विललास । तदालोक्य वणिक्पुत्रश्चित्रलिखित इवे-
on a sofa her - with sported. That seeing the merchant's-son picture - like

तिकर्तव्यतामूढः परं विषादमुपगतः । अतो ऽहं ब्रवीमि । स्वयं
perplexed-what to do to extreme sadness went. Therefore I say: Himself

वीक्ष्येत्यादि । तथा त्वयापि भवितव्यमिति । तद्धितवचनम-
having seen, etc. Thus by thee also will be fared. That friend's-word not

वधीर्य महता भयेन विमुग्ध इव तं जलाशयमुत्सृज्य
regarding with great fear perplexed as it were that water-reservoir having left

मंथरश्चलितः । ते ऽपि हिरण्यकादयः स्नेहादनिष्टं
Manthara went. They also Hiraṇyaka, etc. from affection, (something) unwished

शंकमाना मंथरमनुगच्छंति । ततः स्थले गच्छन्केनापि व्याधेन
apprehending Manthara follow. Then on the land going by some hunter,

कानने पर्यटता मंथरः प्राप्तः । प्राप्य तं गृहीत्वो-
the forest perambulating, Manthara caught. Having caught him, having seized,

त्थाप्य धनुषि बद्ध्वा भ्रमन्क्लेशात्क्षुत्पिपासाकुलः
having lifted, to the bow having bound, walking about, through fatigue by hunger-(and)thirst-troubled

स्वगृहाभिमुखं चलितः। अथ मृगवायसमूषिकाः परं विषादं
towards-his-house (he) went. Now the deer-crow-mouse to extreme grief

गच्छंतस्तमनुजग्मुः। ततो हिरण्यको विलपति।
coming him followed. Then Hiraṇyaka laments:

एकस्य दुःखस्य न यावदंतं गच्छाम्यहं पारमिवार्णवस्य।
Of one trouble not while to the end go I, to the shore as of the ocean,

तावद्द्वितीयं समुपस्थितं मे छिद्रेष्वनर्था बहुलीभवंति ॥ २०३ ॥
then a second approached to me, in damages the evils are multiplied. (203)

स्वाभाविकं तु यन्मित्रं भाग्येनैवाभिजायते।
By his inborn-nature but who a friend, by fortune only he is produced,

तदकृत्रिमसौहार्दमापत्स्वपि न मुंचति ॥ २०४ ॥
therefore one of unfeigned-friendship in misfortunes also not does one give up. (204)

न मातरि न दारेषु न सोदर्ये न चात्मजे।
Not in a mother, not in a wife, not in a brother, not and in one's own offspring,

विश्वासस्तादृशः पुंसां यादृङ्मित्रे स्वभावजे ॥ २०५ ॥
confidence such of men, as in a friend by his inborn-nature-become (one). (205)

इति मुहुर्विचिंत्याहो दुर्दैवं।
Thus repeatedly having thought (he cried out): Oh, the hard-fate!

यतः। स्वकर्मसंतानविचेष्टितानि
For, The by one's own-actions'-spreading-wrought

कालांतरावर्तिशुभाशुभानि।
at other times-reverting-good- (and) evil,

इहैव दृष्टानि मयैव तानि
(are) here already experienced by me at least those,

जन्मांतराणीव दशांतराणि ॥ २०६ ॥
like different-births, different conditions. (206)

अथवेत्थमेवैतत् । कायः संनिहितापायः संपदः पदमापदां ।

Or, thus verily this, The body has destruction-close to it, happiness the place for misfortunes,

समागमाः सापागमाः सर्वमुत्पादि भंगुरं ॥ २०७ ॥

meeting with-departure connected, everything born (is) frail. (207)

पुनर्विमृश्याह । शोकारातिभयत्राणं प्रीतिविश्रंभभाजनं ।

Again having reflected he says: From sorrow-enemies- (and) danger-a protection of affection (and) confidence-a vessel,

केन रत्नमिदं सृष्टं मित्रमित्यक्षरद्वयं ॥ २०८ ॥

by whom jewel this created, '*Mitra*' thus the syllable-couple? (208)

किंच । मित्रं प्रीतिरसायनं नयनयोरानंदनं चेतसः

Moreover: A friend, a pleasure-elixir of the eyes, a delight of the mind,

पात्रं यत्सुखदुःखयोः सह भवेन्मित्रेण तद्दुर्लभं ।

a vessel that in happiness-(and) trouble together might be with the friend, that hard-to find;

ये चान्ये सुहृदः समृद्धिसमये द्रव्याभिलाषाकुलाः

And what other friends in success-time, with wealth-desire-filled,

ते सर्वत्र मिलंति तत्त्वनिकषग्रावा तु तेषां विपत् ॥ २०९ ॥

they everywhere meet (us); but the truth-touch stone of them (is) adversity. (209)

इति बहु विलप्य हिरण्यकश्चित्रांगलघुपतनकावाह । यावदयं

Thus much having lamented Hiranyaka to Chitrânga-(and) Laghup. says: So long as this

व्याधो वनान्न निःसरति तावन्मंथरं मोचयितुं

hunter from the forest not goes away, so long Manthara to rescue

यत्नः क्रियतां । तावूचतुः । सत्वरं कार्यमुच्यतां ।

an effort may be made. They both said: With-haste what to be done may be told.

हिरण्यको ब्रूते । चित्रांगो जलसमीपं गत्वा मृतमिवात्मानं

Hiranyaka says: Chitrânga to the water-near having gone dead-like himself

दर्शयतु काकश्च तस्योपरि स्थित्वा चंच्वा किमपि विलिखतु ।

may show, the crow and over him standing with the beak somewhat may peck.

नूनमनेन लुब्धकेन तत्र कच्छपं परित्यज्य मृगमांसार्थिना

Now by that hunter there, the tortoise having left, for the deer's-flesh-desirous,

सत्वरं गंतव्यं। ततो ऽहं मंथरस्य बंधनं छेत्स्यामि संनिहिते

with-haste will be gone. Then I of Manthara the tie shall cut; having approached

लुब्धके भवद्भ्यां पलायितव्यं। चित्रांगलघुपतनकाभ्यां शीघ्रं

the hunter, by you to be fled. By Chitrâṅga- (and) Laghupatanaka, quickly

गत्वा तथानुष्ठिते सति स व्याधः श्रांतः पानीयं पीत्वा

having gone, thus accomplished being, that hunter, tired, water having drunk,

तरोरधस्तादुपविष्टस्तथाविधं मृगमपश्यत्। ततः कर्तरिकामादाय

under a tree seated in such a condition the deer saw. Then the knife having taken,

प्रहृष्टमना मृगांतिकं चलितः। तत्रांतरे हिरण्यके-

with rejoicing-mind near to the deer proceeded. There meanwhile by Hiraṇyaka

नागत्य मंथरस्य बंधनं छिन्नं। स कूर्मः सत्वरं

having approached, of Manthara the tie cut. That tortoise with-haste

जलाशयं प्रविवेश। स मृग आसन्नं तं व्याधं विलोक्योत्थाय

the water-reservoir entered. That deer near that hunter perceiving, rising,

पलायितः। प्रत्यावृत्य लुब्धको यावत्तरुतलमायाति तावत्कूर्मम-

escaped. Returning the hunter while the tree-foot he approaches, then the tortoise

पश्यन्नचिंतयत्। उचितमेवैतन्ममासमीक्ष्यकारिणः।

not-seeing, reflected: Proper only this for me, not-circumspectly-acting.

यतः। यो ध्रुवाणि परित्यज्य अध्रुवाणि निषेवते।

For, He who certain (things) forsaking uncertain (things) attends to,

ध्रुवाणि तस्य नश्यंति अध्रुवं नष्टमेव हि ॥ २१० ॥

the certain (things) of him perish, the uncertain is perished already. (210)

ततो ऽसौ स्वकर्मवशान्निराशः कटकं प्रविष्टः। मंथरादयः

Then he through-his own-action disappointed the camp entered. Manthara, etc.

सर्वे त्यक्तापदः स्वस्थानं गत्वा यथासुखमास्थिताः ॥

all freed-from misfortune to their-place having gone happily remained.

अथ राजपुत्रैः सानंदमुक्तं । सर्वं श्रुतवंतः सुखिनो वयं ।

Then by the princes with-joy said: All having heard pleased we.

सिद्धं नः समीहितं । विष्णुशर्मोवाच । एतावता भवताम-

Accomplished of us what (was) desired. Vishṇuśarman said: With so much of you

भिलषितं संपन्नं । अपरमपीदमस्तु ।

the desire fulfilled, further also this may be:

मित्रं प्राप्नुत सज्जना जनपदैर्लक्ष्मीः समालंबतां

A friend acquire ye, O, good-men; with the nations Lakshmî may dwell;

भूपालाः परिपालयंतु वसुधां शश्वत्स्वधर्मे स्थिताः ।

Princes may protect the earth, constantly in their-duty standing;

आस्तां मानसतुष्टये सुकृतिनां नीतिर्नवोढेव वः

it may remain for the mind-gratification of the virtuous Nîti, a new-bride-like, of you;

कल्याणं कुरुतां जनस्य भगवांश्चंद्रार्धचूडामणिः ॥ २११ ॥

prosperity may cause of the people the venerable, who has the moon's-half-for his crest-jewel. (211)

॥ इति हितोपदेशे मित्रलाभो नाम प्रथमकथासंग्रहः समाप्तः ॥

Thus in the Hitopadeśa, Friend-acquisition by name the first-story-collection finished.

www.ingramcontent.com/pod-product-compliance
Lightning Source LLC
Chambersburg PA
CBHW032152010726
47493CB00008BA/2666
* 9 7 8 3 3 3 7 1 8 8 5 7 3 *